Also by Angelo Loukakis

For the Patriarch

Norfolk: an island and its people

The Greeks

Vernacular Dreams

Messenger

Who Do You Think You Are?

The Memory of Tides

HOUDINI'S FLIGHT

Sometimes you need to disappear
to find yourself

ANGELO LOUKAKIS

Fourth Estate • *London, New York, Sydney* and *Auckland*

Fourth Estate

An imprint of HarperCollins*Publishers*, Australia

First published in Australia in 2010
by HarperCollins*Publishers* Australia Pty Limited
ABN 36 009 913 517
harpercollins.com.au

HarperCollins*Publishers*

25 Ryde Road, Pymble, Sydney, NSW 2073, Australia
31 View Road, Glenfield, Auckland 0627, New Zealand
A 53, Sector 57, Noida, UP, India
77–85 Fulham Palace Road, London, W6 8JB, United Kingdom
2 Bloor Street East, 20th floor, Toronto, Ontario M4W 1A8, Canada
10 East 53rd Street, New York NY 10022, United States of America

National Library of Australia Cataloguing-in-Publication data:

Loukakis, Angelo, 1951– .
   Houdini's Flight / Angelo Loukakis
   ISBN 978 0 7322 8065 9 (pbk.).
   Houdini, Harry, 1874–1926 — Fiction
   I. Title.
A823.3

Cover design by Christa Moffitt, Christabella Designs
Cover images: plane by Apic/Getty Images; all other images by istockphoto.com
Typeset in Adobe Caslon by Kirby Jones
Printed and bound in Australia by Griffin Press.
60gsm Hi Bulk Book Cream used by HarperCollins*Publishers* is a natural, recyclable product
made from wood grown in sustainable forests. The manufacturing processes conform to the
environmental regulations in the country of origin, Finland.

5 4 3 2 1   10 11 12 13

To Ann, Nicholas and Christopher

with love and admiration

CONTENTS

In the *Discovery of Witchcraft*, published in 1584, Reginald Scot wrote that conjurers have a place so long as '... they abuse not the name of God nor make the people attribute onto them his power, but always acknowledge wherein the art consisteth, so as thereby other unlawfull and impious arts may be by them the rather detected and betrayed'.

PART ONE
ESCAPE

1
Old Magic

Terry paused to remove his dinner jacket. He took his time and folded it neatly before laying it along the back of a chair. He swung his arms once, twice, and ended the preparation by shaking his hands freely at his sides, as if this final trick needed some extra, physical effort and for which he needed to be loose and ready.

Looking across his ancient audience, lined up on three rows of folding metal chairs in the recreation room, he took care to smile and make plenty of eye contact. Next, he reached across to his table of props and took up a shiny, black top hat. He passed it to his left hand, turning it over so that they could see it was empty inside, leaving his right hand free to work the trick.

'Ladies and gentleman,' he said — and no mistake there, because he had only been able to spot one old bloke in the audience at the Banjo Paterson Memorial Home this night — 'ladies and gentleman, and I do use the word advisedly, bear with me as I explore the wonders of this amazing hat ...' And so he began, slowly pulling out over five metres of multicoloured silk from the mysterious receptacle.

Being the fourth occasion he had performed the trick, the banter had come easily — 'Look at all the pretty colours! Are you keeping up?' — he was more confident, the pulling motion sweeping and generous. He had time, for once, to look up and enjoy the disbelief on the faces of those in the front row.

Untroubled in working his hand in and out of the hat — the whole thing took almost a minute from start to finish — Terry also had time to notice that his performance was reflected in the windows that faced the garden, a doubling of the act. It was unsettling to see himself repeated there, as if some ghost were in the glass, imitating his motions. But here was an opportunity to check how he was doing — was he standing straight? Did his somewhat short and round figure make a sufficient impression in formal dress? Everything appeared to be in order, though he did feel something was still missing.

He was careful not to lose contact with the audience and kept an ear on the oohing and ahhing and the sound of clapping until it became loud enough to require a response. The trick completed, the stage in front of him strewn with coloured cloth, Terry returned everyone as wide a smile as he could, waved the hat in a triumphant circle and turned its inside towards the front. To all intents, there was nothing to be seen but the regular interior of a hat.

'Now where could all that have come from, folks?' he asked. 'Well, what can I say — that's the wonder of magic, isn't it?'

He ended with a deep bow, a wave, and a final hearty thank you to 'all the ladies — and the gentleman'. But as he scanned the room one last time, he saw he'd been mistaken about that. Sometime during the performance, another mature gent had arrived and was standing at the back, gazing earnestly at him over the heads of those seated; a tall, untidy sort of character in an overcoat who didn't look to be one of the residents (these being mainly scrubbed and collared and cardiganed).

'Sorry! Gentle*men*, I should have said — I see we have the pleasure of another, someone at the back there who …' Terry nodded and smiled at him, tried to make eye contact, but before he could connect the fellow turned and quickly left the room.

'Never mind, he mustn't have liked the show!'

All done now, Terry moved off to wait behind the makeshift curtain, which had been hung as a kind of backdrop for his act, to allow the staff to lead the residents away and back to their rooms.

Until he could come out again, he reviewed things. Overall, he was pleased with the show. The patter was still a bit corny, sure — he was not completely satisfied with himself on that score yet. That was okay. Most of the effort had gone into learning the tricks themselves; his presentation was a work in progress and would be for some time yet. The important thing was that he had pulled off six tricks in a row without muffing any of them.

What he had mastered so far was simple enough; this was pre-packaged magic, after all, where he only had to repeat the steps that were outlined in the instruction sheet that came with the box. The greater achievement was in finding and delivering the right gestures — the way he needed to lean forward to illustrate or highlight something, the way he needed to occasionally sweep an arm across his body to create drama or distraction, or with studied deliberation lay down an item of clothing to suggest something else was happening when it was not.

The night had been a triumph, from the Vanishing Bird Cage (would have been better had he also had the bird — you could get them in look-alike plastic complete with beating wings) to the Dancing Cane illusion, to the best of the lot (for a novice like him, anyway) — the Endless Scarf from the Top Hat trick. Unleashing some of his scarier routines might have been good — say, the needle through the arm trick — but he had deemed that one inadvisable. Just as well he had checked with the staff beforehand. The residents were frequently given needles of one kind or another, he had been informed, and it was unlikely they would see any fun in even a pretend version of the same thing.

When the room was at last empty, Terry emerged to pack his bags and fold his portable table. He carried everything to the entrance, then went to see the night manager to collect his fee. She told him they were very satisfied with his contribution — in the days ahead of each performance, she said, some of the residents spoke of nothing else. That was good to know, and he would be more than happy to return, he said, and then left for the carpark with his gear.

At the car, Terry put his hand in his coat pocket for his keys, but they were not there. A worry, as he kept them nowhere else. He searched through all his pockets but with no luck. Thinking they might have accidentally fallen into one of his bags, he shook each of them, listening for the distinctive sound. Again no luck. There was nothing for it but to open the two large sports bags that held his array of tricks. He did that, but the area was dimly lit and he could not see detail. So he emptied them out, arranging the contents in a circle around each bag. Still they were nowhere to be found. He would have to go back and ask for help.

The night manager was not in her office. She had been called away on an emergency, said the hastily written sign on her door.

But dozing on a chair beside the door was one of tonight's two male audience members, the chap who had been there from the start. He seemed to have been left to mind the fort.

Before Terry could rouse him to ask when the night manager might be back, the man came to and recognised him.

'Mr Voulos!' He stood up immediately. 'Loved your show, great stuff!'

'Thanks for that, Mr …?'

'Call me Frederick, just Frederick,' he said, and put out a hand to shake.

'Look, I'm having a bit of trouble getting into my car and I was going to ask the lady here for some help, maybe …'

'Ooh, that's no good. Like the sign says, she's not here. But I can help you. I'll get a hanger.'

He shuffled away quickly and just as quickly returned with a coathanger, waving it triumphantly.

Terry didn't have the heart to refuse the old gent, so led him outside to the car. He would have company, at least, until the office was attended again.

At the car, the aged Frederick straightened out the hanger, pushed it through the rubber seal and began to jiggle it.

'Bit of a hoodlum in my youth, I was, as you can see,' he said.

While Frederick was fiddling with the hanger, Terry looked away so as not to embarrass him. He knew he was going to take over any second. Just then, he caught some movement near the entrance. Someone was in the shadows next to the door. He recognised him. The same chap who had come in to hang around at the back of the recreation room. The tall, thin, rather miserable-looking bloke in the greatcoat. He saw that he had been noticed and came out into the light, then walked over to them.

'Having trouble there?' he asked when he saw what was happening.

'Yes, mate,' said Terry without acknowledging him directly. He didn't need another complication right now.

'Maybe I can help.'

The bloke gently edged his way between Frederick and the door, so deftly that Terry marvelled at the movement. Next he pulled some small object out of his pocket, while at the same time trying, it seemed, to keep it hidden from view. He inserted it into the lock. A twist, then another twist to which he added a pulling action, and the driver-side door opened.

Frederick stepped back, all the while nodding to acknowledge his rival's superiority. Terry said, 'Many thanks, mate. You're a lifesaver.'

'No trouble,' the fellow said. He put away his pick or whatever it was and took out a piece of paper, which he handed to Terry. 'Take this,' he said. 'There's an address. Might be able to help you, with your magic act and such.'

Terry took the piece of paper, unsure what was meant, but not really caring at this moment. 'Thanks to you both,' he said. 'I'd have been lost without you.' He patted Frederick on the shoulder and shook the tall bloke's hand.

'No worries, no worries,' his rescuer said. 'Glad to be of service. I'll send you the bill!'

Terry watched as the two old men headed off, Frederick back to the door of the home, the other into the night.

As soon as he was inside the car, Terry saw his keys on the

floor in front of the brake pedal. They must have fallen from his pocket when he'd got out earlier this evening. They were not needed to lock the car. An old Corolla such as this, all he had to do was push the button down and swing the door shut to lock it all up. Which was what he had done.

Terry put the key in the ignition, then paused. Motionless, he let a few moments pass in the dark, composing himself, looking to recall his earlier satisfaction. It wasn't easy; any time on his own and he was soon diverted to how fragile things were on other fronts.

He turned to a more pleasant topic: the question of finding a name to go by. Every good magician needed a proper name; he couldn't go on being announced as 'Mr Terry Voulos'. But what? 'The Great Voulos'? 'Terry the Terrific'? Like others that had come to mind, they were way too corny. He would give up for now and try again later. He started the car.

*

That night Terry Voulos arrived home a little after ten to a darkened house. Ricky would have gone to bed a couple of hours earlier and Jenny — who made a point of being the first to get to her practice in the morning and always hit the sack early — was asleep. He stepped quietly down the hall, conscious of the warmth of the air. Early May now, the nights were beginning to chill off properly — but as per the annual ritual, his wife was already turning the heaters up full blast and the place was stuffy.

Terry knew he would not be able to get to sleep at this hour, high as he was on the evening's small success. He thought to watch some muted television until he felt less wired, so poured himself a glass of red wine, then went to the living room where he opened a window slightly and began flicking the remote, looking for something to help him wind down.

With nothing but late-night talking heads on most channels, he ended up at a subtitled Middle Eastern drama on SBS. The thing had started and he had no idea what was happening, but was intrigued by the shots of jellaba-clad merchants haggling in a market, of mysterious women in chadors, the jerky cutting between some seedy city cafe and a landscape of anonymous sand dunes and desert tents. All until a woman passing by was grabbed by one of the coffee shop men and dragged into a back room, where her headgear was pulled off and she was summarily beaten.

At that, he sank his head into his hands and heard someone speak the word for mother in Greek out loud. He was surprised at himself, but only for a moment. He had been thinking of his mother a lot lately; he needed only the slightest spur to bring back to consciousness his few memories of her. An exaggerated assault on some lame TV drama was more than enough.

Switching the television off, he stood up with an idea of retreating to the shed for a while, until he heard footsteps coming down the hall. The light went on and Jenny was there, staring at him, as much cross as concerned.

'Terry, it's you … What was that about?'

'Nothing,' he said. 'Sorry I woke you.'

She kept staring at him. 'You need to get some counselling.'

He waited for a moment in case she had anything more to say. Nothing came. 'Maybe I've got a better plan.'

She shook her head, turned and left him to go back to bed.

2

Ancestor Worship

Terry's rostered day off, and he was giving the morning over to a round of the magic shops. But he was curious about the character he had encountered the previous evening and so thought to take a closer look at the piece of paper he had been handed outside the old folks' home.

He went to the laundry and yesterday's shirt, from which he pulled out the note: a lined page, folded into quarters, and headed 'Josephs — Ironmongers'. On the facing quarter the name 'Hal Sargeson' was written in biro, in a nice old-style cursive, and below that was an address — 'off Wentworth Avenue, at 221c'. There was something about the way the man had waited, stared at him so intently. He was curious about the offer of help; he would detour briefly to this address.

Terry spent the bus ride into town dwelling on his progress in magic. The most money he had made so far was $100, which was what he'd been paid for each performance at the Banjo Paterson Home at Gladesville (as much as they could afford, or so he'd been told). The money didn't matter for the moment. He had originally taken to doing a few tricks as a hobby in the privacy of his shed; with a basic grip and a small repertoire, it had become a way of entertaining young Ricky and his mates — first at home on otherwise boring weekend afternoons, then this year at the school concert as well as the annual fete. He had now notched up four performances at the old people's home in the past couple of months. He wondered again if he could take it further.

The arrangement had come about accidentally. He had been told by the welfare officer, one of his regulars on the 440 bus, that the pensioner chap who used to come and sing every third Thursday night had sadly shuffled off and the entertainment was consequently a bit thin. Terry had surprised himself by offering to come in and do some tricks. Since then, and as each show seemed to be received better than the previous one, he'd allowed himself to believe he could take the thing a lot further. To become a professional magician, now that would be something!

Terry got off the bus at Chinatown and headed to where he thought he was meant to go — except things weren't exactly clear at the street number he'd been given. At 221 Wentworth Avenue he saw only a large, anonymous-looking office block, its frontage ending at the corner of a lane. He walked down the lane, past some crumbling, late-Victorian warehouses, and arrived at a dead end.

There, facing him and almost filling the narrow space but for a small opening to a side passage, was what looked like an old meeting hall. A brass plate that said '221c' was screwed to the front wall to the left of two boarded-up doors. Above, where the entrance arch ended at a Gothic point, a series of fading Chinese characters was painted on a cracking wooden panel fixed to the stonework.

Terry stood and stared for a moment to try to make sense of it — the place was well-hidden, the meaning of that script even more so. There was no entrance from here, it seemed, so he made his way around the back, following the narrow passage that separated the structure from the foundries or warehouses or whatever they had once been, hidden behind the main street. He came to a plywood door with a string of modern latches and deadlocks tattooed along one edge. He knocked a couple of times, but it was opened a crack before he could knock a third. When the man in the slit recognised him, he pulled it all the way open.

'So …! Come in! Name's Sargeson, Hal Sargeson.'

'You were the man at the home.'

'Yes.'

'Hi. I'm Terry Voulos. You wanted to talk to me about magic, right?'

'I do, come in.'

Terry followed the man into a rectangular space, about twenty-five metres long by six or seven wide. On the wall to the right as he came in were two large wooden plaques bearing lists of names in faded gold lettering — all Anglo-Saxon, none of them obviously Chinese. A meeting hall? A masonic lodge?

'What is this place, Hal?'

'Been lots of things over the years, which I'll tell you about later. There's something left up the other end worth a look though.'

'How is it that you're —?'

'It's abandoned, friend. I live here, have done for years.'

'Anyone —?'

'No. Nobody gives a stuff. Been caught up in some development shenanigans for years, it has. Zoning … whatnot. Never sorted.'

Terry followed Hal as he headed further in, looking around as they went. Overhead, a single globe burned. The centre of the space was bare but for a couple of obviously scavenged director's chairs. A battered wooden table with cut-down legs made for a sort of coffee table against one long wall, and a couple of chipboard bookshelves filled with books stood next to it — Hal Sargeson's library and reading room, he supposed.

Against the other long wall was a single bed with a pillow and a couple of blankets neatly folded at one end. Hal saw that Terry had noticed.

'That's the sleeping arrangements, son. Basic, but what do I need?'

Hal stopped abruptly before they got to the far end. In the dim light, and with cartons and junk in the way, Terry did not immediately register what he had been brought to. A large, box-like contraption reared up in front of him.

'This was the altar.'

Terry scanned the ornately carved and filigreed arrangement, but again could not make much sense of what he was looking at.

'If you say so. Looks Chinese …'

'Hard for us Westerners to get — I mean, ancestor worship is not big with us, right? This was Confucian mainly, with some Taoist luck worship too … Bring on the luck, eh mate?'

'And they just up and left?'

'They built a bigger and better one not far away. Have a look at this.'

Sargeson retrieved one of two similar-shaped objects standing atop the altar, a cylindrical container of some kind. He handed it to Terry.

'It's a fortune-stick holder. The priest would shake them around, spread them out, you'd take one. And you would know your luck!'

'As random as that?'

Hal looked out from under his brows. 'Not much use to the magician that, is it? Leave nothing to chance, more like it! Now I want to show you something else …'

Terry started to frame a question or two — the first of which was how Hal had come to live here — but before he could speak he felt Hal's hand on his elbow. Next he was being steered across the room. Running almost the length of the long wall that the bed was pushed against was an arrangement of wooden tea chests and blue plastic milk crates — holding the guy's belongings, Terry assumed. Hanging above these was a line of photos, making a kind of gallery.

Here was a series of black-and-white images of a man escaping various shackles, restraints and bonds. Mostly taken outdoors; all pretty much early twentieth century, from what Terry could tell by the clothes and setting. He was willing to guess that he was looking at an escape artist. Studying the round, large head, the face with its intense and confident gaze that gave way to an occasional wry smile in some photos, he deduced this had to be the most famous of them all.

'Houdini?'

Hal slapped him gently on the back. 'Well done! Indeed it is Houdini.'

Terry scanned the photos again. There were large numbers of people in the background of some of the shots. Only Houdini would have been famous enough to draw such crowds.

'How did you get hold of these?'

'They're only copies. Part of my private collection. There are more in the boxes …'

Now Hal pointed to the blue plastic crates arranged beyond his bed.

'Are you a fan, Hal?'

'Ha! Come over here with me for a minute.'

Hal quickly gathered two of his director's chairs and arranged them in front of the display.

'Explanation, maybe?' Hal offered, in a voice Terry heard as distinctly younger, excited almost. Terry nodded.

'Must be curious as to what you're doing here … a bit? Okay, Terry, two things. First, I've known you for years.'

Hal saw Terry tense at this and said, 'Nothing nasty. Only that I've caught your buses lots of times — but I wouldn't expect you to remember me.'

Terry tried to recall whether he had ever seen him before, and couldn't honestly say he had. He shook his head.

'Never mind that, just listen. The second thing — the second thing is much more important — is on that wall and in those boxes.'

'Okay, I've got a minute. What are we looking at here?'

'These photos, they're photos of Houdini all right. And most of them were taken right here, in Australia. In Melbourne and Sydney in early 1910. Go up closer and have another look. There's a man nearby in some of them, keeping the great Harry

Houdini close company. Houdini toured the world in those days. The chap with him, who went with him almost everywhere, was my father.'

Terry stepped across to look at the pictures more closely. The same man indeed appeared in a few of the images. A tall thin fellow, always a few steps behind or to the side of Houdini. 'That's not him, is it, this guy with the seaman's hat? He looks a bit like you.'

'That's him.'

'Tall too, like you … Well, how about that?' Terry was quietly intrigued.

'No,' Hal replied loudly. '"How about that" is not enough. There's more to this, as you may find out.'

Terry was surprised at the irritation in his voice, even as it died away almost as quickly as it had appeared. Terry would be more cautious with him.

'Go on. Sorry. Tell me what it is you want to say,' he said softly.

'Didn't mean to shout. You know something about Houdini?'

'Sure. Everybody's heard of Houdini. Could get out of anything, right? The magic shops I go to have books about him. And there was a movie, wasn't there? But big escapes like these …' Terry lightly touched the picture of a suspended Houdini '… they're way out of my league.'

Hal nodded, seemingly pleased that his visitor knew at least something. 'For now, maybe,' he muttered. Then more loudly said, 'That movie was rubbish, by the way. Tony Curtis as Houdini — they had to be kidding!'

'Tony Curtis, that's right. But, hey, what was that about your father again? Or no, wait — before that tell me a bit about yourself … in case you're an axe murderer or something,' Terry said, only half joking.

'My life's not worth talking about. But there's something else here for you, for us both possibly. If you would hear me out, that is.'

'Okay, I'm listening.'

Barely waiting for him to finish, Hal started talking again. 'Because for a story to make sense is like for a trick to work; the audience has to be ready and ripe for it. The audience has to need this for themselves.'

'Don't know about all that, but I'll hear you out.'

'And maybe more than that, when I'm done. I've got an offer to make you. Put yourself in my hands, and I'll turn you into a magician. A real one.'

Terry wondered what he had let himself in for, but he was here and now truly interested. Hal pointed to the chairs and motioned that they should sit; he squared his chair up to face Terry more or less directly. He was keen, Terry noticed, for some serious eye contact. He obliged.

'Bit hard for people to understand today, but early twentieth century, Harry Houdini was not only the most famous illusionist, the most famous showman you could name — he was huge. Up there with Sarah Bernhardt, Teddy Roosevelt, the Kaiser … He pulled gigantic crowds, everybody wanted a piece of him. He was making more money than any other performer, including stage, music — enormous piles of dough. Before TV, before radio, people would crowd the wharves to see his ship come in, thousands of them. And his name lives on. Think how many times you hear someone say so and so has "done a Houdini" or whatever. That's not celebrity, mate, that's fame!'

'And your father was with him? That's pretty amazing,' Terry said, catching Hal's enthusiasm.

'Yes. My old man was American-born. He came to Australia with Harry, as I say, and then, after that tour, he stayed on here. And what he learned from Houdini are things that are absolute gold. And which I'd like to tell you about.'

'And which I'd like to hear. Before you do that, small question: what were you doing at the Banjo Paterson Home the other night?'

'Oh, a couple of things,' Hal said, waving his arm to suggest what would follow was not important. 'Wanted to see what an old folks' home is like — some care worker was telling me to start thinking about it … not that I've got the money anyway. I saw the poster about you on the notice board. And when you're talking magic, mate, you're talking me! Magic can be a wonderful thing.' He smiled broadly.

'Agreed,' Terry replied. 'So what's the story? Better start at the start.'

'I will. But this story is as it was told to me, first off.'

'Go right ahead.'

'My father … my father's name was Francis. He liked to be called Frank and he liked to tell stories. He was very good at it, better than I could ever be. I remember when I was a little chap he would put me on his knee and tell me tall tales and silly stuff, things to make a kid laugh. He had one very big story, though.

'I was probably eight or nine when I first heard about how he had come out with Harry Houdini. Later, when I was older, he told me more and more of the details … everything. But this is going to take some time, and I don't know if I can get to the important stuff in one go, just one sitting, Terry. Do you mind if it takes longer?'

'Mmm, depends on how appealing you make it,' Terry tried to joke. But Hal looked down at the floor, his expression beginning to sour.

'This will be worth your while. This is much more important than just tales, Terry.'

'All right, tell me what you can today and I'll see if I can come back. Must have been amazing to work with someone like that — what was your father's job?'

'No fancy title. An "assistant" was how he described himself. Harry had lots of those. Some were just muscle, you know, for the lifting and toting — and he didn't travel light. But my father was one of the important ones, that I know, and not just from his say-so. Harry told the trusted ones things he never told the blokes who just helped with the acts, the set-ups for shows and such.

'Francis Sargeson was right there, with Harry on his boat, when they came over by ship in 1910. He first told me about it when, as I say, I was just a kid, then at other times later on. I know it well, very well, even some of the dates. How about the third of February 1910, for starters?'

'Which was?'

'The date Harry Houdini's ship, the P&O *Malwa*, first entered Port Phillip Bay. My old man was standing right next to Harry and saw the look on his face when he heard the sound again — the sound the ship made when it shifted to half-speed, a sort of groan which also meant you were approaching a port. It was a welcome noise, the only good one that boat apparently ever made.

'They were at sea for six weeks. Steamed through Suez round to Bombay, across the Indian Ocean to Fremantle, in all kinds of seas and weather, docking in all types of ports. My father was familiar with each of the main commands — Full Ahead, Full Astern, Dead Slow — and all the ones between, as each shift of gear had its own special effect on the hull or keel, he said.

'But Houdini was way ahead of him. Mostly people only notice the obvious; same goes at sea — like changes in the wake, or the breeze coming at you on the foredeck. But Houdini, he always paid attention, everything big and small. Stored it all up in here …'

Hal paused to point to his temple, waited until Terry nodded before he continued. 'It was his style to listen and listen hard, to watch carefully, master the little things that mattered. Staying alive depended on being very, very careful … So there they were, heading into Melbourne. The tugs come alongside, and then a deckhand sends a hawser flying up to the men waiting at the bow bollard. Harry watches that coil of rope come flying up — you know the sort of thing, as thick as your wrist, three inches easy — a rope made of jute and flax as they used to be, and calls out, "Say, boys, got a length I can use in my act?" Typical Harry, that.

'Must have been a strange thing to stand and wait and look out to landfall that day, Terry, don't you think? Everything flat and featureless as far as you could see. But anyway, somewhere beyond the cranes and docks slowly becoming visible was the city of Melbourne. They were going to be performing there for six weeks, before Sydney, where it was to be another six.'

'Why here?' Terry asked with interest.

'Why Australia? Different theories. Some said it was the flattery that brought him all this way. Rickards, Harry S., was the promoter for this trip and he had agreed that Houdini would be paid even for the time he spent at sea. And no performer had ever been paid higher fees than he was offering.

'Harry didn't need more money — he was the highest paid performer in the world back then — but he was restless, hugely restless, all the time looking for the next big thing and then the next after that. He'd been that way since he was a little boy, they reckon. Anyway, late 1909, he and his group were in Europe looking round for some new engagements, but only in a half-hearted way; what they were really thinking was that maybe they should get back home — home in those days being New York City. They'd already been on a long tour.

'There were a lot of people, he had a big team, probably all sick of the travel. The top hands were …' Here Hal paused to count them off on his fingers, '… Kukol, Vickery, Brassac and my father — Frank Sargeson. A show like Houdini's took a lot of organising, it was like a military affair. They got on with each other and only argued sometimes and then only about small things, but they were all pretty much of one voice in late 1909.

'By then they'd been on the road for the past eighteen months. No performer had ever done a tour like that. They spent a whole eight months of 1908, from January to August, in England, before moving on to Europe. From September they played Germany, then England again, then back to Germany, then France. They weren't meant to go to France at all, but for Houdini seeing a biplane in Germany for the first time, and then being bitten by the flying bug. Which was a new and big thing back then.

'It was in Hamburg that they first heard about the Voisin plane, which was being built by a couple of boys by that name outside Paris. So instead of going home for a break before the next tour, Harry bought a plane and spent many days learning to fly. This was one of the first aeroplanes in the whole world; they had only made maybe five or six different kinds all up, and of course Harry had to have one.

'But then, as Harry said, "Why not? It seems that man is meant to fly after all." He told his crew that no-one had officially flown in Australia to that date. We're talking late 1909. And then what does Harry Houdini say next? "I mean to be the first," is what he says.'

'Good story so far, Hal. You must have paid attention to your old man.'

'Oh yes, I listened all right. And I learned, too. Now, where was I …? Oh, about that trip, coming into Port Phillip Bay … One of the men who couldn't wait to get off was Antonio Brassac. Antonio was a Frenchman, he was the aeroplane expert. Apparently he'd been a shade of green ever since they left Marseilles. But young Antonio was a good stick, according to my father.

'Antonio was keen on the plane, as you can imagine, but Harry loved it so much you couldn't keep him away from it, even on board ship. He was always hanging around it, always saying to whoever was handy, "Come on, let's see how she is," and he'd take them to that end of the deck and make them stand there and stare at it with him.

'That plane, they had protected it with tarpaulins against the weather and lashed it down. It was only the outline you could actually see, what with the way it was covered. Although Harry, he would stand there and see through all the angles and points in the canvas as if that cover just wasn't there … I'm no expert on those old planes, but it was said that this French job could not do as many things as the one the Wright brothers had made — but it was perfect for Houdini, who at that time considered himself still a novice.

'My father said, "You never saw a man get so much pleasure out of something," as Houdini did from that thing. When he got off the ground for the first time, which was in Germany and for a few seconds only, you never could believe such exhilaration possible. That a man could leave the earth at last … now that was really something! The thing couldn't be done without that Brassac though. He knew everything there was to know about those contraptions — he was vital if Harry was going to try for the local record. Which they did and which they got. At Diggers Rest, outside Melbourne. March 1910, it was.'

Terry was impressed at the amount of detail Hal had about Houdini — and he hadn't even landed him in Australia yet — and wondered how long this story might take. As he was looking at one flushed, not especially healthy-appearing older gent, he thought to ease him down for a moment or two.

'Hal, you know, you haven't said anything about yourself. You're retired, I guess. What did you do for a crust?'

'Definitely retired. Had lots of lousy jobs when I was young — and then the one, true vocation.'

'Which was?'

'I was a magician myself. An illusionist to be exact. In the game for years.'

'That's great! The Houdini connection, right? Why didn't you tell me earlier? Did you do escapes?'

'Yes, I did,' he said, with an effort at modesty. 'I studied them, collected a lot of information and plans. The big ones take a lot of doing, the good ones. But there's more to my telling you about Harry Houdini than escapes. Terry, it is my belief that all a man needs to learn about how to live can be learned from Harry Houdini. But, as my old man used to say, to learn from Houdini you have to know him first.'

'Right,' said Terry lightly, not wishing to sound any doubtful note. 'But on the other subject, do you seriously want to take me on?' This seemed an easier question than any he might ask about what Hal meant by what he had just said.

'To become a professional magician is a big thing, boy,' Hal answered earnestly. 'You've got to be trained, starting with the simple, then moving up. And that's not the whole story either because there are the realms … The most important thing of all, you've got to stick to the code … I've developed a few techniques of my own that I can explain to you, if you're willing.

'But here's the point, Terry: I will need twelve weeks. Give me twelve weeks. And give yourself twelve weeks. Because I reckon that's all I need to get you across the line …'

'What line, Hal?'

'The line that says you're well under way, that you've got the foundations. To being a professional magician. Right now, you're not even an apprentice, you're a baby. Interested?'

Terry did not have to think. 'Yes, I am.' He was more than ready to learn from someone who had practised the art to which he aspired.

'Good. Excellent. But you know something? I'm going to stop right here today, because there are a million things for you to take in and this is enough for now.' He pointed a bony finger at Terry. 'And you shouldn't think this is going to be in any way easy. Understood?'

Before Terry could answer, Hal abruptly got up from his chair and repeated, almost to himself, 'Enough for now, and maybe you need to think about this some more. Whether you want to come back.'

Terry studied the expression on Hal Sargeson's face. He saw some kind of yearning mixed with uncertainty, and something else he couldn't quite name, an odd kind of friendliness, some eagerness to please or help … Whatever it was, he would not disappoint him.

'Don't need to think about it. I'll absolutely come back if you want me to. I'm always ready to learn from an expert.'

The agreement was struck with a handshake as Hal walked Terry back to the door. He would turn up at Hal Sargeson's place after work each Wednesday and take instruction. Hal would work on a program for him.

3

A Real Magician

To have encountered a real magician the way he had, Terry took to be a mighty stroke of good luck. Even better, this Hal Sargeson had a connection to probably the best of the best, to Houdini himself. As to his grip on the art and craft of magic, Terry knew that Hal was much more knowledgeable than himself — and to learn from such a person would be far better than trying to follow the steps laid down in magic magazines. There was a question or two, however. Having taken almost a year to acquire his own meagre skills, twelve weeks did not seem a long enough period to get to a professional base. And there was the matter of how fair dinkum this Sargeson was — even if so far he hadn't asked for money or put anything to him that sounded like a scam.

Terry listened to the gears of his bus grind down as he pulled into the Town Hall stop. He waited for the last few stragglers to jump on board. Other days these delays would get to him, especially late in a shift when he was tired; today the rag-tag crew trundling up the bus's steps seemed more amusing than annoying. They took so long, he had plenty of time to drift. He recalled the success of the other night: pleasing to think his technique had so improved that he had quite usefully entertained that ailing bunch of old people. (A couple of whom he knew from when they'd been regular passengers of his.)

But as for these buses — after twenty years of driving them for a living, Terry was over the whole deal. The misery of endlessly steering a gas-powered Mercedes loaded with 50-plus passengers (wage slaves, pregnant women, shaky geriatrics, delinquents, idiots, complainers …) around the inner west of Sydney had got to be too much. Thank God he had found new occupations and interests in the past year, of which magic was the most recent and by far the best.

When he was at last able to close the door, Terry checked in his mirror that everyone was more or less in place. He was struck by how glum the passengers looked, a bunch of sad sacks. Possibly they needed some change in their lives too. Or some entertainment. He switched the engine off, then turned his head and called out, 'All settled?' When no-one answered, he was provoked to go a step further. 'Too bad. Bus has broken down …'

That stirred them up and various loud groans rolled towards him. At which he stood up and faced the throng. 'I'll give it one last go.' He sat down again, hit the ignition, and the engine started. Raising his hands in the air, he half turned, grinned and shouted 'Hooray!' and heard that repeated by one or two passengers, even somebody clapping. He set off again, thinking, *Yes, we all need a show* …

Moving once more down George Street, Terry looked at his watch: five pm and not too much longer before he would be back at the depot to clock off. As to getting home, he was in two minds.

Keen as he was to see Ricky, there was the distinct possibility that Jenny was gearing up to talk about her 'feelings' again. She had been doing that increasingly lately; the silence this morning had been ominous. Arguments between them were more frequent and Jenny was ever more agitated about what she called his 'future'.

Terry would agree that serious change — a job other than driving a bus — was proving hard to engineer, but there were one or two bright spots. If loath to say as much to Jenny, the magic was adding up to real pleasure, a change that had somehow authorised him to pursue other diversions and bits of fun as well. He now had a growing collection of exotic fish in a tank in the hall (recalling here that he had forgotten to feed them this morning). He had even gone back to his stamp collecting.

That evening, when it became clear that Jenny wasn't going to bail him up on their problems, Terry told her about the plan with Sargeson. 'If it works out,' he said breezily, 'it'll be a regular thing for a while. I'll just go and listen and see if there's anything to learn.' But Jenny was hardly thrilled to hear of this development, nor was Ricky when he told him. He looked forward to having his dad around on Wednesdays when he got home from school; he liked to join him in his shed where he was allowed to watch him working at his tricks or act as a pretend audience member. Terry was disappointed with their reaction. But he would keep his appointment with Hal.

*

Terry arrived at Sargeson's hall on the appointed Wednesday at the agreed time, mid-afternoon.

'Well,' Terry said, as soon as he had been let inside, 'your pupil's here! What are you going to teach me today, my man? Maybe there's something in one of those boxes that a learner could use?'

The older man waved this cheek away. 'In good time. We'll get to that and more, but the lesson begins today with Harry again. Are you ready for that?'

'I'm up for it, yes,' Terry said.

'So let's sit.'

Terry rubbed his hands together to suggest enthusiasm as Hal led him to his little arrangement of director's chairs and coffee table. Terry noticed that Hal was holding a piece of folded paper.

'What's that you've got there?'

Hal opened it out, then held it up for Terry to see. It was an antique theatre poster with the words 'The Great Houdini' arcing in old type across the top quarter. Underneath was an image of a very large, old-style metal milk can.

'Impressive! Tell me more.'

'Well, like it says here, this is a poster from what they called the New Opera House. In Melbourne. Early February 1910, Houdini and his team were there, my father with them.'

Hal handed it over for Terry to look at more closely.

'The old man used to say that nothing ever happens, or has happened, in this country. But wherever human beings live, things happen, no question. Look at the date on that poster. Just a few years before that the place was federated — and a few years later sent all those boys to the dreadful first war. My opinion is there was more taking place here than people elsewhere liked to admit, things that few would credit even today. My father was wrong about that, I reckon.

'But Frank called Houdini, Harry Houdini, a friend. And I don't believe he was mistaken about that. They'd spent months travelling the country, mounting the shows, performing, bumping them out again —'

'Bumping?' Terry interrupted, unsure about that word.

'Show talk for clearing out a production — there's a lot of work involved, you see. Something you'll learn if we kick on with this plan.

'Anyway, the pattern for Houdini was that everything had to be right for the first routine or there would be hell to pay. Things would just keep going wrong. The team had to go over the gear while Harry stood in front of the limelights and watched. They used to lay everything out on stage that was needed for the evening's performance.

'Their first show was at this Opera House of Mr Rickards, as I said. Everything was ready for the milk-can escape, the straitjacket escape and the coffin. Harry always required the right order to be observed.

'By the way, with the milk-can escape, they had to make a slight alteration. The cans Harry knew from America, as on the poster, were not available; but they'd found another kind of can here, called a Furphy, a kind of farm watering tank on wheels. It would do, and Harry himself was apparently impressed by the motto raised on one end — "Good, better, best, Never let it rest. Till your good is better, And your better best." Could have been Houdini's own motto, that.

'As for the set-up, some of those early stages were very rough. They used to put ground sheets out and roll them across. One of his assistants, could have been Kukol, would then pull open the lid on this can with the funny name, and Harry would climb in. After that, Kukol would set six padlocks for locking him in — "One, two, three, four, five, six …" Houdini would listen as each of those heavy locks was pushed home. Then Kukol had this technique of looking up, a question on his face like some faithful mutt. "Yes," Houdini would say from inside the can. "Loud enough."

'Then Kukol would come forward, put his fingernails under the edge and try to lift the lid. He'd get practically no movement, only the hard rattle of those locks hitting the sides of the can.'

'So,' Terry interrupted, 'how did Houdini get out of the thing?'

Hal gave him a thin, odd smile. 'He kept that to himself as you can imagine. Call it a professional secret … although I do happen to know.'

Seeing that Terry was a little disappointed, Hal said, 'Look, that's for later, Terry.' He picked up again quickly.

'That first night went well, so my old man said. After the show was over, Rickards, who was a bit of a character, came in and said, in this big voice he had, "Mr Houdini, they loved you!" "I'll bet they never saw one of those cans used like that before," Harry said in turn.

'In the dressing room afterwards, it was a huge crush — you can imagine. The biggest showman in the world is there and everybody wants a piece of him. They're bringing in flowers, cards, people are trying to get a private audience, you name it. Don't forget, at that time, no-one was more famous than Harry Houdini.'

'I knew he was big, but —'

'Oh yes, he was that and more. As you're going to find out! Anyway, that night my father himself learned some more about him. Once they'd cleared everyone out — Bess, Harry's wife, was there doing plenty of the pushing out too, by the way — Harry sits on a stool and asks if any mail has arrived from home. "We had the first today," Bess tells him.

'"Did she write? Did Mother write?" he asks. "Yes, she did," says Bess.

'When he hears this Harry stands straight up, like the energy had come back into him again. All excited he asks, "Where is it? Did you bring it?"

'Bess tells him that the letter, along with some others, is back at the hotel. And then Houdini did a strange thing. Not two seconds later, he grabs his coat, grabs each of them there by a hand, gives that killer smile of his, and starts dragging them off to leave the theatre …

'Harry could be what is called manic today — a word I don't like, but never mind. Imagine what it was to be with him when he was charging up. What could you do except go along with it? Nothing! So they trailed after him and at the stage door the manager asked them to wait because a path had to be cleared through fans outside. And there's Harry, holding his wife's hand, holding Frank Sargeson's hand, both tightly, and then he starts to dance on the balls of his feet — as if he's about to run a foot race.

'"Harry, Harry, when are you going to stop?" Bess asks him. "Never," he replies. But she's irritable at having been pulled along like a child, and says, "You will when you die, Harry!"

'Now that must have hurt. Houdini stops and stares at her. "Don't say that, Bess. Why do you have to say that?"

'A bad mood lasted until they'd gone some way towards the hotel, the Windsor, and then he says, Harry does, "Let's go somewhere else, I want to go for a decent walk with you, Bess, with my pal …"

'Something was always eating at Houdini, but he also had a big heart. He gave out to everybody, which I suppose was one reason his wife put up with him. So there he is and he grabs their hands even tighter and he asks directions of the man at the door. Next thing you know, he has them heading towards the Queens Bridge.

'After such a draining night, that particular walk was a relief, my father said. They marvelled at how warm it was, and Frank said how if this was New York, most probably it would be very bitter this time of the year. Going down Russell Street, Bess pronounced that Melbourne looked a bit like Philadelphia, only not so big. Houdini agreed with her whenever she spoke, but said not much. That was a man who really loved his wife!

'Eventually they got to the approaches to the bridge. "Looks kind of different at night," Harry says.'

'Had they been there before?' Terry asked.

'Oh sorry, forgot that. Yes, they'd done a reconnoitre earlier in the day because that bridge was meant to figure in the tour a few days later. So now they're on the bridge and Harry does another strange thing. He grips Bess's arm even more tightly and he increases the pace. "Let's go to the middle," he says.

'But then it seemed that Bess did not want to go out there. There were no other people, just the three of them, and I reckon she must have felt exposed, maybe even scared. My father remembered looking up at the sky, saw clouds racing, now covering the moon, now revealing it. It was eerie — and Harry did not like that moon, the way it was split exactly in half.

'At a certain point Harry stops, looks around for his bearings. "This is about it," he says.

'"What? Where you are going to jump?"

'"Yes …" he replies.

'Next he turns and takes Bess in his arms and kisses her hard. Right in front of my father — I mean the man was not shy when it came to his feelings. She wanted to respond but was a little embarrassed, as you can imagine. He's there, still holding her, and then he says, "Bess, I don't want you to die." And to my father he says, "Or you, Frank. Or anybody! Not you, not my mother, not anybody …"'

Hal stopped there, blew a long sigh. 'But, that's got to be enough for one day, Terry, wouldn't you say? Done enough talking.'

'That's some story, Hal. Christ. And you're talking about your very own father there?'

Hal did not reply but kept stock still, as if too deep in thought to respond. Terry got up and took a couple of slow steps to stretch his legs. He felt he had been given a glimpse, a personal, private glimpse, into the heart of one of magic's true royals. This Hal was gold. How amazing to have fallen in like this with a man connected to the best of the best. Even if it was his father who had featured, the way Hal told the tale had made the distance nothing at all.

Now Hal got up. 'Right!' he said briskly and unexpectedly. 'Time to show you a little something, as I promised.'

'Sure you want to?' Terry asked.

'Absolutely.'

Hal had to get his bearings for a moment. He stared at his storage crates and after a time said, 'Ah yes, I know …' then went to look through one of them. There was some rattling around, then he pulled out a number of large metal rings. There were eight of them in all, each about twenty-five centimetres across. He turned to face Terry.

'Okay. Seen the linking rings illusion?'

'Only on television once. Never done it myself.'

'So then, watch, and I'll explain later.'

Hal put the rings on the floor momentarily so as to roll up his sleeves.

'Never forget to do this, eh? There's an expectation of honest toil in rolled up sleeves — oldest trick in the book.'

Hal took up the rings and with precision began to move them about — one into the other, then out again, somehow joining and unjoining them in a way that defied the unity and integrity of each. Terry was as pleased to watch him work as anyone else would have been, magician or not. It was a satisfying spectacle, made the more so by the loud clink of the rings as they appeared to do the impossible.

As he found his rhythm and began to move them ever more swiftly, a smile widened on Hal's face. 'Ha! Doesn't take long for it to come back,' he said. Then, with a circling of his arms and a flourish, he ended with all eight rings being joined in the one instant. 'And there you have it!'

Terry clapped enthusiastically. 'Well done, mate. I'd be keen to use those myself.'

'I'm sure you would, Terry. The linking of things is a common theme in magic. There could be more of it in life, too. Now come closer and you can have a go.'

Hal handed the rings to Terry. 'Simple enough, aren't they? Even Houdini used these when he was starting out. Surprised you haven't got a set already.'

Terry gripped the cold, smooth, hardened steel in his hands tightly. He felt a touch embarrassed — of course he should have had a set of these by now. 'Well, I haven't been at it that long …'

'You need to learn the art and the craft,' Hal said softly. 'Every magician is an apprentice for a time. Has to be. But the magician's master doesn't have to be alive. Thanks to my old man, Houdini became mine — and he was long dead when I got started.' He looked at Terry intently. 'I knew when I first saw you that you needed a model too.' When he spoke next, it was almost with a religious passion. 'Houdini, Terry. I'm absolutely convinced he is the one for you, as he was for me. Let him be your teacher. For blokes like us, who better to learn from in the whole wide world?'

Terry listened hard. He opened his mouth as if to answer, but stopped himself. The feeling of animation and more, of excitement, that had come over him could not be denied. The idea was so grand, improbable, he thought he should get his head together before he said anything or it would sound stupid. The life, the work of Houdini — as he was coming to learn of it so directly — was extraordinary, brilliant even. He felt as if he should have known far more about the man than he did, even as a novice. Now something came to mind to ask.

'Obviously Harry was the king, but what about local magicians, Hal? Any worth following here?'

Hal snorted. 'Locals? Plenty of them, but all deadbeats. No imagination. You always have to look beyond little old Aussie to become the genuine article, I say.'

'Where was he from, do you know?'

'That's another thing — he was an American Jew, out of Hungary originally. A mongrel, bit like you and me. But Terry, Houdini never lined up in anybody's army. He was from everywhere and nowhere, mate. Houdini was Houdini!'

Terry waited while Hal drew some deep breaths. He gave the impression that he knew he'd become overexcited and needed to calm down. One, two, three, and he next spoke in a more measured way.

'Sorry, I get carried away sometimes. Anyway, that's a start on Harry. I learned from him, direct and indirect, Terry. And you will too. But there's the practical work, much practical work in this profession. And you being a baby at all this, there's plenty for you to learn.'

'I'm beginning to get that,' Terry replied. 'The shops are full of tricks and —'

'Stop right there!' Hal cut him off, sounding frustrated. 'That's exactly what I mean about you being a baby! To be a true magician, which means to be an illusionist, you need a special kind of *real* knowledge, which is art and craft and more. It's about what you pick up from those who went before and then it's about what you do with that, how you shape it so that you become your own man. As for me, I stayed a novice until I worked my way through the four realms.'

Now Hal held up one hand and, extending one finger after another, intoned loudly:

'Lowest is Escape.

'Next comes Disappearance.

'Third is Levitation.

'Fourth is Metamorphosis … big one that, because some say metamorphosis is something that's inside and outside the knowledge. I reckon it's more about where you finish up than what you're capable of. And then, along with the realms, there's our code of behaviour too. So you see, you got a long way to go, Terry. But one day, who knows …? We'll see.'

Conscious that the rings he still held had warmed in his hands, Terry shifted his grip. Hal noticed.

'Want to have a go?' he asked.

'Not just yet,' Terry said and smiled. 'Not just yet.'

Terry handed the rings back to Hal and was starting to feel overloaded but wanted to make something clear. 'What you're offering is great, and generous. And yes, I'll take Harry Houdini as my guide too, if you show me how. But it's a big ask … and I'm no great student.'

'Excellent! I mean that you're willing. Won't be easy, but so what?' Hal grinned at him.

Conscious that the rings he still held had warmed in his hands, Terry shifted his grip. Hal noticed.

'Want to have a go?' he asked.

'Not just yet,' Terry said and smiled. 'Not just yet.'

Terry handed the rings back to Hal and committed to come back for a further 'introductory session' as Hal suggested, then made to leave. He stopped briefly at the door.

'By the way, that thing with the rings — which realm was that?'

'That? None of them — it's just a cheap trick.'

Out in the cool air and heading to Goulburn Street, Terry couldn't understand why this Hal Sargeson wanted to make such an effort with him, someone he hardly knew. He got into his car and paused to weigh up the attractions. They were considerable. But how could a part-timer, an amateur like himself, make the leap to professional magic, let alone aspire to Houdini's model? He had no support at home or anywhere else much. And yet there was this ex-pro …

Terry sat a minute longer, then asked himself a simple 'Why not?' What if this turned out to be the one big thing for him, the thing he had been unable to find so far? He was forty years old, practically middle-aged; how much longer did he have to get on a path that he could tread well, that led somewhere or to something of use or pleasing to others? He'd had a taste of the possibilities of magic already, even if his steps so far had been low-key and stumbling. In magic, you tell your audience that amazing things can happen. Then you make them happen. He could begin by believing this himself.

He turned on the ignition and with it the radio. An Abba song: 'I had a dream …' Terry turned up the volume and drove into the traffic, whistling as he went, smiling at how right and how stupid the lyrics were.

4

The Right Order of Things

Terry stopped working for a moment. In the din he had been making, he wondered whether he might have missed a call from the house. The shed was a good ten metres from the back door that led to the kitchen, and he would not have heard if Jenny (or young Ricky either) had been calling him for dinner. Probably wasn't a good time to be in here, early Saturday evening as it now was, but there were few other opportunities. He had begun this project since last seeing Hal and was determined that this chance didn't slip away.

He was planning for the training ahead. In anticipation of the second of Hal's realms he would build his own magician's cabinet: the style of cabinet that was needed to make objects disappear — inanimate objects in the first instance (making an assistant disappear was, he believed, a long way off). He did not have the money to buy a cabinet, as the professional type came at considerable cost and usually had to be imported from overseas. And then, although they were not struggling, there was no way to convince Jenny it was anything other than an extravagance. He'd eventually found on the net some diagrams for a homemade version, using cheap pine and bits and pieces from the local timber yard.

When he'd described this alternative, Jenny was all raised eyebrows and mutterings (and a shake of the head when she thought he wasn't looking). But he was unwilling to give up on it, and had taken it on as a DIY, low-cost shed 'project'. This afternoon's effort had involved fitting one of the sides to the box, which meant the power saw and a lot of noisy hammering.

But now, nearing six o'clock, Terry was too tired to keep going. He wiped his forehead on his sleeve and put his tools away, listening all the while for sounds from the house. Still no summons came from inside.

He closed his eyes tightly, so as to squeeze out some of the sweat that had run down over his brows. He would keep them shut for as long as it took, waiting for the stinging to subside; he concentrated on the back of his eyelids to block out the discomfort. Only to be struck by something that began to form there in the swirling patterns of blood and nerve discharges.

Terry tried to bring the image up more distinctly. He scanned what he thought he could see, panning across, then up and down. No doubt about the setting, the scene. A beautiful blue sky, the blue almost thrillingly intense, over some lush green fields. Pastures? He looked to see if there were animals, cows or sheep. None of those, but some creatures were evident in the foreground, towards the bottom left of this vision. They were moving about, but what were they?

His eyes still shut Terry tried to identify those dark shapes, recognise those movements. The moment he thought he had made sense of things was the moment he opened his eyes again in fright. His pulse had risen almost instantly, he could feel it pounding in his ears. He stumbled back a step, almost falling over the saw horse behind him.

The shapes were human, a man and a woman, each dressed in black, arms and legs covered; they had been gripping each other and pulling one way then the other. Two people wrestling, fighting. He was certain they were his mother and father. The third figure, also in black but standing back from the other two, he apprehended in that same instant. It was a teenage boy, it was him. He felt a jolt in his chest.

He straightaway went to the work bench, looking for distraction. He would occupy himself somehow. He picked up a stray hammer to hang on the pegboard behind the bench.

No use. His hands had begun to shake and he kept missing the hook. 'Oh for fuck's sake ...' As broad as the curve of the claw was, he was unable to get it to sit on the board. After a couple more attempts he threw the hammer down on the benchtop, where it clanged loudly.

He heard the back door open and close, then the light footsteps of his son tapping along the concrete path towards the shed.

Terry turned towards the shed door, working up his best evil grin to surprise Ricky.

The boy entered, and Terry called out to him. 'Ta, da!' he boomed, his mouth contorted, his lips spread as far as he was able. 'And who does this remind you of?'

Ricky looked confused, unable to recognise the expression of evil sarcasm.

'I heard a noise before.'

'It's nothing ... I dropped something. Go on, guess!'

'Um … is it Batman? No wait, Spiderman?'

'Batman was close — it's meant to be the Joker.' Terry stood aside to reveal what he'd been working on.

'Wow,' Ricky said as soon as he saw the unfinished cabinet. 'You've done heaps, Dad.'

'Do you like it?' Terry asked, relieved by his son's reaction.

'Yeah!'

'Not finished yet, but getting there. Look, if I show you how it's going to work, you won't tell anyone, will you?'

'No way!'

Terry pulled open the front door, which he had not yet hinged, only propped in place. 'See how it's open at the back? It's going to have mirrors inside connected to the two back corners and a black cloth there that looks like wood, so that my assistant — maybe you! — can get out when I give the signal.'

'Would I be able to do that?'

'You would, it's not hard — just another trick really. If you learn the steps, the right order of doing things, anyone can do it.'

Ricky came closer, inspected the front and both sides, then went to the open rear. 'But where do you go when you come out the back of it?'

'Good question. Depends a bit on how the stage is set up — you know, the place where you do it. On some stages for magic, there'd be a trapdoor, but mostly they don't have them so you have to set up curtains and stuff around the cabinet and use mirrors and make the space inside look like it's deep, when it's not really because the space is divided …'

Ricky tried to take in what his father was saying for a moment or two, but looked confused.

'Hard to get your head around, isn't it? Never mind, I'm not that sure myself. Something we can learn together, eh?'

Preoccupied as he was, Terry did not hear the next set of footsteps on the path. The shed door was pulled open all of a sudden, startling him. He spun around to see Jenny backlit in the last of the light. She did not move but stood gazing into the shed's interior. Terry felt pinned in place, somehow diminished, as her eyes settled on the mess still on the floor. He did not believe he was fooling himself or anyone else with this magic and began to feel resentful. Jenny said nothing but kept standing there, the silence growing until Ricky, sensing something wrong between his parents, broke it.

'Look what Dad's built, Mum! Isn't it great?'

'I'm sure it is, Ricky, but I wouldn't mind if you came inside and helped me set the table.'

'Let him be. I'll do it,' Terry said.

'No, Ricky can do it. You've obviously got plenty to be going on with here.'

Ricky stalled any further talk by skipping past his mother to do as he'd been asked. The speed with which he left made Terry feel worse. Did he have any real pull with the boy, other than as occasional entertainment value?

As for things between him and Jenny, he knew their differences were becoming more pronounced. Each had a pretty good idea what was happening, even if they hadn't stated as much to each other. They both understood that some of the difficulties had arisen from the changes in her — not the least being that she had so determinedly forged ahead with a career in dentistry.

Jenny had worked part-time as a dental technician for years before Ricky was born. Once he had started school, she had enrolled at university as a mature age student. Clever and no slouch, she whizzed through her studies, graduated, and had found a position without trouble. She had been working professionally for the past year in a practice at Five Dock. As if to make her choices even clearer to the world, a shingle had gone up at the practice announcing her as 'Jennifer Anagnos'. Hardly anybody knew her anymore by her Greek first and married name, Eugenia Voulos.

The other problem between him and Jenny, Terry knew, was decidedly himself.

A few more minutes passed before he heard Ricky call him from the back door of the house: 'Dad! Dinner's ready!'

The sound of his voice was a small joy, energising him. He quickly swept the off-cuts and sawdust lying on the floor into a pile and dumped it in the bin, then turned off power switches and threw a sheet of canvas over his unfinished work.

They ate in tense silence, Terry and Jenny avoiding eye contact. Terry could see that Ricky knew something was wrong from the way he looked out from under his brows at each of them.

'Hey Rick, wassup? What's been happening at school?' he spoke up brightly. The boy turned to him, seemed relieved that someone had finally said something.

'Nothing much. Mrs Waterford started crying in our room, we don't know why. Then she went outside and left us on our own.'

'From putting up with you lot, probably ... Joking!' Terry said and reached across to give him a little shove.

When she saw a cheeky expression forming on Ricky's face,

Jenny sent his father a look that said 'stop it'. She was of the view that teachers and schools should not have to put up with bad behaviour; she had never had much time for Terry's anti-teacher subversiveness.

'Maybe if kids didn't muck up so much, the teachers could do their jobs better, Terry,' she said, mainly for the boy's benefit.

'Maybe, yes,' he replied quietly, hoping he still had Ricky's sympathy in the matter. But the boy looked torn now.

'Hey, help me clean up, Ricky,' Terry said, 'and afterwards I want to show you a magazine I got in the mail.'

'What magazine?' asked Ricky as he followed his father around picking up plates and cutlery. 'Dad, Dad, tell me!'

'You'll just have to wait,' his father teased.

A little later, when Jenny had gone to her home office, Terry sat down with the copy of *Just Magic* and patted the sofa next to him where he wanted Ricky to sit.

Ricky did not hesitate and immediately leaned across his father to stare at the pages he'd opened.

'Have a look at this,' Terry said. 'Isn't it great? All the latest stuff. All the gear you need for magic tricks, all the best techniques, they're right here …'

Ricky looked on intently, trying to catch something on each page before his father turned to the next. Terry was pleased that the boy seemed interested. But then, before he'd got to the end, Ricky stood up abruptly and said, 'That's great, Dad, but got to do my project now.'

Terry was about to get up himself when Jenny reappeared. She came in bearing a handful of colour brochures which she placed squarely on the coffee table in front of Terry.

'I want you to take a look at these please, Terry.'

Real estate brochures. Knowing straightaway what these meant, Terry had no desire to pick them up. Jenny tried not to react to his usual resistance. In a level voice she said, 'I want us — you — to get serious about what I've been telling you.'

'About what?' he replied, regretting the words immediately.

Jenny snapped. 'Oh, don't start. You know very well. My parents can't keep living on their own in that big old place of theirs. We need to trade up. We need a bigger place to take them in. Especially my mother.' Jenny scanned the room quickly, as if measuring it up. 'These Ashfield houses are just not big enough.'

'No, Ashfield's definitely not big enough,' he muttered.

'Terry, stop that. This is serious.'

'Okay, Okay.' He put his hands up in mock surrender. 'But really, what's the problem? They've got dough, they're still living in Bellevue Hill. She's independent. She's still driving, for Pete's sake …'

At that, Jenny leaned forward and snatched up the brochures. 'Right! That's your attitude. Looks like I'm going to be organising this on my own then, doesn't it?' She stamped off, spinning around for a moment to face him before leaving the room. 'Because you, Terry, are completely useless.'

Terry took up his magazine again, trying to focus on the cover, the title. It was pointless. She had got past him, so far past him that these days he only ever felt he was bobbing in her wake. Besides the very average wage he drew from the buses, he had felt for a long time that there was little of his own that he could add, that made any sort of positive difference, to how things worked around here — certainly little that was acceptable to Jenny.

An inability to 'better himself', as Jenny termed it, was conceded. The tension over housing also had a history. Not so long ago her father had dropped in one day when his daughter was out, to tell Terry that he had been looking around the local real estate agents for the sort of place that his Eugenia was interested in. That had come as complete news to Terry. She had described it to him, his father-in-law said, and he had gone looking: something on a quarter-acre block at least, renovated rather than original Federation, and with a lockup garage for two cars if possible. Terry did not blame her father, he liked him as it happened. He was a quiet, peaceful man who doted on his daughter and would do anything for her.

Feeling bypassed, rejected, on that occasion Terry had shouted at Jenny across the dinner table, something about irrelevant snobbery and wasting money, all the while clenching his fists and once or twice hitting the table — a tirade she had met impassively and which had succeeded only in upsetting the child. He had felt terrible afterwards, frightened that he had been close to violence.

Ever since, whenever he felt inclined to anger, even if only verbal, Terry was reminded of the pact he'd made with himself. His father had been a belter and a slapper, his mouth nasty along with it — all of which he'd applied not for serious harm, but to bring quick, stinging humiliation. Through the years of his marriage to Jenny, before and after they'd had a child, in moments of heat or irritation, what it was like to be on the receiving end had never been far from Terry's mind. Whatever mess he made of things, he would never harm his family, never give in and hurt someone.

He had overreacted to those brochures, he told himself. He could live with his in-laws, if that was what Jenny really wanted. No, there was another spur in the resistance he had put up. He believed he had already begun to ask something more of himself, he had already begun to better himself. But the form of this was still secret, unacknowledged, and definitely not something he had shared with Jenny.

Yes, things were changing, Terry was convinced. He could see a way forward. A new idea was taking shape for him, an idea that would have a productive outcome for himself and for everyone else. He simply needed a bit more time to make it all real.

5

Queens Bridge

At their next session Hal Sargeson's earlier fervour was quickly reignited. 'Are you ready for a further instalment?'

'Ready and willing, Hal.'

Hal smiled at him so magnanimously, inclusively, that Terry felt he was truly being offered something special. A gift in some form. He returned a small grin of his own in appreciation.

'Good,' said Hal, still watching Terry's face. 'Good,' he said once more, then lightly tapped him on one shoulder to turn him towards the director's chairs.

'So continue,' said Terry. 'Your father and Houdini were on that bridge …'

'They were, they were. You see, they had decided on a bridge jump to get the locals' attention. Harry had come to dislike that escape to the point of truly hating it; he had performed it that many times, he saw it as nothing more than a stunt. But that was always a crowd-puller, that was. There was a season ahead and expectations were high for the usual success, and for big numbers.

'To settle the location they'd asked Rickards's advice. Rickards recommended a bridge on the Yarra — which, as you know, runs through the city itself. And specifically mentioned a bridge where, on any work day, you could always expect crowds of people. If it was announced that Houdini was to perform one of his famous escapes, you could expect, he had said, a crowd of at least ten thousand.

'So they get to that bridge that day and look in both directions and see the Australian promoter had done his job well — a huge crowd had gathered. The police had closed the approaches to the bridge to all vehicular traffic. Everyone was waiting to see what the great Houdini would do. Harry might not have had much time for that stunt anymore — would have performed it dozens of times already — but he also knew that everyone expected him to do this very thing. That he would risk his life for them, for their viewing.

'So everyone who went there, all these men and women and children who were there, crushing against the barriers, you could say were in a kind of pact with Harry …

'What does he do next? He pulls the cord of his gown — which was a bit like a prizefighter's, only nicer — tighter round his waist and climbs the steps to a platform the team had put up against part of the bridge railing. There he stands and waits for Kukol. Kukol is busy untying the straps of a burlap bag. When he eventually has them loose, he pushes the sides down to reveal the object the master has to defeat. A 75-pound iron ball and chain.

'Kukol lifts the ball and, with both arms wrapped tightly around it, takes the steps, slowly, with difficulty.

'Then it's Rickards's turn. He comes up, megaphone in one hand, and shouts, "Ladies and gentlemen! Step up, step up!" You can imagine. Everybody would have been startled at that noise.

Apparently the chap had a voice like a klaxon; no wonder he had made his name as a fight promoter.

'Rickards drones, he bellows, his voice runs up and down a scale all of his own. As for Houdini, he would have been paying no attention to what he was saying, he would have been going through the steps in his mind as he stood against the barrier. Try to picture it: there he is, staring directly out over the river — you could see a blue, smoky haze hovering over the water, blue skies above, green banks beyond. He's a guy who's arrived at the threshold, again.'

'Threshold?' Terry asked.

'Think about it. What happens if he gets it wrong …?'

'He dies,' said Terry.

'Yes, he dies,' said Hal. 'So now Harry takes off his robe and hands it to Kukol. Kukol places it to one side, then goes down on one knee for the next part — clamping the chain brace around the boss's ankle. The boss would never look at him when he did that. And nor did he look when a young boy came up behind him to pull on and test that chain.

'I can hear the boy's voice, Terry. You can too, if you listen in your head. Through the megaphone the kid would have shouted out something like, "It's real all right, everybody!"

'Then Rickards calls for a volunteer. "Could we have a gentleman come up, please? A gentleman, please. Ladies, with your indulgence, as this is a delicate matter …" And with that, some fool of a young bloke comes up and stares at Harry stupidly.

'Houdini opens the gown and allows himself to be touched and prodded.

'"Has he concealed anything, sir?" Rickards asks.

'"No, he's got nothing …"

'"Thank you. And before you go, sir, the great Houdini has informed me he wishes to be further bound. Would you do the honours?"

'Kukol hands this guy a length of chain, shows him how to pull it around Houdini tightly, and where to secure it with three padlocks. Then all the coming and going ends and Kukol is on his knees again.

'Harry's set himself and needs only to hear the command. It comes. "Mr Houdini, when you are ready, sir!" says Kukol and slowly passes him the ball. The chain falls hard against Harry's leg and he holds the ball tight against his chest, takes the short step up to the rail. One leg, then the other. He balances on the edge for as long as it takes to find perfect stillness. Three, four, five seconds. And then to move away from the bridge as quickly as possible, he bends his legs, then straightens them with all the effort of which he is capable.

'Looking down, this was particularly grey and muddy water … Have you ever taken a good look at the Yarra, Terry? Looks like sewage, plain and simple. Can you visualise him falling into that?'

'I can, Hal, yes,' said Terry, more engrossed in this story by the minute.

'As usual, he disappears. As usual, the waiting starts.'

'That's bloody scary, Hal. So what did he do down there?' Terry asked. 'How did he get free?'

'Details in a minute, but I can tell you what had to be done first,' Hal replied. 'Releasing air slowly, a few bubbles at a time as was his method, he began working away at the locks and chains.

'Meantime, people on that bridge would have been afraid, wondering what was happening, calling out. He was under there for over a minute and a half, after all. But those who knew, his crew, they would have seen that everything was fine from the bubbles, all being as it should. And then, after a few small twists this way and that, he was free.

'So Harry turns toward the light above and strokes for the surface. He breaks through, finds the air his body sorely needs, looks around. The roar goes up all right, but this time there's no joy in it. There are gasps, and then someone lets out a long, horrible cry.

'Harry shields his eyes with one hand, waves with the other, smiles. But still nothing comes of what he was used to — laughter, relief, hoorays. What was wrong? Those against the rails, on the river shore too, were pointing, waving down at something; what more could they want, he must have been thinking.

'But as he turns to swim to the nearest bank, he sees. There beside him, not three yards away, is some white and shining thing. He can't tell at first, but then it rolls and a face looks across at him, teeth bared, like it's grinning at him. Another moment and it turns away, as if in disgust at *him*. He's disturbed a dead body, it's floated to the surface …'

Terry contemplated the image Hal had just presented him. Whatever else his father had been, he could obviously paint a picture with words. And what a frightening picture it had been.

'Jesus … and you tell me that really did happen?'

'Yep. Don't take my old man's word for it — it was in the newspapers at the time. Now, remember what I mentioned to you last time? The four realms? Let's see what sort of a student you are. Which one are we talking about here?'

Terry did not have to think too long. 'The first I guess … Escape?'

'Well done, escape it was. Notice how I mentioned Harry seemed to be bored with this version of it, too? That's what my father reckoned and it makes sense. Harry was moving on to greater things. It's what happens as you progress. You can't just be satisfied with what you know, Terry, you've got to be always moving on.'

'So go on — tell me more about how he did it. How did he get out of all that?'

'Well, until he got it down pat, it would have been a very risky exercise, I know that. There were no trick locks, he had to physically release himself. He used a pick, a small turning tool like a key.'

'Which was where? I thought he had hardly any clothes on?'

'Where? I could say modesty forbids, Terry, but use your imagination. Where could you hide an implement like that and not have it be seen? Just inside your costume, it would show. Had to be further down, and below, right?'

Terry's eyes opened wide: 'You're kidding! How did he get it out of there?'

'Nothing much to it, just amazing physical dexterity and split-second timing. There's a pact here, see. Harry's part was that he would risk his life this way; the audience's part was that they were prepared to hold their breath to see whether he survived — most of them, no doubt, wanted to see him survive, some probably hoped he would die … But, sooner or later, escape was never going to be enough for Harry Houdini.'

Terry mulled over those last words — and concluded it would be some time, if ever, before he reached such a stage.

'Hal, you haven't told me about your own career.'

Hal did not answer immediately, looked as if he wasn't sure at all that he should until he relented with, 'Oh, I suppose you should know …' He slowly went over to his blue crates. 'Need to consult my files first,' he called to Terry, then began lifting one box off another. He eventually pulled out what he was looking for — a small stack of bill posters — and came back to show them to Terry. 'There you go, that was me in my heyday,' he said with some self-mockery.

Terry leafed through the posters. Prominent on each was a photo of a much younger Hal, sometimes in dress tails and top hat, with the words 'Hal Sargeson, Master of the Realms. A Show of Magic like No Other' arranged above and below in a swirling typeface.

'You look pretty good, Hal,' Terrry said, grinning. 'So, how did you go back then?' Terry tried to gauge the date of the posters — he guessed they were mainly from the 1960s and '70s. 'Did people come to see you?'

'They did. Until about the mid-seventies. Then they went off. And I went off too.'

'Off?'

'That's another story.'

6

The Westering Sun

A few minutes after three in the afternoon, an early June day. To look west along Alistair Road was to be blinded by the dust-magnified glare of the lowering sun. Drivers heading in that direction at that time of the day routinely slowed. Anyone standing by the side of the road could see them pulling visors down, raising a hand to deflect the still potent rays. Those who were cautious by nature anyway, those who knew there was a school at the intersection of Johnston Street and Alistair Road.

At this time, the pupils of Alistair Road Primary School would exit by the side gate to go home. The lollipop man would steer them to the north–south pedestrian crossing — those whose homes were on the north side at least. Today, Ricky Voulos, with two of his mates, Tony and Em, made their own little gang as they waited to be told when to cross. As no-one was waiting to pick him up from the school gate, Ricky thought he would walk home by himself. Why not? He was not a little kid anymore, but eight, going on nine, years old.

His *yaya*, his grandmother Anastasia, was in fact on her way to pick him up and walk him home. It was a change of plans as

Terry had mistakenly thought he was rostered off and would be able to collect Ricky. He had called Anastasia from the depot and she was happy to oblige.

Anastasia knew the drill. She had often met Ricky after school and always enjoyed seeing the boy — she had only one grandchild after all — but with her hip playing up she could not drive and had struggled with the trip from Bellevue Hill to get to the Ashfield school on time. A person whose health was beginning to fail and given to nervousness on a good day, she had been more than usually preoccupied this afternoon.

That no-one was there for Ricky at the bell was one thing: it was also windy and dusty and he and the other kids were impatient, fractious. Em jostled Tony, Tony gave Ricky a little shove. Ricky had not been watching the lollipop man, did not bother to look around, and took the push to mean they should go. He stepped onto the bitumen.

At that moment his grandmother, arriving flustered and in some pain at the opposite corner, saw him and panicked. Sure he was going to run into the road, she took three steps forward herself, holding her arm out in front, trying to get him to stop. No sooner was she on the roadway than the boy wheeled around and scampered back to the footpath. He turned again to look at her: wide-eyed, open-mouthed, he had spotted his *yaya*. She smiled and waved to suggest he was not in any trouble, everything was all right. In that same instant she saw the lollipop man reach an arm across him, to hold him on the kerb, and was relieved.

Anastasia did not see the car that hit her. She was facing the other way and did not see the mountain of steel and rubber and glass that bore down on her, that compressed her 68-year-old body into half its size at the moment of impact. That threw her six metres into the air and sent her landing in a crumpled heap in the middle of the road. She did not see the car that killed her.

But Ricky Voulos did. There and then as it happened.

Free of the lollipop man, Ricky launched himself onto the road. But Ricky could do nothing to change anything. All he could do was stagger, then hurry — halt, hurry, halt, his hands to his ears, to his mouth, his eyes — towards the prone body that seemed to be lying so far, so very far away. The body of his grandmother, Terry's mother-in-law, Jenny's mother, limp and bent and bloodied, had already gone further again.

*

The following Tuesday it was done. A body had been interred. Anastasia's funeral was over. Terry stood looking down at the sheet of green plastic turf thrown over the hole — a neat cover until everyone was gone and the gravediggers could return to pile the earth in over that small coffin. He felt the spaces around him; fifty or more people stood here, but the distances seemed to grow ever larger. No-one was close. No-one was coming close. What was he meant to do?

Paralysed himself, he saw Jenny make a move towards him. She had stood opposite him at the graveside, across that tear in the earth. She had shown no inclination to be near him, had taken instead a position among her own family. Her distraught, haunted-looking father, her two stumbling, trying to be brave sisters. He looked across at her as they tried to distract her, tried to take her arm and lead her away.

Apart from letting him know what arrangements she and her family had made for her mother's funeral, Jenny had not spoken to him since the day of the accident. Now she would not be held back. She came around quickly and her breath was warm against the side of his face. 'You bastard, Terry, you bastard …' Her voice was a tumble of small gravel off a metal barrow.

'Jenny …'

'How could you not have got there? How come you are never there when you're needed?'

'Jenny, what's that got to do with —'

'You said you would pick him up and you didn't. And the sum total, the end result, is you've killed my mother and traumatised my son.'

'For God's … you don't think I wanted …'

Jenny did not move away but put a hand up to say 'stop'. He may have been standing next to her and speaking but she was not going to listen to what he had to say at this moment.

Jenny had closed him out to give herself time to think, Terry told himself. He knew she was exhausted, distraught, but also that she could not have stopped herself blurting out those words. His distractedness, his 'not-there'-ness that she'd put up with for so long had contributed, in her view, to the disaster.

He had given her reason before this terrible event to lash out from time to time, complain at the way he was and the effect it had on her. He knew she had felt let down. Worse was that she seemed to believe she had somehow *allowed* Terry to let himself and her down over their time together. In permitting him to go on the way he had, not insisting he get help, or laying down the law, issuing an ultimatum or two. Forcing him to confront himself.

What had been his problem, what was his problem, he could never exactly put his finger on. He could never say; she could never say. Terry knew he was not a bastard, he was a kind enough person in his own way, but this was probably the best that could be said for him. He also knew he was a man uncomfortable in his skin and that had had so many negative effects. To have taken his issues on with greater focus might have helped, or it might not. Now Jenny seemed set on a separate path, for herself and for their son, convinced she was doing the right thing.

'Jenny?' Terry said, trying to break through. She heard him, but the insistent note in his voice added to her distress. She swung round, anger rising. 'Forget it, Terry! Forget me, forget everything. Okay? Look what you've done to your own father.'

Terry did not have the strength to ignore her pointing finger, the way she directed him to consider his old man, the pile of skin and bones standing there in his one and only crumpled grey suit. Terry saw the vacant, downcast stare, the handkerchief clutched in his hand and felt the blows multiply upon his own skull.

Her sisters caught up to Jenny, and again gently tried to lead her away. Only when she had begun to cry once more could they ease her from the graveside. Not before the eldest, Diana, had turned to give Terry one last dark look.

He thought to go after her, to say something, but found his path blocked almost straightaway. Margot from the depot office was in front of him, looking up at him. Margot, good pal that she was, had come to Rookwood to support him, he knew, although she had not yet spoken to him. She was saying something now, something consoling. He heard only words, noises on the wind, things to nod at before accepting her squeeze of his forearm, before taking himself away.

In the end, Jenny insisted on going home with her father and sisters. Terry did not immediately leave but wandered to another part of the cemetery. He found himself in a section where death was no longer fresh and real, but took the form of faded lettering on crumbling and lichen-covered stone, a corner of aged and broken sandstone angels, columns, plinths. He would wait until everyone else had left before returning to the carpark.

In the car, he sat for a long time before putting the key into the ignition. He felt immobilised, obliged to wait just where he was. Do nothing for a time longer. There was nothing to be done that made any sense. Nothing worth doing.

The thought came to Terry that he might stay here. Get out of the car and go back into this heartland, into the growing dark, among these trees and shrubs and plantings, until he might somehow disappear into the earth himself. An elderly woman had died. Friends, people they knew and people they didn't, would learn of her fate and accuse him, or pity him or hate him.

Maybe he knew he hadn't committed the deed himself, but maybe what Jenny had said was right. Her mother's death was real, and somehow at this moment he felt responsible. Why did he feel this way? Why not? was the better question. What was he but an unimaginative dud of a human being? A failure. Why shouldn't he feel that a good person, otherwise unnoticed, minding her business, trying to look after his son, had met her end because of an idiot like him who couldn't organise a simple timetable properly? That was the reality. And against that measure, he didn't believe he squared up at all. Any plans he might have been developing at this instant made no sense whatsoever.

As for the bright, gentle little boy who was his son, something had happened to him. Ricky didn't seem to want to speak to him. What had his mother said to him? What did he himself think? He refused to say. Was he still in shock? But if he felt his father was responsible for his grandmother's death, why would he ever want to talk to Terry again?

In the days that had followed Anastasia's death, Terry had felt that his life had become even more indistinct, that it had the consistency and shape of smoke. He was barely hanging on to any picture at all of himself in the world. Nothing was in the slightest way real. A feeling only made worse by what they were meant to do next — hold a wake for his mother-in-law.

*

Jenny had wanted to spare her father the agony of holding the event at Bellevue Hill, in a house filled with memories of his wife, so it was organised for their place at Ashfield. As much as he was allowed, Terry helped with the preparations. Finger food was passed around. A sad toast was proposed by his wife's father, who, with as much dignity and composure as he could muster in his devastation, spoke movingly in Greek, then bravely in English. The halting words in a language that was not his own, the affection he clearly had for the woman who had been his wife and the mother of his daughters, were desolating.

People skirted around each other, around Terry and Jenny, as they always do at such things, not wishing to exacerbate the hurt, aiming to project some sort of calm or acceptance. Stavros, Terry's father and Ricky's other *papou*, stood in a corner for a good half-hour after the formalities had finished, ignoring entreaties to come and say hello to this one and that one, to join in somehow; his demeanour told anyone who approached that he wanted to be anywhere but here. He could never connect with the family his son had married into anyway, these 'nose-in-the-air types' as he had called them in earlier days; this was another, even more excruciating instance of feeling alienated in their company.

It was some relief to Terry when he saw his father finally give in to his exhaustion and sit down. He let him settle, then went over to him.

What on earth could he do for him? Once large as well as tall, a good six inches taller than Terry, Stavros had shrunk with age; sitting bent forward, his hands clasped and elbows on his knees, his proportions looked all wrong. A frail and fragile man, out of place, wanting to be somewhere else. And waiting. An air of waiting. But for what?

There was something that could be done for him, it occurred to Terry then. He could take him home. There was nothing his father would gain from staying among this lot much longer. It was not as if anyone could say or do anything that would make any difference to how he was feeling. He at least wouldn't have to listen to Jenny's Aussie friends declaiming at him — or her own father for that matter — as if he was deaf.

Terry spoke softly. 'If you want to go home I'll give you a lift.'

'I do,' he replied. 'I do want to go home … I can walk.'

'No you can't.'

Lacking the will or the energy to argue such a small point in the circumstances, Stavros got up slowly to follow his son out to the car. As they moved to the front door, Terry glanced at Jenny and caught her eye. He signalled that he was giving his father a lift, saw her nod coolly.

Out in the driveway, Stavros insisted once more, 'Is not far. Let me walk.'

A few years earlier, once he was too old to run his cleaning empire, Stavros had moved back to the inner west from Rose Bay. 'To be close to my son,' or so he had told Terry. They lived about a kilometre apart, but Terry was not happy to let him walk the distance alone tonight. 'No, come on. Hop in,' he said.

At his father's flat, one of six in a three-storey walk-up block, Terry stepped slowly up the stairs behind him, then waited patiently while Stavros fiddled with his key and the door. Inside, he asked his father if he'd like a cup of tea.

'Tea? No. Nothing. Just leave me, you go back.'

Terry didn't want to leave him in this state. 'Do you want a sleeping pill?'

The offer angered Stavros. 'What for? I don't want to sleep, boy. This, what happened, is too terrible for sleep.'

To try to distract him, Terry went to the kitchenette and clattered a few cups around, began fiddling with the hot-water jug.

'Think I'll make a coffee. Sure you don't want one?'

'No. I don't want,' Stavros replied, then started to wander, agitatedly, aimlessly, around the small space of his living room.

Terry kept an eye on him as he paced about. He eventually stopped to remove his jacket, only to get himself tangled up in one of the sleeves.

'Here,' said Terry, leaving what he was doing to straighten his father out, 'let me help you with that.'

Stavros brushed him away, finally extricating himself. And the relief of removing that constriction seemed to release something else in him. He said, 'Now sorry, Terry, but I have to speak to you straight. All right?'

'Say whatever you like, *Baba*.'

'In the old country … in the old country we never let such things happen to our people. You know that?'

'What do you mean, "never let such things happen"? Nobody *let* anything happen to Anastasia.'

Facing him squarely, his father punched his right fist into the open palm of his other hand. 'Mother look after the children, father get the money — for everything! Not the *yaya* have to go and get the child from the school! And then an old woman has an accident! Not such things! Mother's job, that one!'

Terry took a step towards him. 'Hey, hey, calm down, calm down … I know you're feeling awful. But blame doesn't help. Jenny did nothing wrong.'

'Bullshit! Bullshit, Terry. Everybody done wrong. You listen to me, okay? I tell you straight. Where is the mother? She must get the boy, this is her job.'

'It wasn't her fault. She was at work. I know you've never really liked her, but —'

'Doesn't matter! Doesn't matter if I like or I don't like!'

'It wasn't her fault that she couldn't be there.'

'So whose fault? Your fault? No! Anyway …' Exhausted, Stavros sat in one of two mock-leather armchairs. 'Empty words

… I say empty words because I know the answer. I know whose fault — *my* fault. I should be there because Anastasia, everybody knows her legs no good anymore!' With this Stavros began to slap the side of his head with one hand — one open-palmed, loud smack followed by another, then another.

Terry went to his side, kneeled next to the chair and took hold of his hand.

'Please, *Baba*, you didn't do anything wrong either. Stop it now.'

'Oh I did wrong, plenty wrong. I come here to this stupid country, that's one thing.' He allowed Terry to put his hand back on the armrest then turned his head slightly towards him. 'Your mother never want to come here — but good that she is gone, not to see this drama.'

Terry got up, not wanting to be near him while his father was on this path. He had hated these diatribes when he was a kid, having to listen in silence at the dinner table to his father spewing out all manner of resentment and bile — Australia was always second-rate. Australia was bad. Greece was better. Greeks were too good for this place. And he hated them even more now — so undignified and futile in a man of seventy-plus. He found he could not hold his own tongue.

'Oh for God's sake. Do you really have to start up with the ethnic whinge? And at a time like this?'

'Ethnic? Whinge? That's what you call it, eh Terry, this tragedy?'

'No. It's what I call the things you are saying. This blaming everyone stuff.'

'Ha!' Stavros gave a short, bitter laugh. 'You the one to know about that! You, the mister bus driver fella. What you know? You just a bloody bus driver!'

'You're right. I don't know anything,' he said resignedly, lowering his voice, hoping his father would take the hint and cease.

'That for sure. You know nothing.'

Terry spun around. 'Great! Thanks for the insults and abuse, *Baba*. You've been good at that, haven't you?' He began his own pacing now. 'What was I doing when it happened, does anyone care? I was doing my job.'

Stavros stared at his son, tried to follow what he was saying. In his lexicon, 'insults, abuse, doing my job' were part of a language he took to be entirely beside the point.

'Not much of a job, I know, if anyone cares. But I was on duty.'

'Duty, duty ...' Stavros repeated. If nothing else, this word he understood. This word and its meaning he was convinced he understood better than anybody. 'My boy, you don't know duty. Nobody here in this country know duty, believe me. Not the woman you marry, not you, not me, not nobody.'

With that, Terry had heard enough. Of all the things his father might have said or done in the situation, this was the killer. A lecture on obligation, in case he didn't already feel like complete garbage. He grabbed his car keys and slammed the flat door behind him.

7
Just for Fun

Terry shifted on the garden bench, slapped at his arms. At ten pm, the air was chilly, his chest constricted. So hard was it to breathe, it felt as if he had come into contact with something bitter and astringent. Add the stinging dryness around his eyes, the taste in his mouth, and he could have been drinking laundry bleach.

By the time he had got back from his father's at around eight, everyone had left. The wake was over. He had sat in this corner of the garden for the past two hours, on the bench under the bay tree. He had not moved. The urge was there — but so was the thought that if he did get up to move he just might not stop.

The words 'a family home' intruded as he looked at the dimmed structure beyond; he recalled how his father had spoken of its importance when, long ago, Terry had told him of his and Jenny's plans for the future. Tonight, Jenny had said not a word to him since he had returned; he was not welcome anywhere near her, that was a given.

Those few who had spoken to him at the wake had done so out of Jenny's earshot. He had heard the words of condolence and had tried to say in return the things expected in the circumstances. But conscious of where Jenny believed the blame lay in this disaster, and wary of saying the wrong thing around her, people were afraid to be seen talking to him. A hand would be placed on his shoulder or his arm squeezed, then a forehead would wrinkle and the gaze would be broken — the person would look away from him to check Jenny's whereabouts.

His being an object of pity, he knew, was just the beginning.

*

At midnight Terry went inside to get a thicker jumper. After hours of turning the question over and over again, Terry knew this: the idea that he could change course, throw in his rotten job in pursuit of the magician's life (or any other life but the accidental or given), and have the support of his wife or father or anyone else supposedly close to him, was at best a bad joke. But that was not the whole story; it was an instalment in a much longer one: that he did not feel wanted around here, had not felt wanted for a very long time. In light of that, he believed he had come to an answer — a kind of answer, a first-step answer, but an answer just the same.

Terry went back into the garden and quietly walked along the passage at the side of the house. He let himself out the front gate and began to walk. Unclear where he should or could go, he just kept walking. After a few minutes he was on Parramatta Road, heading towards the city. He thought of the harbour at the end of this road. He was drawn to feel the cool breeze off the night water.

Stumbling along, Terry felt intermittently unanchored to the earth, one moment scuffing his shoes on the path, the next somehow floating through the night above the ground. Two hours later, he ended up at Dawes Point. He sat in the park under the Harbour Bridge and listened to the noise of fruit bats overhead as they squawked and circled one of the giant fig trees nearby. He contemplated maybe going to a hotel but that possibility filled him with dread. He was better off here.

Terry gazed at the blue-black waters of Sydney Cove, heard the stirred-up sea slopping against the retaining wall. The south-easterly breeze was strong, making him shiver. Terry took out his phone and held it for a long time. Eventually he pressed a key to make it light up, then flicked through the numbers until he came to his own. 'His own': how weird was the thought now. About to press it on the off-chance that Ricky might pick up, he only stopped himself when he remembered the time. He put the phone back in his pocket.

Through the early hours, Terry tried to understand his feeling of desolation. He was able to arrive at only one conclusion: it was not about his mother-in-law. He did not really believe he had been responsible for Anastasia's death. There was no logical reason to think so. And still he felt terrible and still he knew something needed to be sorted out. It was not right to feel like this. But nor was it right to act the way he had; if Ricky did not see him this morning, he might take it that his father had run out on him. He wished he knew what the boy might think. He did know he was going to have to fix things with him, short term and long term.

Terry looked at the neon-lit office towers, then at the smaller cluster of highrise buildings across the harbour to the north. He turned to gaze across the near distance again at Luna Park, that crazy place framed by the deck and pylons of the Bridge. Luna Park — 'Just for Fun' — where he had been taken a couple of times as a small kid. All lit up, it was a blaze of coloured lights.

That sickening, thrilling Big Dipper rollercoaster ride. Smashing around in the dodgem cars … the Ghost Train and how those weird arms — mechanical? real? — would lean out, touching you as you went around in the passages and the decapitated heads that jumped up in front and then were gone … The illusions in Coney Island, the peepshow machines in which things that were not real were made to look real.

The memory of a beating came to him, one administered by Stavros after an outing there. He must have done something very bad that time, as it seems he'd done so often, to have caused his old man to punish him so. He looked at the huge grinning face at the entrance of the amusement park, then at the lights of the Opera House across the way.

All had been fine until that last time when, on top of the three and three only rides he'd been allowed, he'd had the cheek to ask for an ice cream. That ice cream had been bought for him (a Drumstick?) and he had gobbled it down and enjoyed it — until told by his father afterwards that it was a waste of money. 'But have you got any money, boy? No! You spending mine!' Then the familiar lecture about having been a factory worker, and nothing more. Stavros was running a successful cleaning business by then, but he was right: there was precious little to be spared 'just for fun', and for a child who was never satisfied. What there was instead was a silent father during the ride home and an unexpected cuff across the back of the head, preliminary to being smacked all the way into his bedroom.

Something else came to Terry as he sat, staring now at the stars. His father calling him to his side one afternoon when Uncle Mylonas was around, to tell him that the old uncle was going to show them something very special. Him dutifully following them both to the shed where his father kept his gear, his paints and poisons and tools for working on the car. And where he kept the drum of kerosene. 'Watch this, boy. You gonna learn something today!' he had said, or something like it.

And learn he did. Uncle Mylonas — no real uncle, just an old man from the same village back in Greece who had fallen in with his parents here — took a teaspoon out of his pocket, slowly opened the tap at the bottom of the drum and, with much care, filled the spoon. He then put the thing into his mouth and swallowed. And then he did it once more.

Terry had cried out in horror, only to be told not to be such a girl. 'Uncle says it good for the stomach — fix you up inside.' His father had grinned at him. 'Not just for fun, he do this, ha ha ha!'

But what did 'just for fun' ever mean?

Terry stretched a little and realised the ache in his legs had begun to subside, enough for him to be able to lie flat on his back. At last sleep came to him.

*

Terry came to feeling as if someone had hit him. As if he had received an almighty punch in the head that had brought him around rather than knocked him out. He understood he had not

74

been felled when he was able to gain focus by staring at the ground next to him. He noticed a bump and moved his hand over it, some thin sliver of root from a nearby tree snaking past. He scratched away at the grass and soil and exposed it, a woody finger seemingly without start or end, a couple of centimetres thick, looking for water.

Now he tilted his head back and stared at the first sliver of early morning light in the east, the darker sky still overhead. The cold had begun to bite. He was trying to do up the zip of his jumper when he heard a piercing animal shriek, the sound of a wild beast cornered and wounded, but defiant. He did not at first realise where it had come from; but then, when he recognised the cry as his own, he jumped up, suddenly desperate to get moving.

The effort it took to stop himself from heading off randomly was enormous, but he managed it and sat again. By six-thirty he had concluded this: he could not just turn around and go back to Ashfield. There was another path and he would take it, embrace it just as he had recently planned. He would go to Chinatown and find Hal.

Terry stumbled down the grassy slope to the roadway under the Harbour Bridge, aware of the sound of the air entering and leaving his mouth, the rise and fall of his chest, abdomen, the swing of his arms. He would not run. It was enough that his body was in motion taking him somewhere. Perhaps it would take him away and beyond what he had learned over these past five days, these ten, twenty, forty days, months, years … If he pushed on far enough, hard enough, where might he finish? He was going to find out.

The leaves of the trees began to turn green as the light grew around him. Though proper daylight was a few minutes away, there must have been people about — this was the city, the CBD — but he couldn't identify any, none possessing any singularity. None had the form, the status of individual for him. Not at this moment.

A few more steps and Terry concentrated on the pulsing of blood at his temples and nothing more. Until he became conscious of a shadow, a darkening presence somewhere to his left. And then saw an arm stretch across in front of him.

He looked down at the arm and the hand at the end of it — brown, wrinkled, an older man's, but with skin that was smooth, shiny.

'Heavy weather …' Terry heard a voice say. A quiet voice. He stopped and looked to his side. Hal Sargeson.

He felt a wave of relief. 'It's you.' He looked at Hal's lined and weathered face, striking in its own way.

'It is,' Hal replied calmly. 'Sorry, didn't mean to scare you.'

'You won't believe this but I was heading your way,' Terry said.

'Were you now? Good. I'm glad.'

'So how come you're here?' Terry asked.

'It's interesting, isn't it?' Hal paused to look up at the huge webs of steel, the bridge understorey, that hung overhead. 'Look at that.' He pointed above him. 'We've met under a bridge. A span that joins two otherwise unconnected things. Just like magic …'

He placed one hand in the small of Terry's back and turned him gently towards the roadway with the other. They walked side by side along George Street, heading in the direction of Circular Quay. After a few minutes Hal steered towards a stand of trees in a small park near the water's edge.

'Nice under here,' he said, angling below the giant canopy of a Moreton Bay fig. As they settled themselves, Terry noticed how agile Hal was for an ageing coot, the way he folded his legs neatly beneath him. He was weather-beaten but obviously not arthritic.

'How old do you reckon this is? This tree?' Hal asked.

They were each leaning against a separate tangle of root tendrils and sinewed trunk, Terry forgetting himself long enough to look up at the expanse overhead.

'Don't know. Couple of hundred years maybe.'

Hal said no more for a very long stretch. In the silence, Terry looked at him closely, trying not to draw his attention. He had a long, mournful-looking face and, though ringed by wrinkles, alert, bright blue eyes. Not unfriendly eyes.

'Well, Terry, I reckon you could do with something to drink. Wait here and I'll get you some water.'

Hal went away in the direction of a nearby cafe. A couple of minutes later he returned with two plastic cups of water.

'They've got free water in there.' He smiled. 'Chaps like me are always annoying them … Look, I don't know what's happened, but maybe I can help, eh?'

'Truth is I've got some decisions to make. I've walked out of home,' Terry mumbled.

Hal nodded as if he understood and accepted these things without question. 'Come down to my place if you like. Plenty of room. I was wondering why you didn't show last week, Terry. And from what you're telling me —'

'I needed some time, Hal,' Terry cut him off, not wanting to go into detail. 'Are you okay for a visit?'

'The offer stands.' Hal got up to go.

Again they walked together. At each instant that the pain started to come back at Terry — trying to get hold of his throat, his heart, his head — he breathed deeply. He tried to keep filling his lungs as rhythmically as he could.

Terry knew that at this hour he was meant to be at work and on the road. He took out his phone and called the depot, getting through to Margot immediately. He told her he wasn't feeling well, although there was nothing seriously wrong, and he would probably be back in a day or two. Keen not to ring any alarm bells, he repeated that everything was all right — until Margot broke in to say there was no need to go on, she would sort things out with the roster manager.

Would Jenny try to contact him today, he wondered. There had been no calls or texts since he had disappeared — or was it escaped? — from home. She was probably thinking good riddance.

8

The Trick

As soon as Hal closed the door to his eccentric abode, Terry spoke. 'Hal, I want you to answer a question for me.'

'Do my best. What is it?'

'What were you doing down at Dawes Point? You weren't tracking me, were you?'

Hal let a few seconds pass, then said, 'Bit paranoid, aren't you? I spend a lot of time around those parts.'

'Which parts?'

'Dawes Point. The Botanic Gardens. The Domain … colonial Sydney. You know, all the good bits that got stolen from the blackfellas. There's something special about that foreshore. I'm down there every day.'

Terry looked away, not knowing whether to accept this as truth. Hal was not that easy to read. He tacked instead to the more immediate question. 'You said I could maybe stay for a while?'

'I did. Are you feeling a bit better?'

'Better than what?' Terry asked.

Hal saw his discomfort. 'Never mind, I know you're doing it tough. How about a little show? Get your mind off things.'

Hal nudged his guest towards one of the director's chairs. Terry was content to be told what to do, not have to make any decisions right now. He watched as Hal fished theatrically around in his coat pockets, one then another, until eventually he brought forth a pair of shiny metal handcuffs.

'This might interest you …'

He swung the cuffs over his wrists, one hook at a time, leaving them to dangle unlocked. Terry wondered whether there was coincidence or design in what he had produced from his pocket.

'Here,' Hal said as he thrust his hands in front of Terry's face. 'You can do the honours.'

Terry touched the cuffs gingerly. They felt heavy, not fake at all.

'Haven't used these myself, yet,' he said. 'You can show me how they work.'

Hal didn't answer at first, but presented again his surprisingly appealing grin. Terry thought that whatever else, he was an unrepentant showman.

'So, what are you waiting for? Snap them shut,' Hal said.

Terry hesitated for a second, looking at Hal for reassurance.

'Don't worry, I know what I'm doing.'

Intrigued, Terry snapped one of the cuffs shut, then the other. There was a solid click each time. Terry had a fleeting sense of how satisfying it might be to throw these onto someone, an enemy, someone you hated, someone prepared to hurt you.

He watched attentively as Hal, after a few flicks of his wrists this way and that and what appeared to be some real struggle, somehow released himself from the cuffs.

'You're still the pro, Hal. Also borrowed from Harry?'

'You could say that … though handcuffs were the least of it with him. And I know *that* for a fact. Take a look at these and see if you can find the answer.'

He handed the cuffs to Terry, who turned them over, examining them closely. 'Some of them have a trick button somewhere …'

'Psshaw! Amateursville. Can you find a button?'

Terry looked once more but couldn't find a release button or catch.

'Nothing there because this is done the old-fashioned way.' Hal shook his sleeve, and a tiny pick appeared on a very fine thread. Just as quickly he somehow made it disappear. 'The art was that you didn't see me do it, did you?'

'No, you're good all right.'

'Okay. Quick revision. Which realm?'

'Escape?' Terry replied.

'Still Escape, yes. See? You're learning!'

Terry wondered what he had let himself in for, signing up like this with Hal Sargeson. How could the man possibly help with his life and situation? He wondered whether staying with him was a sensible move. Good magician he might once have been, but at this moment he looked like nothing so much as an obsessive eccentric, who was maybe just a little mad with it.

Terry shifted and began to stand up.

Instantly, Hal's hand was on his shoulder. 'Settle! Show's not over yet!'

'Maybe this isn't such a good idea …' Terry murmured, getting to his feet anyway.

'Don't go, Terry. What's your hurry?'

'What do you mean?'

'Oh, you could run off, I guess,' Hal said softly. 'But where would that get you?'

Taking it that Hal was needling him deliberately, trying to gee him up, Terry didn't respond.

'Hey, come on. I showed you a trick. Why don't you do something for me?' Hal broke the silence.

'Like what?'

'Oh, you could tell me a story, for instance. Doesn't have to be yours. Tell me about your people. What's your background? Ancient Greek glories, no doubt?'

Terry was in no mood for telling stories. He had never felt so intensely that everything was beyond his powers, his capacities. And yet he had been shown some kindness, and more. He relented.

'All right. What do you want me to tell you?'

'Indulge me a bit, is all I'm saying. Poor old derelict that I am,' Hal said with a grin. 'Just tell me a story — I've told you one or two, haven't I?'

'My people … okay. From Greece, yes they were. The Peloponnese. Know where that is?'

'I do. The bit at the bottom.'

Terry watched as Hal used a finger to draw a shape in the air.

'That's right. Something like that. Came out after the civil war over there. Father, Stavros, started out working at the old Sunbeam factory.'

'Appliance factory?'

'Yep, then he had a cleaning business until he retired. That was about ten years ago. *Mama* was on home duties, as it goes, all through until she died. Died young. And me, sole heir and survivor. The flower of their efforts, Hal old son. The bus driver in the family. But my real achievement, the big thing I've done with my life, apparently, is kill my mother-in-law.'

Terry stopped, expecting Hal might want to say something about that. But he kept looking into the distance, and seemed not to be paying attention. It was as if he hadn't heard a thing — or had heard it all before.

'Hello? Don't you want to know what happened?' Terry asked. 'You did say you wanted me to tell you a story.'

Hal seemed to be brewing an answer but said nothing for a while. Eventually he spoke up. 'I know you're in trouble. The details don't concern me. Plenty of room here if you'd like somewhere to clear your head for a few days. And didn't I have a plan for you? You're supposed to be in training. Terry, you've got to take charge of this.'

'Agreed. But I need to sort a few other things first.'

Hal nodded and headed across to the other side of the hall where he began absentmindedly looking for something in one of his piles of boxes. Terry wondered how old he was. Agile yes, but he had to be sixty and more with that skin. He also had some trajectory that was hard to fathom, Terry thought. What was he doing moving from one place to another around the city, on some imaginary journey or path? Trying to stay ahead of the mission vans and the do-gooders, perhaps?

But his own trajectory was troubling Terry more. He was starting to feel some guilt. Whatever Jenny thought about him, he was concerned to make contact with Ricky, let him know that he was all right, that although he would not be around for a while his son wasn't to worry. He felt in his pocket for his mobile phone and went out into the lane to make a call.

He tapped in the number for home, strange idea as that was becoming, and hoped that Ricky would pick up. He didn't, but he had half expected that. It was a school day, after all, and Ricky was probably rushing through breakfast, looking for his sport socks, packing up his homework. When Jenny answered he launched straight in: 'Jenny, I want you to tell Ricky that I'm all right.'

A large, sarcastic sigh came down the line before she spoke.

'It looks like you've made some sort of decision, Terry. But if you're not going to be around, then don't be around, okay? I can't understand how you can just run off like this. Where are you anyway?'

'Nowhere …'

'Suit yourself. Just that if that's how you want to do things, please don't all of a sudden feel free to make calls or whatever. If you want to abandon your child, that's fine, you have to live with it.'

'Is that what I've done?'

'Pretty much, Terry. As for me, there's nothing to abandon.'

'Jenny … I'm sorry.'

'Don't sorry me. And in fact I'm glad you rang in a way. The police say that we're going to hear about a trial date within a couple of months.'

'Trial date?'

'Some poor woman's been charged with negligent driving, occasioning death … All thanks to you.'

Terry heard Jenny's voice catch as she spoke those words, then a pause.

'Jenny?'

Her voice came back stronger than ever. 'Hopeless. Hopeless situation … She's another old woman. But it doesn't matter, does it? This has got to be done. This nightmare has to be gone through.'

Terry said nothing.

'With or without you, Terry. Just thought I'd let you know. You might want to turn up for the proceedings.'

Terry was trying to come up with something to say, some way of responding, when Jenny hung up. He was annoyed at himself for being slow, for missing the chance to speak to Ricky. He would have to find some other way of reaching him.

'Look, I'm not entirely sure why I'm here …' Terry said when he went back inside. 'But I will take you up on a night or two. Just until I get sorted. I don't believe I can go home … and I'm worried about my son … Ricky.'

Hal raised a hand. 'Don't need to say anything. Only thing I would say to you is be careful about your kid, Terry. One thing I know is, never leave your kid behind …' Hal pointed to a pile in one corner. 'I've got some spare blankets and there's a camp bed buried in that midden somewhere.'

'I'm always worried about Ricky, Hal. So, where can I …?'

'Here if you like,' Hal replied, pointing to some space beneath the altar. 'Your luck might turn.'

'Thanks,' Terry said and went to pull the bed into place.

'Sorry, it's a bit rough. We can do something about that if you stay.'

'Doesn't matter to me,' Terry said, as he sat down on the edge of the bed.

Hal stood looking down at him for a moment. He reached into his pocket, fumbling for something. 'Here,' he said, bringing out a small bottle. 'Drink this. Might help.'

'What is it?' Terry looked up, at the same time trying to identify the liquid himself.

Hal smiled. 'Lime cordial … for a toast, let's say!'

Terry unscrewed the cap on the small bottle and brought it close to his face to make sure he wasn't about to swallow a dose of arsenic or whatever; it was some kind of green cordial, he decided, before taking a swig. The sweetness was so unexpectedly satisfying, his eyes welled up with the relief. Hal put a hand on his shoulder.

'Didn't mean to upset you. Sorry, Terry.'

Terry waved the concern away. 'It's not the cordial, Hal,' he said, trying to smile back.

'I know,' Hal said quietly. 'Tomorrow I'll have something more to tell you. Might have something that will help.'

Terry lay back on the bed, but was too agitated to sleep.

*

With no duties or work to do, Terry wandered around the city shops and Hyde Park until early evening, when he and Hal stepped out for a cheap meal in Dixon Street. They were back at the old hall by nine in time for the early night Terry needed.

In the moments before exhaustion carried him off, Terry watched Hal shuffle away to his side of the room. He couldn't help but notice Hal getting ready for bed. Touching it was, too, the way he pulled out a big T-shirt — his only sleepwear it was soon clear — from under the covers and flapped it a couple of times before slowly lowering it over his head.

All done, Hal flicked off the light switch. In the dark, Terry heard the groaning of rusty bed springs as his host settled down. Next came a relaxed sigh and then Hal's voice: 'Right. Are you comfy?'

'Enough, yeah.'

'So, any further questions, as the saying goes?'

'You could tell me what you're doing living in this place. Did you say they were looking for a home or something for you?'

Terry heard a snort, then, 'They can keep looking. I'm perfectly all right here. Suits my temperament and my philosophy, it does.'

'That so?' Terry didn't know whether Hal was being serious or not.

'Been doing it for myself since I was about twenty. Don't remember my mother, she scarpered not long after I was born, left me with Frank. Took a long time to sort myself out, Terry. This joint is part of that. I wasn't much of anything, as I say, until I found magic and my master, yes sir …

'But this place, all sorts of people have used it — to worship something or work something out, you name it. Going right back the Presbyterians had it, then it was a Temperance Union hall — you know, for those against the grog. Then the Chinese took over. Eclectic — is that the word? — eclectic sort of joint. Everybody's been through here. It's all right to be anybody in here. And did I mention it was also the headquarters of the Magicians' Society for a while?'

'What magicians' society?'

'Oh, we had our own organisation once — I'm talking about the days when magicians mattered, by the way. There might still be one somewhere but I don't trouble myself anymore, not interested in politics. Used to come to meetings here, I did.'

'Is that how you first found out about it?'

'Correct, but all that was long gone when I moved in. Might be a dump today but some very good stuff has gone down in a hundred and twenty years here, Terry. Seen all kinds come and go, this joint has. Edwardian days, you had a million different things happening in this town, not like now. If you were a blackfella you'd probably call it a story place. Whatever, there's lots about it that I love.'

'And you've made it your own.'

'My own, yes. Although not all my things are here; got so much gear, I've got to have storage elsewhere too. Nighty nights now …'

Soon there was silence, but for Hal's intermittent snoring. Terry lay awake wondering about him. At least Hal was living indoors rather than out on the streets; he was not entirely down on his luck and seemed to be making do with a pension. He knew his magic and his Houdini and he seemed to have plenty to say … Or was the talk he talked just a way of pretending he had some kind of meaning in his life? Pretending or otherwise, Terry felt Hal was ahead of him in that department.

9

The Escaper's Craft

Terry woke early next morning, thanks to the thin, sharp strip of light flooding his face via the glass panel above the hall's disused front doors. He propped himself up, stiff from having lain on the lumpy camp bed all night. There was no Hal in sight. He felt disoriented, a small panic rising, before he settled himself, thinking there was no reason Hal should not go out first thing in the morning. The man was quite likely on one of his daily circuits, or maybe down at Centrelink.

Hal was back soon enough, clutching a couple of white paper bags. 'Got us some breakfast. Some nice pork buns! Here, have one.'

Terry looked at the pork bun being thrust at him and knew with dazzling clarity that what he needed today certainly wasn't a pork bun.

'Hal, what I want is not to blow the schedule I'm on. That's what I want. And you can pick up where we left off with Harry. Will you do that for me? There must be more you can tell me.'

'There is. Matter of fact, today Harry's going to take us deeper into the art of escape. Which requires first that you and I take a short trip into other parts of this mysterious city …'

Within the hour, the two of them were underground, in arcade land, out of the city's wintry air. This route of tunnels near the northern end of the Queen Victoria Building led anywhere you wanted to go, said Hal, if you knew the way. He picked up the pace, his strides growing longer, Terry following.

They veered deftly this way and that, avoiding the approaching throng, the morning going-to-work crowd. Terry was enjoying this stepping out; to move quickly was to heighten things. The buzz of neon, the flashes and pricks of light, multicoloured and garish, came at him from the displays on either side; the faster he went, the more pronounced the sensory effect.

He felt light, easy, a touch manic. A touch manic was a useful kind of manic — it helped get things done — and it was a feeling Terry was prepared to go with in this environment. Here were the arteries of the speedy, for the speedy, running through a thousand shopping vaults festooned with myriad crazy images and icons. He put out of mind the tremendous layers of bitumen, steel and concrete capping all this — and the fact that it was closer, stuffier down here than it was up on the streets. But this was no kind of hell.

'I love this city,' Terry announced. 'Don't you?'

'Great to be under the road for a change, I'll tell you that!' Hal replied. 'What I say is that above and below ground, in no part of Sydney do you wander lonely as a cloud, or lonely as a crowd, or however that line goes …'

The buzz of the crowd was all the better, Terry felt, for thinking in. Maybe things had spun out in a way that would allow him to grab the controls again in a different orientation, and not ever return to where he'd been. The old route would be no more, would be cancelled; communications along the previous frequency would no longer be possible.

But he would have to be active in his own fate, he knew. He could start by trying to tip out the dregs, and fill his cup again with something fresh. When he looked around, though, it occurred to him that maybe the change he dreamed of was impossible: people were everywhere stitched into their armour. All these blokes in suits, the usual greys, blues and blacks, the collars, ties. And the women were just as bad, with all that material draped over them, the jackets and coats and scarves and whatnot.

He saw himself reflected in a men's store window and was not pleased. It was hard to accept his appearance as anything other than a reprimand. He noticed the stoop to his shoulders, the hair in need of a cut, flying out at the sides over his ears; enough to frighten a small child. Alternately, he might simply adjust his point of view: this was merely a mirage floating on glass, an instance of the basic principle of so much stage illusion — the principle of reflection.

Terry stared at his shadowy likeness, until a rush of sadness so sudden it was almost overwhelming washed through him. He felt his eyes sting. He could deny or try to avoid his situation as long as he liked, but it was not going to go away of its own accord.

'Stop dawdling, Terry, we're nearly there,' Hal called out to him. In a moment they were outside the famous Maxwell's, where a neon sign shouted from the front window: 'Everything for the Professional Magician'.

Terry had been here once before, but had only looked in the window and walked on. This was the real thing, heavy duty, not kids' stuff. He had not felt authorised to enter. Now Hal led him inside, veering to a book rack close to the door.

'Look at this, Terry.' He handed him a copy of *How to Levitate*. 'But this is down the track for you, for a day to come.'

Terry opened the book and peered at the numbered diagrams and schematic cross-sections of various boxes and other constructions — all as complicated as he'd expected. Like someone excited by a new language but with so far only the first words in his head, he put the book back on the shelf.

Hal had moved along to a display of photos and posters and stood before a small, framed black-and-white image. He beckoned Terry over. 'Take a look here,' he said. Terry had to lean close to make out the detail. A disturbing scene. Someone suspended upside down from a huge crane. And some time ago from the look of the crane and the surroundings.

The background was all masonry and brick, early model cars and trucks, men in heavy, solid clothes coming and going; here was a city pushing upwards, a strong feeling of energy and purpose.

But then there was this human being, trussed up, if he wasn't wrong, in a straitjacket … and what an item that was — large buckles, straps and belts fastened across his body. And the man's predicament an entertainment to the hundreds of onlookers. Although if that *was* Houdini, Terry wondered how much of a predicament it could actually have been.

Taking a closer look still, he saw the men in the crowd wore old-fashioned collars and the women long, fitted dresses and that it was definitely a steam crane, a turn-of-the-twentieth-century job, all steel plates and rivets, from which the man was hanging.

The buildings in the background were tall, imposing — they did not look English or Australian.

Terry turned to Hal. 'Houdini?'

'Correct.'

'I think I want to buy that, Hal.'

'Good decision!'

The parcel under Terry's arm, they left the shop and emerged from the underground world at George Street.

'Where to now, Hal?'

'State Library, for today's lesson.'

Twenty minutes later, the two of them were at the entrance to the State Library of New South Wales. Terry checked his parcel, then followed Hal, who seemed to know his way around. Terry pointed to the computer terminals. 'No need,' said Hal. 'I know where everything is, don't worry about them.'

Hal went to a desk where he requested a number of items. As they waited for the books to be retrieved from the stacks, Terry gazed around uncomfortably. Here was a place dedicated to, a repository of … what exactly? Libraries made him uneasy, reminded him of failure, with making a hash of his Higher School Certificate because he had never bothered to visit them. He hadn't been inside this building before.

Hal had ordered up a couple of biographies of Harry Houdini, including Houdini's own account — *A Magician Among the Spirits*. He took them to a desk and began to flick quickly through them. Among the hundreds of images of daring escapes and posed publicity shots illustrating the texts, it wasn't long before he came across the very same reproduction Terry had bought. He passed the volume across to him.

Terry inspected the print once more. 'So where was this, any idea?'

'New York. A place where people were always taking risks. Question is, will you?'

'Yes, I will —'

'Good, I'm very pleased to hear it.'

'— so long as we start on the ground first.'

10

Callan Park

The next day Hal had a large vinyl sports bag packed and was ready to go before Terry was awake. 'Terry, listen,' he said excitedly, as soon as Terry opened his eyes. 'Pertaining to yesterday's introduction, we follow up today with an adventure!' He explained they would be making a trip to one of the locales that had featured in Harry Houdini's tour of 1910.

Once he had processed this, Terry was quick to rise. He would ignore other realities for a moment — easily done now that he had committed to go down Hal's path. Still, to apply the old rules and measures of his life — as husband, householder, bus driver — it was unnerving to think he had turned as quickly as he had. Yet the prospect of advancing himself in magic was drawing him on, reviving him. It was good also not to be bound to anybody else's schedule, particularly Sydney Buses'.

The thing that continued to trouble him was his one true obligation — to the son he had fathered. He had still to figure out a way of reconnecting with Ricky and staying close to him. Compared to that, his only other responsibilities were minor: he had agreed to listen to a story — one that some might think preposterous but that for him had a strange and growing appeal — and to take a magician's instruction. He could have done a lot worse, he told himself, with these past few days than to have spent them with Hal Sargeson.

He also knew that his taking Hal as a mentor might be seen by others as a stupid or reckless move. He expected Jenny to count it as further proof of her view of him, and his father as more evidence of his failure and everything that was wrong about Australia — but all that was too bad.

'According to my old man, Terry,' Hal began as they boarded a bus heading to Rozelle, 'Harry opened his Sydney season at Rickards's Tivoli Theatre on April tenth. That must have been the same Tivoli from when I was a boy — it's not there anymore. Do you remember it, Terry?'

'No, don't think I do,' he replied.

'Haymarket it was, not far from where I am, around the corner from the Capitol. Huge, 2000-plus seater it must have been.'

Hal saw that he was continuing to draw a blank with Terry. 'Terry, to be a magician, you have to know your history. What happened when they got to Sydney was that the first few evenings went well enough — the newspaper crits showed that — though Harry was not in especially good form. Something was missing, something making it hard for him to reach across to his audiences. After a few of those early shows, my father overheard him tell Bess one morning what he thought the matter was. What he said was: "I'm not seeing the people in this town. I don't know who they are."

'Bess chipped him about that. "See the people? You can see them in the street any time you like!" she said. But that's not what Harry meant. What he meant was, you don't get to know anybody until you've seen them in their troubles, do you? Bess would have understood that all right. "People and their troubles" was something her husband always brought up when he had one of his charity shows in mind.

'And so, Terry, eleven days after the first show in Sydney, Harry and his team took a short trip from the city to Callan Park Hospital for the Insane at Rozelle, which is where we are headed today … Now, you do know where *that* is, right?'

'I know where it is. I've driven this route for years.'

'Yes indeed. Amazing it's still here, what's left of it, in the inner west. The largest asylum in the southern hemisphere once, I heard,' Hal said.

They got off the bus at the Cecily Street stop, entered the old hospital grounds, and cut across overgrown grass through the acres of neglected, once-glorious parkland, towards the original Kirkbride complex. The array of gloomy Victorian sandstone wards up ahead, once the very latest in lunatic facilities, appeared more ominous to Terry the closer they got. It seemed like nothing so much as a set for some horror movie.

Terry followed Hal to a small enclosed courtyard at the back of one of the disused wards. Hal went to an unlocked, rusty wrought-iron gate, pulled it open and they entered.

'Right. We're now standing in the exercise area of Ward 21. For an outdoor show, which is what it would have been, Harry and his crew could not have asked for a finer morning. This space is about fifteen metres by fifteen to my eye, and the only prop he had, by the way, was a wooden chair in the middle there.'

Hal stepped across to where he estimated the centre of the yard to be. He looked around, then shifted about until he was satisfied he was in the right place. Next, he pointed down to his left, to the imaginary chair.

'Harry sits down here, more or less, closes his eyes and begins that drifting, that falling he always did. He would go down into some kind of quiet place inside him that he liked to visit before a test such as this.

'He was on his own, and waiting for the authorities to bring him the straitjacket for which he'd asked. He'd already explained to them that it'd be better for him to be on his own like this for the effect. He didn't mean the theatrical effect, Terry. What he had in mind was something else.

'Picture the scene. When he opens his eyes again, there are all the inmates assembled before him; they'd lined them up like it was some kind of army roll call. He glances from face to face, tries to hold this or that person's gaze for a few moments, smiles at them. Such suffering humanity, you couldn't help but be moved; but Harry felt the pity of it all more than most.

'You can imagine the misery he would have gazed out on here, Terry, can't you? Crazy people walking in tiny circles, poor bastards banging their heads against these walls …'

'He liked to do events in places like this?' Terry asked.

'Habit of Houdini's, it was. He never could explain what it was, he just knew that it was important for him to do this. For six or seven years past, every place they went, he gave performances for the unfortunate. Hospitals, orphanages, homes for destitute men, lunatic asylums — from Hamburg to Edinburgh to New York. Every place he went they clapped or cheered or roared, they cried or they smiled or they laughed. But each place was different and no-one could tell for sure how he would be received.

'Oddly enough, he never had any trouble convincing the authorities to allow the test he liked to propose — a straitjacket of their choice, to be fitted to him by the strongest attendants they could find. You would think they might object.

'In this case, the superintendent — a Dr Ogilvie apparently — and three orderlies brought the item he had requested. It was half hidden, but there was no difficulty picking the dreadful thing for what it was, as you'll see for yourself in a minute. Now imagine the scene, Harry speaks loudly, in his usual manner: "May I have your attention, please —"'

'Stop there, Hal. So what was that, how he was talking? What kind of voice did he use?'

'Well, he didn't like the usual spruiking at all. Not many people realise that Harry didn't have the sideshow-alley style. Promoters and impresarios were always surprised when they first heard him. They always wanted him to speak more, do the "Roll up, roll up!" thing. Not that he ever did. That day in 1910 he was as patient as usual; he would have known that some of the sick people needed time to collect their attention, such as it was; never mind the others, the ones who had to be prodded or turned in the right direction.

'So what he says is: "Thank you, thank you all … I would like to say to you, before the little show I have for you here today, that I have learned, going around the world as I do, that some good people don't always have the chance to see me …" He pauses, he smiles gently at them before continuing. "I guess some of you gentlemen would be in that position."

'There would have been a few titters about then — and not only from the staff. No surprise really. What was crazy, what wasn't — that was a question Harry had often thought about and talked about. This laughing at themselves was a strange thing he came across in such institutions. Harry found it comforting for some reason.'

Hal stopped for a moment, turned his head towards Terry in search of a response. 'Does that make sense to you?'

Terry nodded. 'Yes, yes it does.'

'Indeed, Terry. So there they are on that day and it's time to begin. Don't know exactly what he said, but something like this would have come next: "Dear friends, for your benefit I will now attempt to demonstrate to you that nothing is impossible. If some of you didn't hear me I'll say it again, loud and clear — *nothing* is impossible. Enough talk for now … oh, except that I hope you enjoy what you are about to see, and get well soon everybody!"

'Would have been more laughs at that — but of a different and mixed kind now — and some howls, some cries. But that wouldn't have been any surprise to him either. And about then, Harry would have turned to the superintendent and said, "Thank you for allowing this, sir."

'You know, you could not do what Harry Houdini was about to do without the co-operation of the top man in a place like this; and Harry would have been able to tell within a minute of walking into his office whether he was going to be onside.

'So Harry becons to the orderlies to come closer, talks to them all gentle-like, as if they're some kind of pet dog, saying, "Hello, fellas," and after that he shakes each one by the hand. I tell you the man could charm the devil out of hell, he was that good with people!

'Next he says, "Ordinarily, I would ask my own assistant to help me with this," pointing to one of his men, "but I've heard you Australian boys are good and strong. Is that right?"

'Harry waits for someone to respond, except nobody appears to have anything to say. But there's always someone willing to come up in the end, isn't there? There's always someone who thinks he can stick it to the great man.

'So Harry then holds his arms out in front of him to allow whoever it is to begin pulling and tightening hard. Nothing strange in that — as I say, it's common for someone you call up from the audience to act like they've got something to prove. There's always the guy who starts tugging and pulling to gain an extra notch here and there, to show that he means business.

'But whoever it was, they couldn't have known you could just as easily jump over the moon as restrain the great Houdini. See, what Houdini learned, among other things, was how to look into men's hearts; from the way a rope was pulled against his flesh, he could read the man, same as he could when they tested a chain around his neck, or hammered too hard the nails into a coffin from which he was required to escape.

'Whatever they were capable of, it was the work of shrivelled spirits, puny souls, Terry! Men who did not know that Harry was capable of a different kind of shrivelling. It was what he did ahead of letting his own spirit swell, which is what I believe he always aimed for in his life. Never mind Sydney, Australia or London, England, he knew what he had to do in this mean world. You see, Terry, Harry Houdini was determined to be free in the face of any odds, and it didn't matter where — a theatre, music hall, opera house, any place at any time the challenge was issued. Even here at the bottom of the world, our hero was ready to fight against — and defeat, Terry! — the things that pin us to the earth.

'Sure, he would get out of this contraption just like he did every other kind. And you'd never have seen an effort like it; left him barely able to walk afterwards. He'd be so tired he couldn't tell if there was anyone beyond the footlights. I don't believe he could hear a thing — the groans and cries of the crowd didn't register with him at all.

'Let's just say this was not a performance, but a man wrestling with something demonic. What Houdini was engaged in was not, most definitely not, an entertainment, Terry.'

Terry wondered at Hal's words. He wouldn't be surprised if Hal had delivered that spiel more than once in his career.

'As to the practicalities, what the guy strapping him in never saw, probably being eager and cocky, was that Harry had slowly expanded the muscles in his chest and upper arms, and in his neck and shoulders. Whatever he was fitted into in that state, there was always slack to be gained by simply untensing. That was technique number one. There were others, but that was the basic job.

'Harry also knew that his sheer strength tended to surprise the little tough guys that liked to volunteer to do the tying up. And in such an escape, other than getting the angles right, strength was the main tool. Oh, and by the way, Harry was a fitness nut — used to keep up his exercise regime even on the boat. Running on the spot, push-ups, skipping with a rope — they were the basics, but there were special routines too. Not a tall man, only five foot three — nearly everyone was taller than him — but he was almost as wide as he was high and had the upper body power of a bullock.

'So on this occasion Harry Houdini would have been ready once again. Always was, always would be. Ready to muscle his way out.'

Here Hal paused to give his impression of the man at work. He spread his legs and began to take slow, noisy breaths, his arms tensed behind his back.

'He begins with the breathing out, deep and steady … Four, five inhalations and exhalations, and he feels a little give at the point of his left elbow. That found, he pauses for a moment to smile and wink at his audience. They were almost all of them watching him now in silence, as if the man had an answer, the single most important answer, to the question they each had in their own hearts and heads.

'They couldn't know yet, but he was well along the path to release. For that was all it ever took — a small space, an angle, something to push against, and he was on his way.

'What was needed next was brute force, and of that he had plenty. Although he begins the struggle with the fingers of his left hand splayed out behind his right armpit, inside five minutes he has his left arm entirely free of its sleeve, even if it's still imprisoned in the body of the jacket.'

'Did the audience know?' Terry interjected. 'I mean, what would they have been seeing?'

'Some at the front would have had an inkling he was making progress in getting out. As for Harry, he would have been looking for inklings of his own.'

'What do you mean?'

'Well, I reckon he would have been listening very hard for a snort or scoffing noise. Not from the patients, the patients gave him strength, but from the others, the orderlies and attendants, any authority types, any of the doubters present. Those sorts of people served to spur him on: because of them, he would try even harder.

'So there he is, and with further pushing and pulling and God almighty effort the other arm is free too. After that, he's able to loosen the lower straps around his waist and begin the final manoeuvre — inching the jacket up over his head. Then, a huge last effort, and he'd have the dreadful thing off.'

Hal was smiling beatifically, as if in some heavenly transport. 'Oh, Terry, I can hear him as if he was here! I can just hear him calling out "Ha!" and waving it over his head.' Hal now waved his arms over his head as if he himself had removed the garment.

'Can you hear the gasps, the shouts of joy, the laughter — the crazy kind and the natural? I can, Terry! I can! All that Houdini himself could ever wish to hear. It was these poor men who knew, who knew the struggle, if any did, and he loved them for that. And he had just shown them not only a struggle but a victory.'

Caught up in Hal's euphoria, Terry asked excitedly: 'And then? What happened then?'

'Well, as he was all done, the audience would have begun to fall apart. We are not talking healthy and sane people after all, Terry. No doubt they would have begun to wander off, drift off in all kinds of haphazard ways, maybe helped away by staff. Some of them would have been laughing happily enough, but only some. Imagine what it was like here in the days when they locked people up. And Harry was not a miracle worker, remember.'

Terry, still buoyed by Hal's vast enthusiasm, took some

moments to find the question he had meant to ask earlier. 'So, tell me, how long did the whole exercise take?'

'According to Frank, in this instance the thing took him fully eleven minutes, which was within the half-minute of his best. He was panting and bathed in sweat, and needed Kukol, ever-ready Kukol, to towel him down apparently … And that, my friend, is the story. Now then, you might like to have a go yourself.'

Without waiting for Terry to respond, Hal opened his bag and took out the unmistakeable, ghastly form of a traditional canvas straitjacket. 'I'm in no shape to try this myself, being a broken-down codger and whatnot these days, but you, you're still a young bloke. And a magician in training.'

Hal held the garment up and brought it closer for Terry to inspect. Terry scanned its shape, then touched it. He was appalled by the stiffness of the fabric, the thickness of the leather straps and buckles. 'Did you use to do this escape yourself?' he asked.

'I did. But …' Here Hal lowered his eyes a little, '…But I was never strong enough to use Harry's original method. You can always get trick releases, of course.'

'Ah!'

'But I'd love it if you would give it a go, the way I've described. Would you?'

Terry hesitated for a second or two, then took the jacket from Hal. He turned it this way and that, but found it difficult to thread his arms through the sleeves.

'Here, let me help,' said Hal.

The basics done, Hal moved behind Terry and set to work on the straps and buckles. 'Not exactly comfortable, is it?' he said, and laughed as if to lighten the proceedings.

'It's truly horrible,' Terry replied. He stood still for a moment, trying to get his bearings, trying not to struggle. He recalled the steady breathing that Hal had mentioned and began to take a few slow, gradually deepening breaths before the final brass buckles were pulled close and tight.

'That's it, that's it, take it steady,' Hal said, watching him carefully. 'Look to make a space … All right, now work it!'

Terry did as directed, sinking his chest and diaphragm, relaxing his arms as best he could. But he felt nothing like the slack that Hal had mentioned anywhere within the contraption. Incredibly well pinioned is what he felt. Instead of persisting with the shallow breathing and relaxing, he decided to try something else — a bigger, deeper breath. Maybe that would force open some space with which he could work.

Hal saw what he was up to and called out firmly, 'No! That's only going to —'

He needn't have bothered. For Terry suddenly felt the full strength of the restraint, as if caught in the gripping coils of a powerful snake.

'Jesus!' he yelled. 'This is …'

Again he did the wrong thing, again he breathed too hard and this time pushed entirely the wrong way. He felt as if his left arm was about to be torn off.

'Christ, Hal. I thought you said …' And now he could hardly breathe.

Hal saw what was happening and took a step forward. 'Hang on, don't … let me …'

But it was too late. Terry was in full panic. He stumbled backwards, trying to wrench his arms from side to side, trying to move the thing up his torso, but getting nowhere. Sweating and red-faced, he pleaded, 'Get me out of this thing, get me out, please.'

'Hang on there, mate,' said Hal. 'Don't panic.'

Terry, however, could hardly hear or see a thing. His one last frustrated and frightened lunge had toppled him over. He landed on his side on the parched earth of the abandoned courtyard with a thump, sending up a small cloud of dust, just as Hal was reaching across to try to stop it happening.

'Shit, Terry. You don't have to get so worked up. I'm here to help, you know.'

Terry managed to roll himself onto his back, and gazed up at Hal. Though still bound tightly, he registered the concern on Hal's face, and tried to look less agitated. 'Sorry, you're right,' he managed, forcing something like a grin. 'Got a bit of a way to go, haven't I?'

'You can say that again.' Hal smiled back at him and reached down a hand. 'Here, get on your feet and I'll help you out of that.'

Dusting him off as he manipulated the buckles, Hal worked his way down the straps, slowly releasing Terry from his torment.

'You'll need a lot more practice to get this under control,' he said, pulling the jacket forward to free Terry entirely. 'But in terms of your act, it doesn't have to be a straitjacket; you can always do other kinds of escapes. But look, escape isn't the ultimate goal, is it? Just a step along the way. A stage. I'm even thinking maybe we can skip it altogether and go direct to Disappearance. What do you reckon?'

'I think that would be a very good idea,' Terry replied quietly.

On the way back to the city, Hal leaned across to Terry. 'My mistake, mate, my mistake. I was pushing you too hard. Straitjacket's very tough work, was so even for Harry himself.'

'Not essential to the craft?' Terry asked.

'No, not essential. We can move on, as I say.'

'Disappearance … Funny, Hal, but it feels to me like I'm already part way there.'

PART TWO
DISAPPEARANCE

11

Biting the Bullet

Back at Wentworth Avenue, Terry concluded there were some things that could no longer be put off. He had to settle the work question once and for all — take extended leave or quit altogether or go back. He also knew he owed Ricky a call; he had not spoken to him in days.

Work was a tough one: on leave, the money would run out eventually and he would have to go back anyway; if he was to quit the buses outright, he would be on skid row soon enough. But if he managed, say, a consistent three small shows a week (unlikely yet, but possible one day) he could be making something respectable. Nothing like what he took home as a driver, but enough to live on. The question that concerned him more was whether he could still contribute to his kid's well-being if he and Jenny split up permanently. It would be tough, but not impossible.

Biting the bullet, Terry called Margot at the depot and told her he needed to take more time off to attend to some personal developments. They agreed he should apply for some long service leave and Margot promised to put together the necessary paperwork. She then told him that Jenny had rung and that it would be a good idea to return her call.

Quickly, before he could think too much about it, Terry dialled his home number. As far as he knew, Jenny still hadn't returned to work following Anastasia's death. She picked up immediately and told him that she wanted to meet — soon. That would be good, Terry said.

When she rang off, Terry realised that if he waited an hour or so, Ricky would be home from school. Jenny would be busy then, organising his afternoon tea, thinking about what to cook for dinner, maybe even ducking out to the corner shop for some ingredient. He figured right. Next time he rang, the boy answered the phone.

Almost as soon as he heard Ricky's voice, Terry thought, *This is not the way to do it, I need to be face to face*, but in his impatience and confusion he found himself pressing on anyway: 'Ricky, how ya doin'? I'm very sorry to be away like this, I really am, and I wanted to talk to you.'

The breeziness with which the boy replied — 'Don't worry about it, Dad' — made it a bit easier to keep going.

'I just want you to know that, that this might be more permanent — not you and me, never that — but ... between me and Mum ... Do you know what I'm saying?'

After a pause, Ricky asked, 'Are you splitting up?'

'I think so, yes,' Terry replied. The relief he felt in the grip that Ricky seemed to have on things did not last. The child's family had been broken up for him — and what he was doing now was handing Ricky the pieces.

In the silence at Ricky's end, Terry began to construct a more detailed explanation of what was going down, along with an assertion of his love for his boy and a promise that he would never abandon him. He had no chance to deliver any of it. Ricky suddenly piped up, 'Okay, Dad. Hope everything works out,' and hung up.

Terry felt as if his heart and guts had been ripped out and thrown away.

*

Two days later, Terry and Jenny were seated at a cafe in Elizabeth Street in the city, neutral territory.

'What's this all about, Terry? Where have you been? You can't just disappear, run away or whatever … How much hurt do you want to spread around? Isn't it enough that my mother is dead?' Jenny said quietly.

Terry put his hands on either side of the small table, gripping the edges with the tips of his fingers. He understood that Jenny would give him no opening. He had been tried and condemned.

Refusing to react, he merely stared at her. She returned the vacant gaze. They were silent, still, two pillars holding up nothing.

'What are you going to do about … I don't know, Terry, you tell me. About anything!'

'I'm working on it,' was as much as he felt he could usefully say.

'"Working on it",' she repeated. '*I'm* the one who has to make the real plans because you never do. And *I'm* the one who has to study to get the decent-paying job and do everything else … Are you even *allowed* to say you're just "working on it"? After what's happened?'

'Obviously not.' Terry took a deep breath, then another. He did not want an argument. He believed he understood what she was feeling. He did not wish to be aggressive towards her.

Jenny stood up.

'I'm going, Terry. You keep "working on it". Maybe procrastination and avoidance are all you're capable of. Call me if anything comes up that you feel you *can* communicate.'

'I can say this, Jenny, and maybe for both of us: I haven't been able to make you happy. There's no point me hanging around.'

Jenny neither replied nor looked at him. Instead she searched her purse and took out a twenty-dollar note, put it on the table and walked away.

Once she was gone, Terry was able to think again. He had never wanted to end up a bus driver — or 'operator' as they were called today. He had done it for income, wanting to contribute to the domestic finances. In his defence he was not work-shy. He had accepted all the aggravation and all the management bullshit that had come with the job over the years. To return to that now, he realised, would be borderline impossible.

Besides work, he would have to do something about getting a place of his own, even if he knew that Ricky might see a further abandonment in that. He was not at all clear as to how he might make things up with his boy, if he ever could.

Terry got up to head to Hal's place. He had hardly left the cafe when he got a call from Jenny.

'Look, Terry, I think we should cut to the chase. Do you have any objections — serious objections, I mean — to putting the house on the market?'

With a shock, Terry realised that no real reflection was required, or even possible. He could not have cared less what happened with their real estate. And it sounded like Jenny had other plans besides.

'No,' he said quietly. 'May as well get rid of it. You don't want to stay on there anyway, do you?'

Jenny waited a moment before answering. 'Well, Terry, it's not part of *your* thinking these days, is it? We haven't seen you in a week. You're gone then, aren't you?'

'Suppose so, yes.'

'And what do you want to do beyond that? Do you want to split things? Which I'm happy to do. I don't want to have a fight about it all, do you?'

'Split things? Haven't thought about it, Jenny.'

'Don't,' she replied, cold fury in her voice. 'Don't make this even harder, Terry.'

'If you want an answer, okay. You can have it all, I mean, because you should. I think something is coming up for me and I'm going to be busy.'

'You haven't mentioned that before.'

'No, because it's not entirely sorted. Work in progress.'

'Suit yourself. So, unless you want to get involved — which it doesn't sound like you do — I'll call the solicitors, shall I?'

'You do it. Fine … And just one other thing.'

'What?'

'Can you put a box of my things out, clothes and bathroom stuff and I'll send a courier.'

'Oh, stop being stupid. Just come and get what you need. And listen, talk to your father. He's calling me twice a day. I've been around to see him. He's not eating. You're treating him very badly.'

12

A Tight Fit

Terry spent a further week at Hal's, but realised he could not stay in his dilapidated hall much longer. Issues of chaos and sanitation — the place had only the original urinal, bowl and basin in a lavatory in one corner — were not the only prompts. He had come to see the importance of a place of his own for another reason: he needed somewhere he could take Ricky in comfort and safety, and with Jenny's approval. By the beginning of the following week, his long-service leave had been approved and he had found a cheap rental flat in Camperdown.

Another three weeks passed, mostly taken up with organising his living arrangements. He had disappointingly missed another couple of Wednesdays with Hal as a result, but life had surprisingly not got any worse. Terry had heard the theories that he would crash and burn, living on his own, as so many other separating males his age seemed to do. Not so. Not only had he not fallen into decline, he had begun to do some rebuilding. Steady as you go, small steps, one at a time, trying to get on top of things slowly — that was the idea. If this was going to be the hardest thing in his life, coming back from the disaster of a collapsed marriage, so be it — hard things can get done.

Or so Terry told himself again on what was shaping up as a pleasant Saturday morning. He quickly got through the clean-up of last night's meal things, the dinner plate and water glass and uneaten bread still in the basket, and went to the kitchen table where he had left his book — the latest in a number of Houdini biographies he'd borrowed. He began to read from the point he'd left off the night before.

Harry Houdini's feelings on the death of his mother can be seen in the public efforts to monumentalise and record her passing, to maintain her memory long into the future. But not only her. His entire family is buried in the same place — father, sister and brothers — and all recorded with a large, curved arrangement in stone, a pillar at each end. His wife's name is there in relief in the stone, too, though Bess was Catholic and so had to be interred elsewhere, as her own family apparently wished. At the foot of the gravesite, you can see the figure of a woman carved in the classical Greek manner, bent over and weeping; she is going to be there forever.

Houdini was a man who had no real grasp on loss, its nature, how to accept and deal with it as an adult. This was also a man who did not have a name that was truly his. He had made up the word 'Houdini' and given it to himself; he had borrowed from one of his heroes, as a sort of tribute to the French illusionist Jean Eugène Robert-Houdin. But then, under the name 'Houdini' on the gravestone is the name

'Weiss'. And as if to remind these people of their true origins, that there are some things entirely inescapable, to call them to account almost, is the epitaph to his failed father:

'Sacred to the memory of Our Dearly Beloved Husband and Father Rev. Dr MAYER SAMUEL WEISS Rabbi & Teacher in Israel 1829–1892 R.I.P.'

That the man had issues was an understatement. The absolute worship of his mother, the childish, obsessional relationship with his wife. Then, as for his father, the rabbi, a mysterious sort of figure — where did his father fit in? With that sort of baggage, Terry mused, just how good was the greatest of all untanglers of knots at unscrambling his own private ones? (If he was inclined to look inside at all, that is, for which there didn't seem to be a lot of evidence …) The more Terry thought about it, the more he thought the best answer was probably 'Not very good at all'.

Depressing as it was to speculate about Houdini's mental state, what this (Norwegian) biographer had put down about the man made a kind of sense. And there were echoes: Terry himself knew well what it was not to go by his original name. He was not really a Terry; his given name was Athanasios. (The difference was that Houdini had deliberately excised his name and given himself a new one.) Terry's own mother and father stuff was also a mess. Not exactly the mess that Harry's was, but a mess just the same.

Terry closed the book to ready himself for the real business of this day. He began to pack his sports bag with gear, all the while indulging in a little daydream. He could see himself performing his magic tricks somewhere on a stage before a great crowd as his young helper, Ricky, stood next to him. They were a father and son combo and the crowd was loving it — puffs of coloured smoke rose from the wings of the stage, doves flew from their cages, the audience clapped and cheered and roared. He saw himself sneaking a quick look at the boy standing next to him — who, after acknowledging the applause with a bow and a wave, beamed that lovely bright smile of his back up at his father. A dream now — but later this afternoon, he hoped to make it real.

Today he would collect Ricky from his mother and they would have lunch together in the city. After that, he would see if they could find a magician's outfit for someone as small as his son, who was not tall for his age. (If not, he would investigate dinner suits in boys' sizes — that was probably the easier option as he'd often seen them worn by kids at weddings and the like.) The plan was for Ricky to be wearing his new outfit before the day was over.

The outing began without any dramas. Jenny hadn't needed the cajoling Terry had expected; instead she wished them both a good time (that being more for Ricky's benefit, Terry thought). The boy was in a great frame of mind and more than happy with the proposed expedition. They left Ashfield and headed into the city by bus — Terry's only mode of transport these days since he had agreed that Jenny needed the car more than he did.

By ten am the two of them were in town and had begun the rounds of the shops. They were in the second of the city's two 'serious' magic shops, as Terry thought of them — Jeremy's Prestidigitation Warehouse — when he floated the idea to Ricky. Taking care not to put pressure on him, Terry said, 'Hey, what do you think of maybe being my partner sometimes when I do my magic show? You could be, like, my assistant!'

'What would I have to do, Dad?' Ricky asked, straightaway warm to the idea.

'Not much to start with — just hand me stuff that I need. Then you could learn some tricks to do all on your own. What do you say?'

'Yeah. That'd be good, Dad.'

Terry savoured these words, before adding, 'You reckon? You sure? You don't have to if you don't want to.'

'I do. That'd be good. But when?'

'Well, we could start this afternoon. I've got a show to do, if you'd like to help.'

'I do, I mean I would!'

Among the things Terry had missed most about his son was the way he had of agreeing to a proposition that took his fancy — he felt revived by the boy's enthusiasm.

The early part of the outing went well, even though neither of the establishments they'd visited carried authentic magician suits in junior sizes. Jeremy's had a version made of cheap material, more in the way of a party costume than a proper suit, and Ricky picked up on it straightaway. 'Dad, it's not the right kind, is it? But it's good enough, isn't it?'

'For now, why not?' Terry replied. 'We've got a show to do.'

They left the shops with Terry promising he'd see a tailor about a genuine suit for Ricky in the not too distant future. Next thing was to grab some lunch and head out to the Gladesville facility where he was booked to do a matinee. 'They're nice old people there, don't worry,' he reasured his son. 'And all you've got to do is hand me the things I ask for. They're in the bag here. I've been practising my escapes … you'll get a big surprise!'

Terry had indeed been practising. He was keen to conquer a lock-and-chain escape, and beyond that, determined to get past his fear of the straitjacket that had caused him such grief.

They arrived at the Banjo Paterson home and found the usual small crowd already assembled in the recreation room. Ricky, pride overcoming his affected nonchalance, trailed after his father as Terry greeted the staff. All was fine until Terry took him to one side and said, 'Time to get into the suit — have to look the part, eh?' As it dawned on Ricky what was being asked of him, that he would need to stand on stage and remember what to do, he stiffened.

'You'll be fine,' said Terry encouragingly, and pointed out the men's toilet where he could get changed.

Ricky returned, looking like the proper magician's offsider, but his nervousness was evident.

'I'm not sure what I have to do, but.'

Terry smiled and patted him on the head. 'Hardly anything. Just stand to one side and look like you're with me! That should be easy. And when I ask you for something, just give it to me, okay? After the hand tricks — which you don't have to help me with — I'm doing three escapes: set of handcuffs, then a lock and chain around my hands and feet, then a straitjacket.'

Ricky nodded as confidently as he could as his father showed him the gear for the first two escapes, but looked confused by the mass of heavy cotton and belts that he held up last. 'What's that?'

Terry shook the flaps and arms out to show the outlines of something like a coat. 'I'm going to put my arms through here, and you're going to do these belts up. And then … I'm going to get out of it!'

Again Ricky nodded, if this time with less enthusiasm.

*

Working his way efficiently through the warm-up tricks, Terry had time to notice that his son was absorbed in the performance. By the end of the first part, he even led the clapping when his father bowed. To Terry, the boy looked more than fine in his outfit. The next part, too, went well. Each time Terry asked, 'Young sir, what cruel trap do you have ready for your master?', Ricky leaned forward, reached into the bag and handed his father the props for the next trick.

Terry had done his homework with the simpler releases. He cranked the drama up by helping Ricky clang and clatter the gear — the cuffs as they were placed on his wrists, the chains as they were wound around his hands and feet. Terry saw some nervousness in Ricky as he did this, but whispered softly, 'Don't worry, I've got keys. Keep smiling.' And the boy dutifully obliged.

The straitjacket escape went well, or so Terry thought as he was working his way out of the thing. He had managed to master this only a week ago and there had been no time or way to make it look smooth or effortless. As he had come to know, it was all sheer and brutal muscle.

Judging by the oohs and ahhs, the act of exiting the contraption was well received, but Ricky's response was something else. In the moments before Terry finally rid himself of the last buckle, which required him to lie on his back on the floor like an upturned turtle, he found himself locking eyes with his son for an instant. Ricky was standing on the other side of the dais with his fists clenched, face blanched and looking anxious.

Terry could not get upright — or through the last part of the proceedings — quickly enough.

Before the clapping had stopped, Terry whisked the boy out of sight and grabbed him in a bear hug. 'Didn't mean to scare you, Ricky. You weren't worried, were you?'

The boy did not answer. Instead his eyes began to well up. Terry was instantly furious with himself. But he would not complicate the boy's pain with his own emotions. He held him closer instead. 'Sorry, Ricky. So sorry, son. Didn't mean for that to happen.'

Terry returned the boy to his mother at five pm. He took another bus to return to the city. He wanted to speak to Hal.

13

Suffer Little Children

'Hal, an unqualified success. Except that I scared the hell out of Ricky. The last thing I wanted.'

Silence. Terry stared at his mentor, seated in his usual director's chair. Hal had listened to his account of the afternoon's events, occasionally murmuring 'mmm', but saying nothing. Terry wondered if he had offended him, or whether he simply had not heard him. Hal's head was bowed so low it was hard to tell what he was thinking. 'You said it was time for the next stage. The next realm, isn't that what you called it? Hal?'

Hal looked up sharply. 'Should have talked to me before you tried something like that. But you've been absent, haven't you?'

'Maybe I was practising being disappeared!' Terry said, a little irritated at being scolded.

'Got a note from your parents? No ...?' Softening, Hal lowered his voice. 'Don't worry about what happened, we can work on that. Children are everything. And I say that as someone who's never had any. Our master never had any either, you know, which reminds me ...' He looked to Terry for a sign that he might continue.

'Go ahead.'

Hal squinted, as if collecting his thoughts. 'What I'm about to tell you happened not long after the challenge at Callan Park. Harry decided he needed to go for another one of his walks. A practical necessity these, because when he was performing there was not much time for his training regime. Walking also relaxed him. So where to go that day was the question. The decision was Paddington. And so, without Bess, but with Frank Sargeson for company, this fine morning Harry left the hotel and set off.

'My father was familiar with the way east from the Australia Hotel, which was where they were staying in Sydney. This was the first time Harry had wandered out alone, more or less, in public in Australia, in daylight. Because whenever word went out, as I say, there was a mob to contend with.

'So it's off up to Oxford Street, the pair of them, on foot. Great day, the sun's shining through the trees in Hyde Park … Just imagine that walk, Terry. You can see large black and white birds, magpies or currawongs, swooping and calling, and Harry, being the crowd pleaser he is, every so often doffing his hat and smiling at the couples, the mothers out with their daughters, waving at the carters going past with their horses and drays.

'Along Oxford Street they go, striding past all the commercial premises: men's tailors and hotels, hardware stores and banks; a busy part of town it was in those days. Stopping briefly to look in a window here and there …'

'What did he make of that street, any idea?'

'Don't know, can't remember my father saying, but I can't think he was impressed. The variety wouldn't have been there. Anyway, they keep going and only pause again when they arrive at the entrance to Victoria Barracks. Think of that long stone wall, the sentries on duty, all very grim-looking. Apparently Harry thought it was a prison compound.

'Up the hill and past another run of shops, then they turn left off Oxford Street and continue down into the twisting, narrow back streets of Paddington. Harry looks at the rows of terrace houses and tries to imagine their occupants. "What kind of people live here?" he asks. "Oh, just working people, I believe," Frank tells him. "Reminds me a little of New Orleans, the fancy iron lace, Frank," Harry remarks. And from the way the houses were all crammed together so tightly, they looked like they'd had the breath squeezed out of them, he says. "A situation with which I am personally only too well acquainted, Frank! Only too well acquainted!"

'If anyone needed plenty of room it was Harry Houdini. In New York, in German Harlem where he and Bess lived in a twelve-roomed apartment, he had space for his library, which was huge, as well as for his servants and assistants. Remember, he'd spent his childhood squeezed into a tiny room with four of his siblings.

'So here he is and looking around as you do. Scanning the distance, Harry sees some children playing a game of chasings on the street up ahead. They are racing madly from one side to the other, trying to touch each other, screaming and shouting.

'But then, when he is near enough, he notices they're poorly dressed, these three children; and what is more, two of them are shoeless. They're very young too, maybe five or six at the most, and it seems peculiar that their mothers would allow them to play outside in such a free, unsupervised way.

'But then they hear a bell ring, a sharp little hand bell, and the children make a mad dash back to one side of the street and disappear from view.'

'Where did they go?'

'Well, a little further on Frank and Harry see that these kids have gone through a gate into a large garden. There's a big rundown stone house in there; at first Harry thinks this is an empty house, or maybe a school of some sort. He looks about for a sign, then sees one hanging over the gate: "St. Anne's Orphanage. Governess Mrs. Chas. Simpson".

'Between the fence's iron railings, Harry sees children bolting from behind the building and assembling in two rows on a wide space in front of the house. A stern-looking woman in a black dress appears a few moments later, then positions herself at the top of the steps leading into the house. Finally, the children are all more or less where they're meant to be. Fifty or sixty in number, according to Frank, and none of them much older than the kids they'd seen playing earlier. All of them were wearing old clothes — some of the boys were in canvas britches, the girls decked out in rough pinafores. And here's the thing, hardly any of them were wearing shoes.

'The woman in charge — if that was what she was — suddenly begins to shout at the assembled group. At which point many of the children hang their heads. Frank and Harry couldn't make out exactly what she was saying, but the angry tone, they couldn't miss that. A young man arrives at her side, and she points out one of the children to him — a boy — and he marches up to him threateningly. Next thing, this enforcer takes hold of the little guy by the upper arms and gives him a mighty shake.

The boy begins to sob loudly — loudly enough for Harry and Frank to hear right there on the street.

'At the sound of that pitiful crying, Harry has to stop himself from charging in. Instead, he grips two of the railings and vents his own anger by first squeezing them, then pulling them, as hard as he can. He turns to my father and says, "Things like this should not be, should never be in the world."

'But to make it worse, it's as if this horrible show will never stop. That character isn't going to let up, it's plain; meanwhile the little boy keeps crying, and the woman stays on the steps, glaring at him.

'Only now Harry has had enough. He throws the gate open and marches in, and comes to the attention of the two adults; they are distracted and the ugly business ends for the moment. By the time he reaches the woman in black, her young helper is back by her side.

'Harry races up the steps, causing the couple to shrink back. All that massive energy released, he's furious; his eyes are all fiery, he's almost tearful. He stares at the harpy; his fists are clenched.

'"Don't you know how to look after children here, ma'am? Don't you know?"

'"I beg your pardon," she replies, "but who do you think you are, talking to me in such a manner?"

'"Who do I think I am? Why, I'll tell you. My name is Harry Houdini. I am visiting from America."

'At this, the young helper moves forward to say something to her, but his mistress raises her palm. Harry's not going to be put off by these types and he continues, cold as ice: "I was passing by, ma'am. I see that your children need shoes. How many children do you have here?"

'Harry's got her fixed and probably frightened; but if she's not going to answer, he's going to make it understood he's not a man who can be ordered away. "Mrs Simpson? Is that your name? Will you answer me, please?"

'"Sixty-two," she says finally. "We have sixty-two children at St Anne's."

'"Sixty-two. All right then. Two pairs each. I want you to buy them two pairs each. A Sunday pair and a common pair."

'How did she react to that?' Terry broke in.

'No doubt as if she now had proof these two were just a pair of nuts on the loose. But Harry Houdini is not to be denied. "I will send you the money today, later today," he says, reaching into a pocket for his notepad and pencil. He writes down the address and then, in a low and deliberate voice, adds, "Do you understand? I am staying in Sydney and I will check. This must be done."

'And that's that. He turns quickly, my father in tow, vaults down the steps; he pauses at the bottom, but only for a moment to smile at the children, then marches purposefully to the gate.'

'And did he do what he said? Did he send the money?' Terry asked.

'Of course. He got one of the team to organise it. Houdini always kept his word. Always. And if you like irony, Terry, I can tell you that Paddington and nearabouts was in those days the centre of the shoe trade in Sydney. There were boot makers and cobblers and shoe factories everywhere ...'

Terry had listened and, in the gloom of the hall, allowed himself to ponder. That business with the children, the shoeless orphans — did Houdini have a thing about poverty in general or did he feel sorry for kids in particular? 'Don't you know how to look after children?' suggested the latter. He began to wonder about Houdini's own upbringing — then turned to think of Hal's, about which he knew practically nothing. The idea of asking Hal occurred to him, but that would have to wait for another time.

Terry looked at his watch. Seven pm. Never mind that it was the weekend, around now Ricky would be being badgered about homework by his mother, just as he would be whining to be allowed to veg out in front of the TV after dinner. What was the boy thinking at this moment? If it was about him, his absent father, Terry hoped it wasn't bad. Whatever had been up with Houdini a hundred years ago — and he was sensing there'd been a lot up with him — Terry had more immediate concerns. Hal's gravelly voice broke into his reverie.

'Hello, Terry? Are you there? We're moving on — today was meant to be about Disappearance, as I recall.' Hal waved a hand in front of his face.

'I'm here, Hal.'

When he next spoke, Hal's voice was softer. 'If you're thinking about kids, I don't know what you can do about your own, Terry. All I know is you've got to look after them, mate. You've just got to look after them.'

'I don't know much either, Hal, but you're right about that.'

'Okay then. About disappearing —'

'Before you go on, I don't want to leave anything out. Shouldn't I know more about escaping?'

'More than you do, correct, but there's plenty of less killing escapes you can learn, whereas straitjackets ... well ...' Hal paused, and waved dismissively. 'Who would know about them these days?'

'Great effect though.'

'Yes, yes,' Hal said impatiently. 'But you're on a crash course, Terry. You've got to move on — and quickly. I told you I want to see you all trained up and with a new act inside three months. Twelve weeks and twelve weeks only. But you're already behind and in danger of blowing that schedule.'

'Sorry, Hal, I know — but with good reason. Can we pick up where we left off? I'll do my best. What's today's lesson, remind me again?'

'Disappearance, my boy. Try to pay attention.'

'Right. You'll be pleased to hear I began building a cabinet of my own a while ago,' Terry said brightly.

Hal looked sceptical. 'Building one? You couldn't possibly. Not the professional version.'

'I got some plans off the internet.'

Hal waved this away. 'Forget that. I've got the real thing, couple of them actually. At my main storage, at Rosehill. See, this is where I live, first. And keep some stuff, second. But twenty years in the game, I built up mountains of gear, and kept most of it too. All my serious stuff and the rest of my archive is in storage out at Rosehill racecourse. Which is where I'm taking you next.'

'Man of mystery you, Hal.'

'Could say that, Terry. Oh, and by the way. Harry stuffed up more than once himself. Got to learn from it, that's all.'

14
Rosehill

The next week, Terry collected Hal and together they got on a western line train heading out to Rosehill racecourse. Terry was having difficulty with the concept of Hal having stuff stored at such a place but resisted the urge to ask him about it. There might be some screamingly obvious answer. You never knew with Hal.

'Stay beside me,' said Hal quietly as they were approaching the main gates to the racecourse. 'And act natural.' Terry thought he was kidding — until he saw the determination and seriousness on Hal's face. He was marching stiffly, staring straight ahead, almost as if he expected to be apprehended at any moment.

Terry wondered why Hal was so tense and secretive. This was a non-race day, and there was no problem getting inside, and even wandering around at will. Track staff and groundspeople were at work. Barriers were being moved about, turf was being rolled, horse trailers were coming and going. There was so much activity that no-one paid them any attention — they were just another couple of visitors perhaps, soaking up the atmosphere.

The wide expanse of track and landscaped surroundings were attractive in a fake-pastoral sort of way — a definite feeling of peace curtained off this green space from the world around. There was plenty of room even now, though the course had slowly been hemmed in by industry and suburban development over the decades. But Terry could imagine what it must have been like ninety and more years ago, with paddocks and green fields beyond the track itself.

'Stay close,' Hal muttered again as he steered Terry over to the oldest-looking grandstand, the one that stood behind the Leger. A string of shed doors lined one side wall of the stand; they looked like the entrances to storage spaces of some kind, confirmed when Hal said, 'I'm in one of those.'

They went around the back of the stand where a set of stairs descended to the basement area. Here, they came to a long corridor with doors almost identical to the ones on the outside wall. Terry was sure he was looking at the same string of enclosed spaces, but from the other side. There was no-one else in the basement and, Terry guessed, no reason for anyone to venture down. It seemed this facility was left over from an earlier age. More modern storage areas were likely to be available elsewhere around the grounds.

'No-one's used these for years,' Hal confirmed. 'They're mainly empty except for one or two down the end with old turf-rolling gear in them.'

Each unit had a pair of tongue and groove doors and a simple latch and bolt arrangement for security, along with a padlock. Hal stopped at one in the middle of the row, took a key from his pocket, gently and quietly opened the lock, then pulled the bolt and opened the doors. Terry followed him in and waited for Hal to turn on the light — a single naked globe overhead. Almost directly inside the door was a desk and a pair of antiquated office chairs; in one corner was a metal filing cabinet, while some pine crates and a few suitcases were stacked in the one pile in the opposite corner. But that was not all. Behind this little office set-up was an array of magic equipment, including at least three cabinets that Terry could identify and maybe one more — if the long object in front wasn't a real coffin, that is …

'Wow, Hal! You weren't kidding about having some serious stuff, were you?'

'No, I was not. I've kept a lot of things, as you can see. Not everything, because that would've needed half-a-dozen shipping containers — just the good stuff. The gear I was most fond of … Have a browse while I get organised.'

Terry stepped around the desk to take a closer look at the cabinets.

'Why this place, Hal?'

'Free. And I hate to see things go to waste. But also this place, Rosehill, was where Harry got ready for his Sydney flight demos back in 1910, after setting the record in Victoria, down at Diggers Rest, like I told you. It's one of my sacred sites, you could say.'

'Racecourse back then?'

'It was, but there was lots of flat land around here — pastures, open fields. Ideal for a flyer.'

Hal took his coat off and went to his desk — he made a show of seating himself, as if to say a magician is required to do office work, too, you know. He started to leaf ostentatiously through a large, bound notebook. 'This is my index. There's a whole bunch of printed stuff on disappearance techniques, vanishing illusions. Got to find what I've filed it under …'

As Hal ran his finger down the pages, Terry began to investigate the largest and most dramatic-looking of the disappearance cabinets.

'Not so fast!' Hal croaked. 'Why don't you have a look through the archive while we're here, son? Got a lot of original Houdini clippings over there, my scrapbooks and such.' Hal pointed Terry to the pile of crates and suitcases.

Terry went to the most accessible crate. It had no lid and seemed to be full of folded newspaper race guides; same with the one below. The only interesting thing was that the papers dated to as recently as a year ago. 'Are you a betting man, Hal?'

'I was — and a lot of other useless things besides.' More softly he added, 'I cleaned myself up … The Houdini stuff is in the cases, if you want to know. First one is good.'

Though tempted to ask Hal about his 'cleaning up', Terry realised now was probably not the time. He focused instead on the top suitcase. This was of a vintage kind, with leather belts wrapped around it and large metal clasps, such as might be found on a sailing ship trunk. He pulled it onto the concrete floor and straightened it up so as to be able to open it. Inside were more newspapers, but this time dated March and April 1910. Here were copies of *The Argus*, the *Australasian* and the *Sydney Morning Herald*. Each had been folded to a page featuring photos and reports of Harry Houdini's exploits in Australia. The interest and curiosity he had aroused all those years ago was plain to see.

'Amazing, all this, Hal. You must have been collecting for years.'

'I have. And sometimes new things turn up and I have to decide whether they're best kept in the city or here.'

Terry briefly scanned the first articles, reading a few sentences of a floridly detailed description of a performance at the Tivoli. Whatever else, these pieces told of a time before radio and television when, the few small and grainy photos notwithstanding, the printed word was pre-eminent.

'Let me know if you find anything that interests you,' Hal said, moving over to the filing cabinet, where he began searching through a drawer full of manila folders.

Terry looked down at the other contents of the case. A pile of ruled notepaper sheets, a couple of unused writing pads, some opened envelopes that looked as if their contents were still inside. As well, there was a child's project book into which some papers had been stuffed, a scrapbook of Hal's, perhaps, started but never finished.

Inside the case, as well, was a set of yellowed pages, ten or twelve, stapled and folded in half, containing notes typed with a manual typewriter. 'Report re Francis Sargeson' was the title, under which was a subheading, 'Sceptics Society, 27th September 1971'. Juggling everything, Terry turned over the first page and was about to read on when his grip loosened and a scrap of paper fell from the report onto the floor. He leaned over to pick it up, a page torn from a small jotter. Before putting it back in place he saw that there was a note scrawled on it — 'Connection at Jordan Street, Marrickville' — nothing more.

This was the suburb where Terry had spent his earliest years. For a few moments he simply stared at the note, wondering what it meant. He was aware that Hal was absorbed in his own concerns, but then sensed him tilt his head slightly in his direction. He could not tell for sure if Hal was watching him. A second or two later and Hal was shifting in agitation from one foot to another.

'What have you got there?'

'Oh, just this piece of paper. The address is familiar, don't know why … And something in this scrapbook about Francis Sargeson … your dad, Frank, right?'

As soon as Hal saw the objects in Terry's hands, he moved across to him and took them with some force, then returned them to the case. 'They're nothing. Everything here needs a bloody good clean-out. Don't worry, there's plenty of stuff more interesting than that to look at!'

He took Terry's elbow and began urging him back towards the cabinets and other equipment. 'Now! Let me introduce you to the next stage of your career.'

Hal pointed first to the smallest cabinet, a box of about a metre square. He swung open the two doors to reveal what looked like a black velvet-lined interior.

'You've seen how these work, right?'

'Read about how they work, yes, and you know I'm trying to make one myself.' Terry stepped forward, excited to be peering inside the red and gold painted box. 'But first one I've ever looked inside … nicely made, isn't it?'

'Nothing special though. The angle of the mirror reflects the black on the opposite wall, the space behind the mirror is where the thing is hidden, whatever it might be — someone's jewellery, a dove, whatever you reckon will work for the particular audience. Good for small, close-up groups. Works well too, all the joins are so neat it's impossible to tell what's going on when it's opened up.'

Hal edged his hand in and swung the diagonal mirror across on its pivot hinge, then back again.

'Very neat.'

'So long as you get the subterfuge right and hide the swinging — which is where practice comes in. Anyway, same principle with all vanishing cabinets. Look at this one.'

Hal bypassed the middle cabinet, which looked as if it was meant for a person, and went to the largest of the three. 'I bought this from America but never got to use it myself. Know what it's for?'

Terry studied it for a time — wider than it was high, about three metres on the horizontal to two on the vertical, and about two metres deep. 'Hmm … not really. A small car?'

'A very famous old illusion — disappearing a whole donkey. First developed by Charles Morritt in the nineteenth century.'

'And you never used it?'

'I bought this not long before I gave it all away, when everything got too much. Couldn't afford the donkey, the handling … in fact, couldn't even afford me …'

Terry was about to ask him to elaborate when Hal shakily spun around and stepped away, as if to remove himself as quickly as possible from what he had just said. He positioned himself on one side of the middle cabinet, and quickly recovered his equilibrium. 'But I'm beginning to think you and I can manage one of these basic disappearances — once I've got you organised, you'll have that in your act as well. All right?'

'Absolutely. But, you know, it's hard to believe you want to do all this for me, Hal.'

Hal smiled. 'Let's just say that I've got a soft spot for … for someone who's battling like you. And you've got potential, Terry, you have.'

Hal dusted off his hands and became particular about packing things away; he insisted they put everything back exactly as they had found it.

Out in the daylight again, Terry felt the blue, clear skies above as a kind of relief. Rounding the corner of the grandstand he saw the expanse of the racecourse, a huge green circle of turf bordered with white pickets, and was drawn to take a closer look.

'Let's go down there, Hal,' he said, pointing to the fence. 'You can tell me about when Harry Houdini came to Rosehill.'

Terry made his way towards the fence, aiming to get as near the track as possible. As usual, Hal was ready with a story.

'Thirteen miles from the city, Terry, that's how far out along Parramatta Road, from their hotel, this track was. Don't know if Harry thought thirteen was bad luck, but he always tried not to be superstitious, so he might have put the distance out of his mind. When they came out to Rosehill back then, their car would have been bumping along on wood, you know.'

'What do you mean?'

'The road surface. True. They used to lay something like railway sleepers for a road back then, tar on top. Harry's crowd must have laughed to see what we called a main road. Coming out here in those days, at around about Homebush you'd be looking at abattoirs, stockyards, farms, long stretches of posts and rails. Could even think you'd hit the country. And you would have in a way. This was the nearest place to the city where there was space for flying.'

'You said about the plane earlier … was it here already?'

'It was. When they turned off the main drag and got down here for their first visit, everything was already set up for their runs. This was a professional outfit, no question. Forget that it was a hundred years ago.'

'Training runs?'

'Yes, then demonstration flights. A great place for that. And the race club mustn't have had any objections. Any rate, I don't think my old man ever mentioned any.'

Terry looked at Hal, waited until he caught his eye. 'Hal, I still can't get my head around the fact that your father was here with Harry Houdini a hundred years ago.'

'Stranger things have happened, Terry, mate. Stranger things have happened.'

'Don't doubt it, but there's something else too — how old was he when you were born? He must have been a bloody great age.'

'Well, I'm no spring chicken and he definitely got started late. Would have been about seventy as far as I can work out … To be a part of that adventure, what I would have given, Terry! What I would have given!'

'The flying?'

'Everything! The way they came at things, those guys: "You say it can't be done? We'll do it! You say it's crazy to fly a plane at the bottom of the effing world? Well, we say, if there's an audience we'll do it, if there's no audience, we'll still do it!" Man, not only was it great showbiz and magic, they knew how to *live* back then. They were giants.'

Terry waited until he was sure Hal had no more to say for the moment. 'Hal, you got me hooked, no question.'

Hal beamed at him.

Something further occurred to Terry. 'He flew …'

He looked up at the skies, Hal following his gaze.

'He did. I once thought I might have a go at it myself — I mean, recreate Harry's record flight. Terry, wouldn't that be something? Maybe worth thinking about …?'

Terry was conscious of Hal looking at him. 'It would. Except it's a very hard kind of thinking,' he replied, trying not to sound dismissive. He turned to face Hal before speaking again.

'What's the third realm you told me about? Levitation, right?'

'You're gettin' it, ain't ya?' Hal seemed pleased. 'Yes, and flight's a form of levitation in my book. Look, Terry, we get the basics under your belt first, then anything's possible.'

Hal checked his watch and gave a little start. 'Jesus. Security start wandering around about now. Can you come back here with me tomorrow? I want to introduce you to the deep art of the vanishing cabinet.'

15
The Cabinet

Hal spread his feet wide, assuming a stance Terry had not seen him adopt before. Next, he leaned to his left at the hips and flung his arms wide, then pointed his right hand dramatically straight at the cabinet. Terry saw the slight wobble as Hal worked to maintain his position. But no matter. This, he understood, was the magician at work. This had been his style.

In a loud and sonorous voice Hal proclaimed: 'Ladies and gentlemen, there is a realm about which we mortals know little. A realm about which, may I respectfully suggest, we really know nothing at all …' He broke the pose to speak to Terry: 'How does that sound? Getting 'em in?'

'You got *me* in, Hal,' Terry replied.

'Okay, down to work.'

Hal's plan was to take Terry through the steps required to make a human being disappear from the interior of an upright magic cabinet. The cabinet itself, Terry thought, had a kind of stark power about it. Nothing like the old-time wooden cabinets he could recall from TV magic shows, or even recent magic magazines; it had no gaudy coach-work paint or gilt, but with its clean modern lines and anodised aluminium-like finish, it almost resembled a giant upright toolbox. There was a mirror 'skirt' around three sides at the base which was so highly polished that it could perfectly reflect adjacent surfaces, according to Hal. 'The audience is looking at that and thinking the thing's off the ground. It's not. With this you step out the back at floor level but nobody can pick it.'

For the first exercise, Terry took the part of the magician, while Hal acted as his assistant. Hal would place himself inside the cabinet, allow some moments to pass, then call Terry to meet him around the back where he would have materialised silently and surreptitiously. He did not show Terry the steps he was taking, but said he wanted this first exercise to be a chance for Terry to 'practise the spiel'.

According to Hal he was making a better fist of it each time. The problem was that he wasn't loud enough, or ominous-sounding enough, and Hal came up to him for a refresher.

'Gotta give a pleasant note on the surface, Terry, but with something scary riding underneath. Go for a light monotone to start, say like: "Until modern physics came along, we believed that matter was solid, constant, you could not break it down or rearrange it …" Then shift to make it sound like you've just been handed a terrible secret which you are obliged to share with the audience: "But, since the advent of subatomic physics and quantum mechanics, we … now … know … better … *don't we?*" And stress the last.'

Terry was impressed, not least by the vocabulary. 'That's great, only where did you learn those big words?'

Hal grinned at him, then thought for a moment. 'Good question. Episode of *The Twilight Zone* maybe?'

Then it was Terry's turn to acquire the knack of silently and quickly disappearing out the back of the cabinet, on cue and as instructed. 'What we really need, of course, is a pretty young lady, but you'll do for now.'

Hal scratched some stage marks in the dust on the floor for Terry, to indicate where he should stand as the victim before he allowed himself to be placed inside the cabinet.

The thing was, Hal hadn't shown him what he was meant to do once inside. 'Shouldn't I know how to get out when you give the word?'

'In good time, Terry. I'll let you know in a minute.'

Hal ran through an abbreviated rapid-fire intro, opened the cabinet and ushered Terry inside.

Terry was immediately disoriented. He was not prepared for the complete and utter darkness, nor for how confined and cramped the interior was. Any movement he made caused him to bump against a rigid, unforgiving surface. Whether shoulders, back, chest, arms or legs, he was never more than a few centimetres from these flat, hard planes. When he heard the clasps clicked shut he felt even more uncomfortable.

'Right, Hal, what's the go?' he called out after a few seconds.

When there was no answer he called once more, louder in case he hadn't been heard: 'Hal, you didn't say what I've got to do!'

Again there was no response, and Terry wondered whether Hal had been caught short and gone to the loo. He certainly hoped he hadn't died on him. He decided to try to muscle his way out, pushing at this or that point but getting nowhere; when he tried to find a latch or tab to pull, he found nothing. Terry felt panic rising. But just as quickly he began to work on himself.

He recalled his reaction when he'd been tied into that straitjacket. A lesson had been learned. This needed calm. This needed concentration, the application of positive and lateral thinking. As sweat began to trickle down his forehead and into his eyes, Terry set himself to work through a few questions. First, what was his main fear? That he'd be locked in forever? That was unlikely. He could feel his movements, constrained as they were, shifting this metal box ever so slightly across the floor.

I can kick and buck and twist and try to topple it over. It could open on impact. Or I could do that and scream and shout as well. Make enough noise and someone would come sooner or later …

With this approach, Terry's breathing and sweating slowed. When the cabinet was eventually and abruptly pulled open at the back, he was already in a calmer place. He climbed out to find a grinning Hal, and immediately felt a little annoyed. 'You could have told me what I was supposed to do first …'

'Oh, look, it's easy,' Hal said and revealed the swing point of the mirror he had pulled across to lock Terry into the tight triangle, and also the release lever behind him.

'What was the point then?'

'Two points. One, to teach you the first reaction people have as they watch someone stuffed into a tight space like this, something that looks sort of like a coffin. *I wouldn't want to be stuck in there!* It's claustrophobia.'

'But doesn't that belong to the escape realm?'

'It does. That's the minor key; there's a major one as well. Now, I want you to put me in one last time. I want you to then imagine me as one of your loved ones. Then see if you can find me. Then tell me how you feel. Okay?'

'Okay.'

They repeated the routine. And when it was time for Hal to vanish, he vanished good and proper. Soundlessly, quickly. Terry went behind the cabinet to see where he had hidden himself, but he was nowhere to be seen. His absence was somehow exciting and unpleasant at the same time.

He sat on one of the old office chairs, to contemplate the vanishing in the terms put to him. He tried to imagine it was Ricky who had been transported beyond this visible and tangible universe, to some place from which he might never return. The thought was ugly, shocking. Even as an exercise, Terry realised he couldn't countenance it, and jumped up to await Hal's reappearance.

When that came, it was a surprise. He appeared out of nothing, directly behind Terry. 'Effective, when you think about it, eh?'

'Where did you —?'

'Nothing to it. I made a route behind the junk here, avoiding the most likely places you'd look, to give myself time to get under the desk.'

Terry looked down and saw the space, so close to where his own feet had been.

'You're kidding me.'

'No, I was there all right.'

'Got a lot to learn, haven't I?'

'You do, but I hope you thought about the effect of disappearance — I mean the effect on the audience. Think about all those people, all the different kinds that might come to your show … an elderly woman whose hubby is maybe on his last legs, a single parent scared of losing her only child … Subconsciously, the vanishing act brings you right up to the doors of loss … I mean in here …' Hal pointed to his head briefly. 'And also here,' he said, gesturing towards his heart. 'For the magician, there's a power in this. And a kind of responsibility. Entertainment is only part of our game. Do you get what I'm saying, Terry?'

Terry nodded. What Hal was teaching him was one thing, where he was taking him, another altogether.

An hour later, after Terry had achieved a reasonably smooth grip on the steps and procedures required to operate the device — he was not perfect yet, but had more or less committed them to memory — Hal clapped his hands and called out: 'Okay. That's enough for starters. Time we finished today.'

Terry saw that he was tiring and did not in any case feel he could hold much more in his own head.

'You should have this at your place, Terry. Got to figure out how to get it there.'

Terry had not expected Hal to make such an offer. 'You don't mean that, do you?'

'Yes I do. I want you to start thinking big, Terry. What's more, I'm going to look around to see if we can't get you some proper gigs.'

Hal's audacity made Terry smile. 'Wait a minute, Hal, you're talking to a guy who hasn't graduated from the old people's home yet!'

Hal held up a hand. 'Stop right there. Now don't make me cross. Twelve weeks I said, didn't I?'

'You did, but that doesn't seem long enough and —'

'Twelve weeks, stick with me and you'll have an act good enough for some of the smaller clubs, believe me. Meanwhile I'll check if my old booking agent is still around …'

16

The Semi-Professional

Small clubs be buggered. Hal had lied. In preparation for this, his first semi-professional performance, Terry stepped onto the stage of the auditorium and scanned the space, the seats. This was a wide, cavernous room with, he was convinced, a holding capacity of a thousand or more. The prospect was so daunting that he went immediately past feeling nervous to doomed resignation: if he was to stuff up, it would be in front of the sort of huge crowd that guaranteed a kind of anonymity. There would be so many, any eye contact would be impossible.

Against Terry's expectations, Hal had been able to engineer this gig for him at the Panania RSL. This 'engagement', as Hal termed it, was a favour to him from one of his old mates, Colin Taylor. Agreeably for Hal, Taylor was still managing entertainment at a venue he himself had performed in many times. He offered Terry a 'semi-professional' try-out in a Friday night slot when the regular magician, Kenny Boon, begged off ill three days out. ('Not surprised,' Hal had said to Terry. 'Was hitting the turps for years and never did a thing about it.') It was, in fact, a discount 'Parents and Kids Night', the club desperate to get audiences any way it could.

That hadn't worried Terry. He also took some consolation in the way the manager and Hal had discussed the show earlier in the evening; no-one was expecting a top flight event, he was a fill-in, a guy starting out, Hal explained. 'He's looking for an opening, Colin.'

Colin seemed wary of all such talk, especially coming from Hal Sargeson, whom he said he hadn't seen around for a dozen years and more. He also seemed a little fazed by the contrasting figures Hal and Terry cut — Terry in his dinner tux; Hal in his dusty old greatcoat over who knew what underneath. He did, however, warm to the idea of only having to pay, in the circumstances, a starter's fee for the Maestro of Magic's services.

Terry had assembled a good selection of gear and workable material, augmented by Hal's precious vanishing cabinet, enough for a show of an hour and a quarter by Hal's timing. They had hired a mini-van for the night to transport everything. Which was no problem except for the cost — Terry had calculated that at best he was going to pocket fifty dollars. He told Hal that he would split that with him, but Hal wouldn't hear of it. 'You need the money more than me,' he said.

As they'd arrived at the club in plenty of time, Hal was adamant that Terry should run through the tricks and illusions he'd be performing ahead of the show's high point — the cabinet vanishing act. That, Hal was satisfied, had been well enough rehearsed off-site. And he was happy enough about the sequence of tricks building up to it. But Terry's patter remained a concern. Although he had written a good deal of it down and practised in front of a mirror as he had been instructed, Hal was not convinced that he had it in hand yet, or that it was pitched correctly.

'Very important to get the words happening right, Terry. Can't emphasise that enough,' he told him behind the curtains.

Terry began his introductory spiel: 'Ladies and gentlemen, boys and girls, welcome to a magic act like no other ... Like no other because I'm going to let you in on the secret — hey, folks, none of what you're about to see is for real or —'

Hal stopped him with a raised hand there and then. 'You've changed it!'

'A bit,' Terry admitted, realising that he had yet to tell Hal.

'No way. Too subversive.'

Terry tried to explain. Folks today, especially the young, appreciated it when you didn't take things too seriously. They could still 'get' the magic, have fun, knowing also that they were being tricked. You couldn't fool kids today, they knew too much.

Hal dismissed the argument with a brisk shake of his head. 'I'm a traditionalist. I appreciate it when people do take things seriously. Gotta aspire to the best, not just cheap laughs. On the A team, you build the illusion, stay with the illusion ... Go back to the original, Terry.'

Terry needn't have worried about being overwhelmed by the numbers. When it was time to go on stage, he bounced out to find maybe twenty-five or thirty customers scattered across the front two or three rows. Some of them looked like they'd just wandered in from the pokies or been shooed away from the bars. The only official-looking audience members were a few parents and their children, whose familiarity with each other said they were the one party, maybe all from the same school.

And so, with a simpler form of banter and starting with the same ten or twelve hand tricks he had perfected and used in the past, Terry got through the first forty minutes of his performance with no hitches. There had been a smattering of applause and, even better, no booing, throughout. Terry retreated to the wings for a short break, hoping the vanishing work to come would bring a stronger reaction. Five minutes and a drink of water later, he was back on stage. He made fleeting eye contact with Hal, who was sitting at the back of the audience, watching intently. So far, Terry had avoided looking in his direction. Now he was about to be part of the show.

'Well, it's time to put aside childish things — oops, sorry, kids, you're not childish, I know!' Terry smiled down at the few kids, making sure he got their attention. 'Because I'm going to need someone from among the more mature members of the audience for what I am about to attempt, someone who is not easily panicked.' He looked this way and that, until he fixed his gaze firmly on Hal. 'You, sir! Would you be my assistant in, shall we say, some most mysterious work …?'

Hal did not speak but got up and moved towards the stage, doing his best to appear uncertain, glancing at this one and that in the audience as he headed up the aisle, shaking his head ruefully, as if seeking their support.

Once on stage, he gave Terry a moment's fright when he proceeded to take off his coat. Terry had anticipated he would leave it on, but was relieved when he saw Hal was wearing an old sports jacket and flannelette shirt underneath.

The routine began as planned. The house lights were dimmed and coloured stage lights — mainly reds and blues —

were brought to bear on the small circle of Terry, Hal and the mysterious-looking metal box. The patter, too, was as arranged — subtle, careful. Terry spoke of the way modern-day lives are managed, when you think about it, via boxes, receptacles and containers of one kind or another, all the way from the cradle to the grave. 'After we're born, we're put in a bassinet; if a child is sick it goes in a humidicrib … right? Then we live in a room, which is a kind of box, isn't it? If we are lucky enough to become an astronaut, we are put in a capsule and sent into space. When we die … well, don't want to upset anybody, but that's another kind of box, isn't it? What happens to people when they die, does anybody know? It's a strange thing. Maybe we just dematerialise, our atoms somehow scatter. Maybe it's a process a bit like this … Sir? Would you stand next to me, please, before I show these good people how something can lead to nothing … a nothing which I sincerely hope we can reverse here tonight!'

Terry opened up the front of the box, one door then the other, revealing a dark interior and nothing else. He spun the cabinet this way and that, turned it right round once, twice, then squared it up to the front of the stage. It was time for the clever arrangement of highly polished mirror panels inside to play their part, and for Hal to play his. To the sound of Terry's CD playing snatches of *Thus Spoke Zarathustra* over the AV system, Hal stepped inside and Terry again spun the box.

'Maybe there's no such thing as death? Have you ever thought of that, folks?'

The box slowed its rotation and Terry began to ease the doors open again, in time with the crescendo building over the speakers. As the music peaked, he flung them wide — there was no human being inside.

'Maybe, just maybe … we all go somewhere else!'

Terry paused, then heard what he wanted to hear: a murmur, a gasp. Not loud, hardly there at all — this was a small crowd — but there just the same.

He waited a few more moments. He pushed his hands into the box, being careful not to disturb the panels in any way. He peered in, calling, 'Sir, are you there?' but there was no answer. He tapped around the box, listening carefully for a response. He shook his head sorrowfully, in a way that suggested real departure, genuine loss. Then, just as mournfully, he closed the box again.

'Where do we all go? It's a question, isn't it? Science says everything is in net equilibrium, all the energy, all the mass, all the molecules … When our bodies break down they become part of new life again through the earth. The nitrogen cycle — you might have studied that in school, kids. Some religions say things come back in another form, reincarnation and all that, so it seems we're never truly gone … Let's see if that's true, shall we?'

Terry bent his head forward, putting his closed fists to his temples — the picture of concentration. Then, all of a sudden, he turned to the doors of the cabinet and swung them open wildly. And there was the man who had gone missing.

Hal stepped out slowly, all the while presenting his best impression of mild disorientation — he had previously told Terry that it didn't do to exaggerate the confusion. He was nothing more than a man seeking to have something — he did not know what — explained to him.

As if apprehending Hal's air of uncertainty, Terry said, 'Don't worry, sir, I'll try to explain what happened later.'

After copious thank yous and bows, Terry bade the audience farewell and goodnight. But instead of disappearing backstage, he couldn't help himself and flew around the wings back into the auditorium to be among the audience as they left. While Hal made himself scarce, waiting in the loo for the audience to dissipate, Terry greeted some of the kids and their parents and autographed the cheap flyers some had brought in from the foyer. He was not surprised to learn they were all year five pupils from the one primary school, whose teacher had started a magic club and who had got together this party as a special treat.

After everyone was gone and he was waiting for Hal to rejoin him, Terry felt a blanket of satisfying calm settle over him. It was the kind of satisfaction he had experienced after his earlier, more junior efforts, only this time much stronger, more distinct. This sensation was better than escaping. Better even than vanishing. On that stage, since plunged into darkness, everything had gone to order. What needed to be done up there, carefully, step by step, to create the illogic of illusion, made an exhilarating, mad kind of sense. And while acknowledging the help he had been given in grasping the art of disappearance, it was ultimately he who had worked the madness.

17

Ghosts

Terry felt lighter than he had for a very long time, so much so that he was confident he could lighten things even further. In magic you used only what was needed and needed only what you used.

The Monday following the Panania show, he hunted around the flat for useless and unused items he might throw away, until he was very soon confronted by one of the realities of his new, bachelor lifestyle: there was little in his current environment that was totally dispensable. There was, however, his mobile phone, an object he had come to loathe. He stared at it sitting on the kitchen table; it represented the last means, he knew, by which he might be assailed by timetables or expectations other than his own.

But as bold as he was feeling, he knew he could not get rid of the thing. What if someone called to book him for a show? He also needed to have a number Ricky could use to call him, and that more than anything made him hang on to it.

Later in the morning, the phone's screen lit up and he heard the text alarm sound. He picked it up, hoping it might be his boy. No such luck. It was, instead, a text from Jenny, reminding him to attend Downing Centre court for the first day of proceedings against the driver who had hit his mother-in-law. He had been aware that this was the day, and resented what he took to be an unfair assumption on her part that he couldn't be relied on to remember anything.

At ten am, Terry joined Jenny in a lawyer's office in Elizabeth Street to listen to Richard Lindeman, BA LLb, explain that, in terms of the case about to get underway, Jenny was most definitely an 'interested party'. But in legal terms not much more. Apparently, Terry also counted as an interested party.

This was a matter of the state prosecuting someone who had been charged with breaking the law, they heard. What were the possible outcomes? Jenny asked. That the person be found guilty of negligent driving occasioning death. Should there be a finding of guilt, there were various possibilities as to potential penalties. But the particular circumstances had to be taken into account. The driver was a woman in her sixties. She had no convictions of any kind. No serious driving infringements either. She had apparently been devastated by the experience and had been on medication, sedatives, ever since. Might she go to gaol? Unlikely. If found guilty, a big fine, a bond perhaps.

Jenny took a breath before she asked whether what the driver had done might also count as manslaughter. Lindeman paused before replying. 'Not in the circumstances.'

Jenny reacted as if someone had grabbed her by the scruff of the neck and was pushing her head under water. 'Well, what am I doing here?' she gasped. 'What is anyone doing here?'

'It's a good question,' Lindeman said soothingly, passing Jenny a box of tissues. 'But sadly we have to go on with it.'

He tried to lift her mood with something he imagined it wouldn't hurt her to hear: 'For what it's worth, we will be pursuing damages …'

Jenny said nothing. There was no need to pursue damages. As far as she was concerned, they had already been delivered to her, and in spades.

*

Terry entered the courtroom at eleven o'clock. As if magnetised, he was pulled towards Jenny's clan. He felt inexplicable relief in seeing her old man nod at him, if only to acknowledge his presence. He could sit anywhere, he told himself, but he was further comforted when his father-in-law beckoned to a seat next to him and close to Jenny — even if they were separated by her sisters.

It took a while for everyone to find their place. The murmur and chatter at the front receded, and the matter was announced suddenly, loudly. No-one could prepare themselves for this, thought Terry. To hear what had happened, and to hear the charges announced, was a shock to everyone. How unfeeling it all was. The defendant and her family quickly began crying. A strangled noise came from Jenny as she swayed towards her father, who put a protective arm around her shoulders. Jenny leaned away again, tilted forward and began rocking slowly with the anguish of it all. The way Terry felt, he may as well have killed someone.

Next they were subjected to the dreary routines of the law. The Crown case was outlined by the prosecution; the defence addressed the judge as to how it would be responding. The points of law, as each side saw them, began to be expounded — traded back and forth, seemingly tit for tat. Terry took it for a game, and the game was on in earnest. He watched and listened intently as the priests of the law reached for their fixes. This was the best, apparently, that the state could say or do about the disaster of a person's life lost. What a ghastly con it all was. It made magic seem infinitely more honest.

It was well after midday when the first part of the proceedings ended. Terry followed his one-time family into the vestibule to await their lawyer who would explain what would happen next. It seemed the substantive issues were not in dispute, as the driver, Lindeman eventually reported to the family, had now decided to plead guilty to the charge of negligent driving causing death. As a result, she would be punished as the judge saw fit, taking into account all the circumstances. She would almost certainly not be imprisoned. Did the family want Lindeman to press on to a civil claim?

Jenny looked at Terry, Terry at Jenny. And still looking at each other, as if still one, as if a couple yet, they understood each other and shook their heads. Then, when Jenny's father said, 'No, no, please, no more of this,' it was settled.

Exiting the building, it crossed Terry's mind to ask if they might like to go somewhere for lunch. But as they moved away ahead of him — Jenny, her sisters and father — barely aware that he was behind them, he thought better of it. They didn't need him right now — what they needed, clearly, was each other.

He veered off, calling out, 'See you later, everybody.'

Jenny turned her head to signal she had heard him, if nothing more. Her father gave no sign but continued on his way, bent forward, resigned.

Terry stopped to take a couple of deep breaths. He raised his head to stare at the cloud-dappled sky above the trees in Hyde Park. Where was Anastasia? Was she up there somewhere? He had never hated her, truth be told he had grown fond of her. Mother-in-law or not, she had always been kind to him, concerned for him. He gritted his teeth, squeezed his hands into fists, wanting to lay into somebody, lash out at something. But who or what? He thought then of his own mother. Dead in her early fifties, it was she he missed as much as anyone or anything; at fifteen, he had been way too young when she died.

Terry was an instant away from shouting aloud at the menace, the demon that was out of reach, beyond his ability to grab hold of and see clearly and do something about. There had to be a reason for the way things had turned out in their lives — his mother's, his own — for what had happened between him and Jenny. But what *had* happened? On days like this, it felt as if a ghost was hanging around the periphery of his vision, the edge of his life, some apparition that had tormented him forever, but which he could not nail down, let alone defeat.

A green pedestrian light flashed up on the opposite corner. The crossing beeper sounded, and he felt pulled by the crowd surging ahead at that signal. Terry followed the stream of people southwards, towards Chinatown.

On the other side of the street, things he had put out of mind the past few days came back to him. The mention of Hal's father in that report — a sceptics society? — and that note that had fallen from it: the address. 'Marrickville' again resonated. He and his mother and father had lived in that same suburb until he was, so he'd been told, around five or six years of age. But where, which street? He had no recollection.

In the bustling street, as others surged this way and that around him, Terry felt an unusually warm winter sun and looked up. There it was, burning away the residual cloud that still hung overhead. No matter that he felt guilty about a lot of things, he was not responsible in the disaster of a car accident, whatever Jenny and others had implied or believed. What had happened was a tragedy; he felt sorry for the woman in court, but what more should he feel? He had done nothing wrong, he had caused nothing to happen. But something more needed his investigation, needed scrutiny; he knew that much.

18

Keepers of the Flame

After such a day as had passed, Terry did not want to spend the night alone in his flat. He made his way to Hal's hall in search of company. But he discovered Hal out of sorts and, exhausted as he was, put aside the questions he had been framing.

It was early evening when Terry fell into a dead sleep, in the same spot that had been reserved for him on previous occasions. Next morning, he would not have woken until much later but for Hal's horrific snoring across the way.

To get away from that adenoidal noise, Terry swung his feet onto the floor and headed for the bathroom, if it could be dignifed with such a name. Spending time in the dilapidated loo to which Hal paid minimal attention was still preferable to listening to him sawing away so lustily. As he splashed water on his face, recollections of the preceding day began to intrude, but he had slept well and had the strength to head them off early.

Surprised at how rested he felt, Terry was able to dress quickly and exit without waking Hal. On the way to his bus stop, he decided to have a coffee at a small cafe in Campbell Street.

There, he idly picked up a couple of the trashy gossip magazines that lay in a pile on one of the tables. Towards the back of each were pages of ads for fortune-tellers, palm-readers, psychics of one kind or another — 'Madame' this and 'Stella' that ... Which was when an idea began to nudge at the edge of his brain. It was maybe better not to mention anything to Hal for the moment — he could make his own enquiries.

Terry got up and asked at the counter for a phone directory. He quickly turned over the thick spread of pages, heading for the S's. There he found what he was looking for. There was indeed a Sceptics Society, with an address in the eastern suburbs, at Waverley.

He made a call and got through to someone who said he was the director. Whoever it was at the other end was cordial, and certainly interested in taking Terry's questions. A time for a visit was arranged.

Instead of going back to his flat, Terry decided to return to Hal's place while it was still early. What a shame he had not turned those pages over at Rosehill and read some more — he could hardly go out there now and start snooping around. Was it possible that Hal's father had been up to no good? That was just speculation. Whatever was in that report might not amount to anything at all, or be just a bunch of bullshit. It might even be a document in praise of Francis Sargeson. Innocent until proven guilty, Terry reminded himself. And yet ...

Hal was surprised by his knocking. He had not heard Terry leave earlier, he explained, then spread his arms wide and grinned at him. 'But hey, you're a chap who's learning to disappear ... I should expect that! So, what's out there this morning?'

'I can report it's definitely a whole other world out there, Hal. And also that I got an idea we might head out to Waverley later in the week. See what's out there … Bronte Beach being nearby and all, we might even have a paddle.'

'Waverley? Why would we want to go there?' Hal asked calmly.

When Terry did not answer, Hal shrugged and muttered something cryptic about dark horses and cold water.

*

Terry spent the next couple of days, on and off, responding to Jenny's urging that they separate their finances, whatever was to happen between them next. They should each have separate bank accounts, she said. The only source of income for Terry was the leave money that had been paid to him by Sydney Buses — that together with the small fees he could command for his magic shows plus, by Jenny's grace and favour, half of the eleven thousand dollars they had held jointly in a savings account at the time Terry moved out. It would have to do for now.

On Friday, Terry turned up at the hall to collect Hal. If he had to kidnap him to take him to Waverley he was prepared to do that. But when Hal came to the door he did not fully open it. Instead, he protested through a narrow crack that he had come down with a heavy cold and was in no shape to be outdoors. Terry offered to get some aspirin for him but Hal said not to worry, he would be all right and just needed to be left alone for a day or two.

Terry had no trouble finding the address in Waverley — a rundown Victorian mansion not far from the cemetery. From outside, this didn't look like it could be the headquarters of something called the Sceptics Society. Not as that organisation had been described to him over the phone at least: 'We are a group whose job is to expose frauds, Mr Voulos — psychics, mediums, fortune-tellers, the whole rotten lot of them,' the director had said.

There was a sign planted prominently in the front yard. It was a kind of send-up, a painted cartoon of an old-time séance, done in purples and reds and blacks. Distressed ladies and walrus-moustached gents were seated in a circle, with spooks and ectoplasm hovering over them in the background. At the rear of the circle the medium sat, beardless, a noble, saint-like figure, obviously tuned in to the higher powers.

Terry knocked twice on a solid entrance door, then opened it and went inside. He entered a room festooned with weird-looking mechanical gadgets and old voice-recording machines, trumpets and shrouds. A bearded middle-aged man sat behind a counter, engrossed in reading.

'Hello,' Terry began. 'I'm Terry Voulos …'

The fellow got up and put out his hand.

'Hello and welcome.'

'Forgive me for saying this, but you don't look like the bloke in the painting.'

This drew a smile. 'Name's Fred Horgan. I'm president here, eastern suburbs branch, the New South Wales Sceptics Society.'

'From the outside I was expecting to find a spirit medium or such.'

'You might have once, before we took the place over. The bloke who used to operate out of here we ran out of town; dead years ago.'

'Did he hold séances here?'

'He did. Full-on materialisation nonsense too, with the help of some of these gadgets.' Horgan waved to the paraphernalia on display. 'But I'm racing ahead. You're not a believer by chance, are you?'

'No, no. But that's where you guys come in? When people who do believe get ripped off?'

'That's where we come in. Most people ignore this stuff, of course, but sadly a few get seriously trapped.' He stopped to scrutinise Terry closely. 'You do know it's all nonsense, don't you?'

'Well, yes, though for a moment … And philosophically speaking, we can't be entirely sure that we've nailed all phenomena in the universe, can we?'

'Uh-oh — sounds like I'm hearing an "open mind" viewpoint.' Horgan sighed.

'What I'm here for is about a name, a person I mean, and whether you know anything about him. He was the father of a friend of mine. He had something to do with Harry Houdini … when Houdini came to Australia, that is. You guys wrote something about him or did a report …?'

Terry's remarks met a blank. 'Houdini? You know, the escapologist?'

'Go on,' Horgan said, still not giving anything away.

'Story goes, my friend's father worked for Harry Houdini early in the twentieth century, when he came to Australia.'

Still nothing from Horgan, but Terry decided to continue anyway. 'Well, I recently came across some report your outfit did, a long time ago. A report about him, I think … name was Sargeson — Francis Sargeson, or Frank.'

Expecting him to reply directly, Terry was a little frustrated when Horgan instead said, 'Have you got time for a walk, Mr Voulos? I've got something to show you.'

'Got all day.'

'Good. It's almost lunchtime, so let me turn the sign in the window. I'd like to take you to the headland. Are you interested?'

'Should I be?'

'You *will* be, I guarantee it.'

With Horgan leading the way, they walked the main road for a stretch before veering off towards the old headland cemetery. Terry didn't mind strolling on such a sunny winter's morning; the light breeze off the ocean made it all the more pleasant, just the sort of day to clear up a niggling doubt or a confusion or two.

Terry followed Horgan through the ornate cemetery gates into the field of headstones, then towards the cliff's edge that overlooked the ocean. He was struck by the extent of stone and marble-commemorated death. The headland location was spectacular, but when he lowered his eyes there was a sea of graves, relieved only by the low shrubs and browning grass that grew between them and in the cracks in the paths. As the vegetation thinned out, Terry realised that Horgan was taking him close to the graveyard's eastern edge with its commanding view of the ocean, north, south and east.

'Lovely up here, isn't it?' Horgan said.

'Beautiful. So long as you overlook the graves.'

Horgan stopped to look at him. 'Sorry. If this is making you uneasy, we can head back.'

'No, let's go on. Show me whatever it is you want to show me.'

Now Horgan led him to a grave with a headstone in the form of some winged Greek goddess.

Terry read the inscription:

FRANCIS SARGESON
12 APRIL 1898 – 3 MARCH 1970
IN THE LIFE BEYOND
A GREAT MEDIUM
ERECTED BY SUBSCRIPTION, HIS FRIENDS & ADMIRERS
1972

'A spirit medium?' Terry asked.

'Yes, and the true believers got together, it seems. No-one who knew him in real life appears to have bothered. Look here …'

At the other end of the grave was a simple sandstone block, the date of his death engraved on it in a plain typeface.

'Notice there's no family mentioned, no wife or children. Speaks volumes, that.'

'So who was he, this character?'

'Another phoney, except for the poor fools — the "friends and admirers" — you see there who bought what he was selling. I remembered this one when you said his name. Arrived here from America when he was still quite young, if I'm recalling right. Australia's bad luck, you might say.'

'Could he have had anything to do with Houdini?' Terry asked as he looked at the dates again. He knew the answer in the same instant. 'Except Houdini was here in 1910 … when this bloke was twelve years old.'

'That's your answer to that,' Horgan said matter-of-factly.

'Let's go back and I'll see what else we've got for you.'

At the office, Horgan wheeled two chairs into position in front of a large desk. 'Take a look at this,' he said, beginning to flip through pages of computer-generated printouts. 'This is the register. Every phoney we've ever come across and investigated. All listed here: names, addresses and phone numbers. Or at least as known at the time we identified them — these ladies and gentlemen have a habit of moving on suddenly! A tendency to disappear, like some of their supposed apparitions.'

Horgan flipped over a few more pages for emphasis. There were dozens of pages, hundreds of listings.

'Francis Sargeson is in there?'

'He is.' Horgan turned the pages until he came to the right one. 'Here. And if you say there's a fuller report on him I believe you, though where it might be I wouldn't know right now … Our filing system needs a bit of work.'

'What do you do with what you've got here?'

'Not a lot we can do. Except to tell people like you, anyone who might be suspicious, what we know. Your Sargeson is a blast from the past, but there's plenty of fresh ones going round today, more so than ever. We like to think of this as a public service. You can have a copy of the register if you want. Cost you $5 for the photocopying.'

'I'd like that, yes. And there's another question you can help me with. Do you know anything about *Hal* Sargeson? Is he in there too?'

'Let me check.' Horgan looked down at the printout. 'No, nothing here. Is there something you want to tell us?'

'Not right now, no,' Terry answered. 'He's the bloke who

reckons his old man worked with Houdini on his tour here a hundred years ago.'

'He might have been told that, you never know. Those old frauds never saw the truth as anything but an option. I'd say they were as happy to lie to their kids as to anyone else.'

Terry thought about this possibility, his heart sinking all the while.

'But he's convinced. And he had me convinced the story was true, and I thought —'

'Well, he would be, and you would be too! Operators like Frank Sargeson were and are very, very good. Some of the people you come across in this game are very plausible. Could be that your bloke — Hal? — like a lot of people, had it sold to him when he was very young. Anyway, you can imagine that anyone who could spin a story well would have been able to influence an impressionable kid. Whatever the truth, it seems the poor bastard bought it.'

For some moments, as Horgan photocopied the printouts, Terry contemplated what he had been presented with so far. He asked himself if everything really was fitting together as well as this sceptic seemed to be suggesting.

On the way back to the city, Terry stared at the photocopied sheets. Whether it was a feeling for Hal or something else, he was having difficulty turning to the page containing Frank Sargeson's name.

The entries were arranged alphabetically, both by name and address, and gave the year of the subject's last known residence at the address as well. Terry guessed this way of doing things suited the detective ambitions — or were these fantasies too? — of the sceptics crew. The entries included the stage monikers of the subjects — or suspects — as well as their real names. They were salutary. '"The Amazing Bandini", aka Arthur Cobcroft, last known 16 September 1981 @ 14 Railway Parade, Carlton.' Then there was the description: 'Presents as "Prestidigitator and Channeller", claims spiritual power. Fees average.'

At S he ran his finger slowly down the list. He found Frank Sargeson. The entry read: 'Arrived from US when young. Claims a Houdini connection (on the dates, may well have seen him perform). Main activities fortune-telling and palm-reading; briefly set up as medium, for which see separate report. Buried Waverley. Nothing else known.' And following that, a street name. Here it was a second time — Jordan Street.

Another relic memory began to surface. Someone else he knew had once lived there, but who was it? He mined the nooks and crannies of his brain for some further connection with that street, but try as he might, Terry could not dredge anything up. Yet something positive had come of this: he no longer felt confused; what he felt instead was some kind of anger.

19

Jordan Street

'You haven't been telling me the whole truth, have you, Hal?' Terry said. He spoke loudly, though doing his best to avoid anger and sarcasm.

Hal had opened the door only a couple of centimetres, showing every sign of barring him entry, when he heard this accusation. He was indignant in an instant and immediately tried to shut it. Too late, as Terry was able to lever his way in.

'What do you mean, saying that to me like that?'

'Your father was never on any tour with Harry Houdini, was he?'

'Yes he was. Who said he wasn't?'

'Well, as this is a world of chance, who should I find at Waverley but a professional sceptic. A spookbuster, as they're called. There's a file on Frank Sargeson. Why is that, do you reckon?'

'Don't know. Why?' Hal replied defiantly. Terry watched him as he made a show of trying to look relaxed and reasonable. 'What are you talking about, Terry? You're confusing me … I've got to sit down.'

Terry followed him as he made his way to one of his broken-down director's chairs. He stood over him and scanned his face. The look of confusion he wore seemed real enough. He wasn't sure what to make of the reaction.

'All right, I've got an easier question. Where were you living, say, thirty or forty years ago? 1960s or '70s.'

Sargeson seemed not to want to answer at first, but in a subdued voice finally said, 'Marrickville.'

'Jordan Street, Marrickville? Same as on the paper I picked up at your shed?'

At this, Hal jumped out of his seat. 'You better leave, Terry. I think that would be for the best.'

'Why do I have this feeling you've not been honest with me, Hal? Tell me I'm wrong.'

'Look, I really don't like what you've been saying. And I don't want to say anything back to upset you. I really don't …'

'Come on, Hal! What the hell's going on?'

'Forget it. I want you to go.'

Hal led Terry to the door, opened it and stood resolutely beside it. 'Maybe I've just been wasting precious time on you, Mr Voulos. Here's me making calls — and I have, you know, talking to Taylor, and another bloke. Could have been real gigs for you, not that silly amateur stuff. But I can see you haven't got the right attitude, mate. Your attitude stinks. You'll never make a professional, I can see that now!'

There was no other option but to leave. Terry pulled the door hard behind him as he exited.

One the way home, Terry felt more stirred up than defeated. He resolved to do something he had not done in weeks. He would call his father. He had a simple question to ask.

Stavros answered the phone promptly. 'So, you call me, eh? Long time, *yeh mou*. What you want?' His father's voice sounded feeble to Terry, weaker than the last time he had spoken to him.

'To see how you are, for one thing …' 'Pshahh!' Terry heard him snort down the line. '… and to ask you something.'

'So ask.'

'Before we moved to the eastern suburbs, when we lived in Marrickville, what was the street?'

'Why you ask that?' Stavros said coldly. And then again, even more blackly, 'Why you ask?'

'Oh, nothing. Just that I think *Mama* told me once but I forgot. Sort of thing a son should know, don't you reckon?'

After a pause, his father said in a firmer voice, 'Okay, if you want to know, so what? Jordan Street. 35 Jordan Street, Marrickville.'

Terry resisted the urge to ask more, to go further. This was as much as he could handle for the moment, the way things were going. 'Thanks,' he said. 'I'll come and see you sometime soon.'

'Don't bother yourself. And, Terry, I tell you one more thing: don't make trouble for yourself. Or me. You understand?'

'Fine,' Terry replied.

He pressed the red button on the mobile.

*

As soon as he got home, Terry realised he had made a serious tactical error. He should have gone back to Hal's after that phone call with his father. With that extra bit of information, he should have pressed him on what more, if anything, he knew. He looked at his watch. It was only four pm. Not too late.

The roads were quiet so Terry was back in the city within twenty minutes. But that was the extent of his progress: knocking again, there was no answer. Terry cursed and sat down on the narrow kerb that ran alongside the hall. Hal was not there, or if he was he wasn't answering. Terry made an effort to calm down and told himself he could just as easily pick this thread up again tomorrow.

Except that when he tried the next day, Hal, again, was not answering. Not a little anxious, Terry gave the door a shove. It opened. He went inside and saw that Hal's much-favoured fake-leather attaché case was gone from next to his bed, along with his alarm clock and the bunch of reading — the pulp novels and magic magazines that usually lay on the floor. The bed had been made.

Terry wondered where he could have gone. He had not mentioned relatives or friends in other places. Terry hoped nothing bad had happened to him. Whether or not Hal had been entirely forthcoming with him — and for the moment he was entitled to the benefit of the doubt — he was worried about him. The way the silly bugger liked to wander around the streets, Chinatown especially, he was an easy target for a mugging or worse. But then, when one other possibility occurred to him, Terry stopped fearing the worst.

20

Something Beautiful

As there was no lock on the inside of Hal's storage unit at Rosehill, Terry had only to gently push at the door to see if he had guessed correctly. He had, but only in part. Hal was curled up on the floor next to his desk, amid newspapers and empty cans and bottles, lying in a puddle of dried piss. Terry went over to him slowly, not sure whether he was even alive.

He needn't have worried on that count for, as he moved close to the prone figure, Hal stirred. He turned his head and opened his eyes and looked up, with a steadiness Terry was not expecting.

'Hal, mate, what's happened?'

He did not respond but rolled over to one side, then slowly righted himself. Now that Terry could get a clearer view, he realised the older man had probably been on a serious bender.

'You're not supposed to be here,' Hal said slowly. 'I don't want you here.'

The care he had taken with those words suggested he was not yet entirely sober. He was red-eyed, bleary and, when he got to his feet, unsteady. Terry watched him make his way around the desk to seat himself, looking for all the world as if he was getting ready to receive a visitor or start a meeting.

It was a brave front. There was a fine tremble about his hands, his left eye every so often showed a tic; usually pretty particular about shaving, he had grey stubble on his cheeks and chin.

'I'm not answering any questions, Terry. Just want you to know that, okay?'

'Not asking any. I'm going to get some water, which I reckon you could do with.'

Hal didn't protest. Had he swallowed as much as those empty cans of mixer drinks and bottles of cheap sherry suggested, he was bound to be dehydrated.

He was not wrong. Handed a bottle refilled with water, Hal could barely wait to start gulping and spilled the liquid over his shirtfront as he drank.

'Needed a wash anyway …'

'What's all this about, Hal?' Terry swept an arm towards the mess. 'How much grog have you had?'

'Never mind that, Terry. This is my joint, I can do as I like. What are *you* doing here?'

'I was concerned about you, truth be known. How smashed have you been?'

Terry's persistence seemed to corner his mentor. He descended into a sullen silence, folding his arms and lowering his head to stare at the desktop.

'If you've had a bucket-load you might need to get to a hospital, mate.'

Hal dropped his defence. He put his hands briefly in the air. 'Oh, what are you worrying about me for, Terry? I'm a wreck and who cares?'

'I do,' Terry said without hesitation.

'Oh yeah?' Hal replied morosely, not yet ready to abandon self-pity.

'Enough to come looking for you, anyway. Look, Hal, this stuff about your father — you don't have to talk if you don't want to, but I know for sure that Francis Sargeson wasn't on tour with Houdini in Australia. What I reckon is *you* made up that story of his.'

Any sharp edge that was left in Hal suddenly went blunt. He looked thoughtful, as if he had no choice but to accept Terry's bona fides and concern, and no choice but to be honest and cordial in return.

'Maybe I did …'

'Why?'

'Possibly … possibly because I'm a broken-down old hack, and didn't think I could get you to listen or believe it was important if it was only me. If it was only something that a bloke like *me* had made up … Because, Terry, the point of it stands. Harry's gotta be your guide here, son. What I learned from him is the best thing I can give you.'

'That's not true, Hal. Stop beating yourself up. What about the magic? The training? The four realms?'

'It's all nothing without Houdini, Terry, believe me!'

That said, Hal's shoulders slumped once again; his already battered face reddened and gave way to quiet tears. Terry went to him, thinking that the alcohol had exacerbated some old miseries. He put a hand on his shoulder. 'Hal, things aren't so bad.'

'Aren't they?'

'If they are, I'll help you. Teacher's pet, me,' Terry said, trying for a laugh. 'What I want you to do is go and wash yourself while I clean up here. All right?'

'All right.'

'Then back to the city for you.'

Hal was more hesitant about that. 'You don't want me to run you through another disappearing illusion for a bit of practice while you're here?'

'I'd rather you ran me through the truth, Hal!'

*

Terry had Hal back at Wentworth Avenue by mid afternoon. He followed him into the hall, partly to encourage him to wash properly and change, partly because he was reluctant to leave him on his own. While Hal was sorting himself out, Terry suggested a meal in Chinatown — an offer the hungry old man accepted without hesitation. They ate at Hal's favourite cheapie, the Hai Ling on Dixon Street, where Hal chomped his way stolidly through a chicken chow mein.

On the street again, Hal picked up his lament one more: 'I wanted to show you something good and beautiful. But I've buggered it up …'

Sorrow and defeat seemed to take hold of Hal as he stood beside Terry in the neon and the noise. Restaurant barkers were shouting up and down the street and the flashing lights, the yellows and blues and reds and greens streaming out of shop windows, added to the general hayhem. When Hal didn't seem to know where to turn or what to do next, Terry gently grasped his elbow.

'Come on, let's go down to the Chinese Gardens for a bit.'

In the way of a small boy, Hal accepted the shepherding and walked mutely beside Terry down to the tranquillity of the commemorative gardens. There, Terry looked for a quiet corner where they might sit.

Terry let Hal settle before speaking, then put to him what he had come to believe was fact: 'You lived in the same street as us, didn't you? When I was a kid … That's right, isn't it?'

He watched Hal's face carefully. He nodded once, that was all. Just once. He looked away as if there was nothing more to be said, then shifted as if all he wanted to do was just walk off.

'No.' Terry put a hand on Hal's arm as he indeed got up to take a first step. 'I want you to tell me more. There's something else you can tell me, isn't there? Please … sit down.'

Hal gave in.

The stillness in the gardens was as soothing as Terry had hoped it would be. He saw from the way Hal was sitting, quietly, passively, that there was scarce resistance left.

'Hal, what's your connection with my family? You know me, don't you? You've known me for a very long time.'

'You've got to believe me, Terry,' Hal said at last. 'I just wanted to help you. I remember you from when you were this big …' He held his hand level, away from his body. 'The Greek kid from next door with curly hair. You were a shy kid, you know.' He smiled at Terry wanly. 'And then the shy kid grows up and has his own troubles and … It was all wrong. No-one should be made to feel the way you did. Your father was a bastard. Is he still alive?'

'He is, yes.'

'I remember how he used to behave, the things he did. One time, I'll never forget it, your mum planted some pansies along the path, purple ones on one side, yellow on the other. And he comes out and starts yelling at her — I was putting out the rubbish and saw this — and I couldn't tell what he was saying except he was very angry. And then a few minutes later I see your mother crying there, on her hands and knees, pulling out the purple ones and putting them where the yellow ones had been, and then moving the yellow ones across to where the purple had been. And he used to chase you around and belt you. I saw him do that too, Terry …'

Terry put his face in his hands, covering his eyes. He worked to stay calm. He had hardly expected to hear what he was hearing, here, now, from this man.

Hal spoke quietly. 'Am I lying?'

Terry uncovered his face. 'No. You're not lying, Hal. You're not lying. But I don't remember much. I couldn't remember you, for instance.'

'You moved away when you were a little chap.'

'Apparently … But you know, it looks like *your* father was a bastard too. Just maybe in a different way. Would you argue with that?'

'No … He told me when I was young that he was a magician. I believed it for a while until I got in the game myself. Then I understood he'd taken the left-hand path.'

'What's that?'

'You really need to be further along to understand about these things, Terry. It's the code I mentioned to you when we started out. Quick version, the right-hand path is the proper path for the decent magician; the left is the dark side, black as against white … The difference between witchcraft and magic. When you become a bullshit medium, a psychic, like my old man did, you've broken it.'

'Then why give *him* that story about Harry Houdini?'

Hal paused. 'I wasn't lying when I told you he liked to tell stories. He told me about Harry when I was a youngster myself and I believed it was true. I was a lot older, working, when I realised it wasn't, it couldn't have been. But I saw something in it that Frank didn't, and that's when I made it my own. Francis Sargeson was a liar, yes, but a liar who told me a beautiful story about a great illusionist. And I still believe you can learn from him, Terry. Houdini. What better path is there to follow for the likes of you and me?'

'How true are the stories, by the way? Did any of those things happen?'

'Some yes, some no. But all true in some way, Terry. All in some way …'

Terry saw Hal's brightening, widening eyes and understood for the first time how close this man danced to delusion. How fervid was his belief in a tale about a tale. How complete was his faith in things that had never happened. And how desperately inspiring was what he had made of it all.

His father was a kook who had been up to who knew what mischief, if the information about him was correct. He'd put out some myths and legends that had become meat and drink for Hal, it seemed. But instead of steering away from them when he discovered their falsity, he had worked to make them his philosophy and Houdini his master.

'And the thing is, if I didn't say it was somebody else's story and true at that, why would you believe it?'

Terry thought about that. He could well understand what it was to never feel authorised, if that was the word; it was a reaction with which he was familiar. Testing his own response, Terry realised that what Hal was saying made sense: he would have given much less credence to tales of a long-ago magician and escapologist if Hal had not also announced the connection to Houdini through his father. That was all very well. But as for Terry, where did he fit in?

'Hal, let's accept all that, but why me? Why did you drag me into this?'

Hal seemed to think for a long time before he responded. 'Well, you're asking and I'll tell you. Trying to learn the art the way you were, I thought you needed help. Real help. I knew my Houdini, had learned some stuff ... I also knew straightaway who you were, from the old days. Simple to start with. Turn you into a proper magician — get in, give you a hand and get out again, out of your life.'

'But the address at Rosehill ... It was almost like you hoped I would find it and when I did ...'

'I started thinking, maybe he should know more. I planted it for you to find all right, so you could sort things out for yourself about the old days. But then it felt like a mistake. You were happy learning the magic and I thought, this is good, this is enough. Couldn't get the stuff out of your hands quick enough though, could I?' He smiled wanly. 'Must be losing my touch.'

Now he turned to look into Terry's eyes. 'When I said twelve weeks at the start I meant it. Only ever wanted to introduce you to the finer points, what you really have to know. Twelve weeks. You wouldn't have to keep driving buses. And everybody's happy. But …'

Terry gazed at the stand of ornamental liquidambars that screened this part of the garden from the next; their composed, compact leaves, the jagged reds and golds hanging on in the deepening winter gloom. Night was closing in around them. 'I didn't want to just tell you, Terry. I wanted to show you how the master did it, and not just some of his routines … Only way we really learn, isn't it? What the teachers say, right?'

'Appreciate the intention, Hal — just don't know about your methods.' Terry smiled as he spoke. 'Let's get onto something else for a minute — tell me what you remember from the Marrickville days. I want to hear more. I've got so few memories from that age. What else can you tell me?'

'He could be very mean and nasty, your father, as you know. He used to get into a lot of neighbourhood fights.'

And then the shock, the next thing Hal told him, that Terry at first found hard to believe. That Stavros had something he was hiding, something he should have let him, Terry, in on long ago: 'Terry, what you don't know is that Stavros got into the fakery too; he went down the left-hand path himself.'

It was Stavros's house in Marrickville they had used, Hal said, to perform 'psychic' readings in the years before Terry was born; and then again, later, when he was a small boy. Hal's own father, Frank, had been the boss. Hal could recall the duped customers' looks of satisfaction, the expressions of gratitude. All that fakery and deception received with awe.

'So somewhere, Terry,' Hal went on, 'your father lost his way, too. Though he was no magician to start with, he strayed from the white to the black side.'

The sincerity with which he spoke gave Terry no choice but to believe him. And he knew that this revelation would have more consequences than poor old Hal could possibly imagine. But ahead of any of that lay a more immediate problem.

'Hal, old son, I have to say this: I reckon you need help. Did you ever —?'

Hal cut him dead with a raised hand. 'Hey, I stopped drinking, all right? I told you that. And I'm on the wagon again, thanks to you. I'm back at AA from tomorrow, I am.'

That he had once been a member did not surprise Terry, after what he had seen. 'And a good thing, for sure, Hal. Anything else need fixing?'

'Well, the doctor wanted to put me on some pills once …'

'Will you let me help you?'

The slight tilt of Hal's head in his direction, the silence that followed, Terry took as some interest.

'You might be a bit better but you're not right yet. Why don't I take you to see a doctor?'

'Maybe,' he replied. 'Might be better if you made sure I got to a meeting.'

It was enough of an answer for the present. Terry reached across and gave the back of Hal's right hand a quick pat. 'Done. Tomorrow.'

21

A Simple Plan

Terry counted the evidence: that Frank Sargeson had been the driver for whatever it was that had been happening around his childhood home, that it was he who had spun the tale about Houdini, he who had been tagged by the psychic busters. But Frank's son had also brought forward a wild card. Stavros Voulos had been seriously involved, maybe even central, to activities that he, Terry, had never heard spoken about and knew nothing of. He wondered whether they were even legal.

But how much did Hal really know? If he had been largely sober in the time Terry had known him, he had also once spent a lot of time drunk. Hal had come to believe in Harry Houdini as a teacher and messenger. No argument with him there — illusionist be damned, he was a model citizen compared to their own fathers. As for himself, had Terry needed any further proof of the difference between white and black, the time he had already spent learning to be a magician had delivered that in spades. There was a ready market in the need to believe. The demand drove a supply of psychics, clairvoyants, channellers, mediums, fortune-tellers, palm-readers, crystal-ball gazers — the lot. Fraudsters and crooks were everywhere.

Terry had not paid much attention to this stuff in the past, but now whenever he opened a newspaper or magazine he consciously turned to the back sections which these types infested in droves — there were hundreds if not thousands of the pests. Small or big time, local and humble or upmarket with media profiles, they were advertising everywhere. Their ads ran to acres of print and web space.

Hal had seen something of his early life, Terry reflected, but he did not know about his teen years, spent in a quiet, supposedly toney suburb the other side of the city. The chief fact about those years was still private to Terry: the Voulos home at Rose Bay was always a place of tension and anxiety. A poisonous atmosphere had hung around his growing-up years.

Though much of Terry's childhood was lost to him, his father's abrasiveness, his mother's sullen resistance, her withdrawals and her silences lived with him yet. The uneasiness between his parents — even when they were getting along, even when there were laughs and good times — had stained his early years. There had ever been an underlying friction, as if some deep disagreement or discord had set in early between his parents, which they had come to accommodate. As to the source of that friction, he had no idea, not then or now.

Eleni had died young, a month after Terry turned fifteen. He had long believed that stress could and did kill, one way or another; he had more than once asked himself whether his mother's early death was related to her brooding unhappiness. He wished he knew what had gone down between Stavros and Eleni, what the slammed doors, the constant comings and goings of his father, had truly been about — assuming always that his mother was the innocent party.

But she may not have known what, if anything, her husband was up to. She was a girl from an isolated village in the Peloponnese who left school when she was fourteen; Terry remembered her clever, questioning eyes. But native intelligence would have been no weapon against an expert in secrets management. Say Stavros had been involved somehow in this shonky business. And say she had known. Had she covered for him? Approved of and supported what he was doing? Or had she disapproved, taken some other position?

More than anything, Terry was frustrated, not knowing where his mother sat — how she fitted in to the psychic landscape of the Voulos household.

Against such imponderables, Terry welcomed concrete tasks. His job right now was to rearrange the furniture in his flat to make room for a sofa-bed he'd bought in the hope Ricky might soon stay some nights with him. Diversions, physical and otherwise, were always good. He sensed he would continue to need them for some time. Whenever a stray memory came up, whenever he thought of his own family, he wished for a thousand diversions, for nothing, he thought, could be done to mend things between him and Jenny.

As this morning drew on, Terry sought consolation in recalling other, better Sundays. Throughout the previous couple of winters he had often been on soccer duty at this time of the day. Ferrying his boy to this or that field, taking part in the not unpleasant rituals of childhood. An image came to him: Ricky looking up at him expectantly, excitedly, as they stood together under a tree at a sportsground in Banksia. The match was to start soon but the kids had been horsing around and his son's favourite ball had been caught in its branches. It was a fair way up and Ricky was worried it might never come down.

But then to see Ricky's face when his father had spotted a handy, broken branch, long and sturdy enough to throw up at the ball to try to dislodge it — he would never forget that. Terry had thrown the stick, hit the ball; by some lucky chance he had even knocked it clear. He had joined in Ricky's yelling and cheering as the ball — a spinning pattern of black and white patches — fell back to earth. A father and a son. Now he enjoyed his regular Saturday outings with the boy, but it wasn't the same and it wasn't enough.

Terry had nowhere particular to go, nothing further in the way of tasks or duties this day — but then came an idea. He went to his old desktop computer. This had once sat in the sunny study at the back of their house. In honour, he had set it up on a garden table in the small enclosed balcony here, cables trailing back into the loungeroom. He started it up and sat down at the keyboard for the first time in two months.

He opened a new file. There was something he wanted to sort out, put down. He started to type.

Method:
1. Avoid direct attack on old man.
2. Useful evidence may be gathered from 'secondary sources'.
3. As most will be elderly, approach potential informants with indirect, 'harmless' questions.

He stopped tapping when he accepted that he was unlikely to strike success. Who on earth was left whom he could usefully ask about those Marrickville days? He had so very few recollections himself. But there were some. The strawberry patch in the backyard of Aunt Julie's place, a few doors up. Aunt Julie — who wasn't his aunt, or perhaps even a Julie. She was just a Greek neighbour, real name … what? A widow or a spinster, at any rate a woman who lived on her own. Might she still be alive, or — and this would be a small blessing — still live there in Jordan Street?

22

Aunt Julie

Monday morning Terry got on a bus and took himself to Marrickville. He got off on the main road at the Jordan Street corner and began the walk downhill. He counted the houses as he passed them, until he was at number thirty-five. Here, he saw nothing special or even mildly familiar. Nothing but a standard, ageing Federation-era, single-fronted, freestanding brick and tile house, one of a dozen like it in the vicinity.

He stared long and hard but simply could not place any of the outside detail, not the curved iron awning over the front porch, nor the brick posts or wooden fretwork at either end, within his childhood memories. It was unsettling that he could not remember what his boyhood home looked like. He stood at the gate for a time, wondering whether, if he went inside, his memory might be jogged; then again, he wasn't sure that coming here was a good idea at all.

Urging himself on, he walked through the small wrought-iron gate and pressed the front-door buzzer. The door opened and he saw a frazzled young mother, small child on her hip. She regarded him suspiciously. To ask to come inside would lead to a door in his face or worse, Terry thought, so he apologised for intruding and instead asked the woman if she knew of an elderly Greek lady, going perhaps by the name Aunt Julie, who lived somewhere around the area. She did. She often saw her at the nearby shops, she replied. But why was he asking?

'Oh, only that I lived here when I was a kid, and I wouldn't mind seeing her again. She was a very nice lady,' Terry said as cheerfully as possible, trying not to cause alarm.

The young woman surprised him by showing interest in his story; she asked when he'd lived in the house.

'Oh, more than thirty years ago.'

Though he could see she was a little uneasy, she asked whether he would like to have a look inside. Terry saw the effort at generosity, but saw also the uncertainty in her eyes. It was not as strong as his own, though. Having gained entry, he realised he could not go through with it. He might have been hazy about the outside of this place, and his memories of what had happened inside were few. But there were some. He saw the hall receding behind the woman and recalled being chased down it. His father was after him; he was due for a belting. He didn't want to recognise anything more here.

'Thanks, but it's okay, I don't want to bother you. I'd be grateful for the old lady's address, if you know it.'

Easy enough, she told him. She lived only a hundred metres or so away, on the same side of the street.

Terry headed along the footpath, stopping and staring outside number seventy-one. A revelation. This house he did remember from the outside. When he tapped at the door knocker and the door was opened, he was remembered in turn.

She dragged Terry to her, this surprisingly strong little old lady, pulled his head down for a kiss and then hugged him to her. Terry looked past her down the hall and felt as if he had walked along it yesterday. And then, as she pulled him further inside and led him by the hand, she said: 'You been gone. But I been in this house, the same house since 1960.'

'And I remember it, Aunt Julie, I remember coming here …'

'Good! Of course! Why not? You come here all the time, every afternoon after you start the school, when your *mama* is working at the factory and can't look after you.'

She did not let go of Terry's hand until she had steered him into the kitchen at the end of the hall and sat him at the table.

'I recognise you straightaway,' Aunt Julie said. 'Straightaway!' She clapped her hands and reached across the laminex table top to touch his.

Terry was moved by her reaction. A small woman with her hair in a bun, a woman who, he'd noticed as he followed her, walked with a pronounced limp. With the brightest of demeanours, this was an ancient Greek charmer of the first order. He marvelled at the life in her. He was sure he could recall the welcoming force of her, the warmth. Much as he tried he could not, however, remember her younger woman's face. He told her this, apologetically.

Aunt Julie waved his mumbling away. 'Oh, that doesn't matter! You were only a very little boy when you all left.'

'That's something I want to ask you, Auntie Julie. Why did we leave? Do you know?'

Aunt Julie's expression clouded. 'Your parents, they never told you?'

She began to shake her head and make 'tsk, tsk' noises.

'If you want to know, I will tell you. But for this I must make the cup of coffee for you, and you, you must have the biscuit and some sweet, all right?'

Terry was not going to argue with such hospitality, he said, so long as she ate something too. Or else, he said, trying to find a little residual Greek in himself, he might just be offended.

'Oh, don't worry, this for you *and* for me,' she said, setting out the biscuits and preserves.

She shoved Terry out of the kitchen and settled him in the living room, a room he couldn't help but secretly smile at, what with the walnut-veneer glass-fronted cabinet filled with the *kala*, the 'best', and the doilies and bits of embroidery and family photos everywhere — walls, sideboard, you name it. Smiles aside, as he settled himself in one of Aunt Julie's tasteless but oh so comfortable armchairs, he felt a keen stab — that there was something seriously missing in him, which this warm, folksy clutter served somehow to highlight.

'There was trouble, my boy,' she said as soon as she sat herself down in the chair opposite him. 'But funny thing, your mother started everything. Your poor mother, she didn't mean anything by it, you know?'

'You better explain, Aunt Julie. I don't really know anything,' he answered, and smiled at her in case she needed reassurance.

'Yes, she was the innocent one, your mother. She used to read the cups, yes. But this she did only for fun, not for money or such. She was not the guilty one.'

When Terry asked her who she did this cup-reading for, she replied, 'Oh for me, for the other Greek ladies. But this only for fun, you see? Look, I will do it for *you* if you like … just a game. Drink and I will show you!'

Terry finished his small cup of Greek coffee, happy for the diversion. He was enjoying her company and was in no hurry to go anywhere, now that he had remade the connection.

Aunt Julie raised the cup and took a quick look inside. He smiled encouragement as she made a show of swirling the dregs around so as to cover the sides of the cup — an odd tradition, he thought, maybe Levantine in origin, but which presumably had spread throughout Greece too. He followed her movements as she quickly turned the cup upside down and placed it on the saucer, all in the one action. She winked at him and said, 'Now, we wait, and after I will tell you your luck, how you say, your …?'

'Fortune?'

'Fortune, that's the word. Yes. Your mother, poor Eleni, she liked to read the cups like I say, just for a game to make us laugh. A big shame, because, after, the men got some very bad ideas.'

'Which men, Aunt Julie? My father? Was he one of them?'

'Yes, your *baba*. But not only him, the bloody bugger who live next door to your house. American fella. Him too.'

'Next door, you say? Do you remember his name? Was it someone called Sargeson?'

'*Ne*, that's the one … I forget until you say it. You know him?'

'I do. His son, actually.'

'I can say many more things about this, but first the cup, yes?'

'Sure, why not?'

Aunt Julie stooped down and turned the small white cup over slowly, then carefully studied the pattern made by the coffee grounds. In all seriousness, she intoned, 'You have the troubles in your life, many troubles … But everything will get better soon. Everything will be all right …'

She looked up at him, searched his face like any concerned mother, and said, 'Please, you believe me, yes?'

'Oh I do, Aunt Julie. Don't worry, I really do!'

Jokes and games aside, Terry thought how much he needed affirmation these days. And coming from this kindly, gentle old dear — one of the few people he remembered warmly from those unlamented years — it seemed to mean much more. The affirmation was welcome for other reasons too. Because Terry would need all his strength to hear and accept what Aunt Julie went on to say.

Sometime during the late 1960s, she told him, his father, together with his neighbour, began to turn the tales and superstitions of the old country, the tricks of the maguses, into a way of making money. Rather, of stealing money, as Julie was at pains to say. From poor Greek people at first. Then anybody they could get inside the house — ignorant people, lonely people. His mother became sad, became ashamed at what his father got up to. And whether it was the shame or something more, she became physically ill, attacked by the cancer that would kill her. Terrible things, but this was the truth.

When Terry asked if she was absolutely certain about what she was saying, she replied, 'Of course I am. You don't know this story, my boy?'

'No, I don't. I never knew of these things.'

Terry tried to imagine what might have passed at the 'psychic' sessions. He could not. He felt an odd embarrassment at having to ask Julie.

'What sort of things did they do, Aunt Julie?'

She reached across to touch his hand.

'Oh … they say maybe sometimes you gonna be lucky in love one day, you gonna have good news soon … But lies, all lies for getting the money.'

He asked her, 'Did you have your fortune read by my father too?'

'Me? No,' she snorted, 'I was not cuckoo, you know! But your *mama*, she was very worried.'

'Because of what Stavros was doing?'

'Yes, he was cruel, he use the hand on you all the time. And your mother … And Sargeson — he was bad man, very bad man. He done other crook things, like he can talk to the dead people. Not right for the orphan, the woman who lose her husband, to hear this rubbish. And your father, he start to play the same game. The dark room, the noises coming from the dead people … But now I ask you something,' she said. 'What work your father do after you all left from here?'

Terry explained how Stavros had started a contract cleaning business. He didn't do any cleaning himself — a fact which brought a small laugh of acknowledgement from Julie — but found and employed people who would. Their work was in homes and offices and shops around the eastern suburbs.

'Good that he did a proper job because, you know, if he keep doing what he was doing … The police one day, they would catch him and …'

Aunt Julie made a throat-cutting gesture. She closed her eyes and tut-tutted, as if not wanting to upset Terry any more with what was obvious: that Stavros Voulos had been engaged in some nasty money-making games. Terry saw that she censored her words, but by now he was beyond shock. From what he had heard his father had been involved in some heartless if not illegal business back then. If anything, he was happy to have that much confirmed.

'That's okay, Aunt Julie. I'm not surprised. But another thing, can you tell me about the neighbour's son? The young man called Hal?'

'The son? Yes, I remember him. He was …' She touched her forehead before continuing, 'not too good here. I think maybe they put him in the house for the drunk people, long time ago. I used to see him sometimes in the front of his place with the beer bottle.' She raised her thumb and tipped it towards her mouth. 'I don't know what happen to him.'

They had been together for over an hour, and Terry became conscious that Aunt Julie was tiring. She had to be eighty at least, spritely as she was.

When Terry asked her if there was anything else shady going on in the house, she looked worried, as well as very tired. She could not answer, she said. She could not remember everything. The only thing more she would say was that those were days long gone, and days not worth remembering. People not worth remembering either.

'That Sargeson, like I tell you, he was dirty, bad man.' This was said with such a twist of her mouth that Terry half-expected her to spit as well.

Much as he would have appreciated further details, he felt it would not be sensible to push her for more. She had told him enough for now, he said, as he got up and prepared to leave. She had cleared up a number of things for him, and he was very grateful. Would he call again some day? she asked. Yes, he would. She could be sure of that.

Terry was happy to return Aunt Julie's hugs and kisses on the doorstep. The question she had left him with was more than rhetorical: what indeed was worth remembering in this life? And what form should that remembrance take?

23

In the Nature of Monuments

The next day Terry got up early and took a train to Rookwood cemetery. At a flower stall near the entrance he bought a bunch of chrysanthemums to place on his mother's grave, and some yellow daisies for his mother-in-law's. He headed over to the Greek Orthodox section where he arranged the white flowers in the cement vase beneath his mother's headstone. As he blinked away the tears, the old reel began to roll again. His father, his mother, a struggle in a green field.

To this day, he could not understand why he had not confronted his father about what he had done, and done more than once. He could not understand his own weakness. At the time of that last assault on his mother he was an adolescent, surely big enough to do something about his father hitting her? But he had never hauled him off or hit him back. Stavros would stop hitting Eleni whenever Terry appeared, but that didn't seem enough, had never seemed enough. Now he was an adult and Stavros no longer physically threatening, why had he still not confronted him about his behaviour? Why had he let it all ride?

It was not true that he had no answer — he knew very well

that he had some approximation; the problem was that it only added to his sense of failure and dissatisfaction. Maybe he had not stood up to the old man's bullying and worse because he felt too alone to alienate the last connection with his original family, as flawed as that family was.

Terry had gone on living with his father until he had a part-time job and, at eighteen, was old enough to move into a flat of his own. What else was he supposed to do? What do kids know except to stay with those who have fed and clothed them, put a roof over their head and, yes, occasionally smiled at them and maybe uttered a word of well-meant advice?

That the recollection of his parents' last fight — he did not know why they had fought but could clearly remember it was during a picnic in Lane Cove National Park, for God's sake — was so vivid, that these thoughts had come to him again today, he put down to tiredness; surely that was it, the fact he hadn't been sleeping well? He wondered whether he should maybe speak to a doctor about his insomnia; he might have another go at getting Hal an appointment too.

He picked up the second bunch of flowers and found his way to his mother-in-law's grave. Someone had placed an arrangement of native blooms there recently. Terry saw there was a card, folded over and held in place among the stems. Jenny's writing. 'To our loved mother, from Jenny.'

Terry folded the note quickly and put it back in place. He looked around for some container to hold his own bunch of flowers. He found a discarded plastic vase lying nearby and worked the daisies into as pleasant a spread as he could, all the while conscious of that piece of white, heavy paper, cut for the occasion, as was Jenny's practice. She did not like to buy the standard greeting card stuff. He felt a warmish sun on the back of his neck; the exposed skin was beginning to tingle with pleasure. The breeze rustling among the graves was calming, soothing, a welcome contrast.

The flowers in place, he moved away to a deserted area of the cemetery and rang Jenny at work. He said there was something he wanted to tell her. She waited for him to go on but there was only a stuttering silence.

'Terry,' she said finally, 'please don't bother me unless you've got something to say.'

*

That night, Terry spent some time notating the steps in one of Houdini's tank escapes, to try to understand it better. Then, after a couple of hours with another of the Houdini books that he had been gradually working through, he sat down at his computer again. He thought he would try writing something other than directions for an escape. Terry knew he wasn't much of a writer (although Miss Morse had praised him in Year 9 for his 'essay stories'). But again, there was Hal's example. Whatever else he had done, he had shown Terry that, like magic, words could reveal what had previously been hidden. It was all a question of the right words and the right order. His fingers moved tentatively across the keyboard. He began.

Samuel Weiss was never able to maintain a temple. He was moved on from five or six places. He couldn't keep a congregation. He was by all accounts a failure as a rabbi. What would it have been like to be the son of such a man? Especially for a boy who was the runt of the litter. He was the smallest, physically the weakest. He was the sensitive one out of all the Weiss children.

Harry Houdini was the alienated son of Jewish immigrants. His people had moved to nineteenth-century America, to a large country town in Wisconsin, of all places. When and how did the parents lose their way? Sooner? Later? They would surely have experienced racism, prejudice and the confusion of other newcomers to the rough and ready society of that time.

Terry stopped tapping for a moment, struck by a realisation. The old master, the great illusionist, had many secrets yet — but not only that. It seemed he had many more lessons to teach. What he now understood was that the learning would take a great deal of effort. He would give it his best shot.

*

The next morning Terry travelled into the city to seek out Hal. He found him at home, fiddling about, still in that waking dream of his. He was busily rearranging his archive for 1926, the year of Houdini's death. Terry launched straight in.

'Hal, the Harry story you said was Frank's we know was yours. Thing is, I'd be happy to help you with it. Write it down, what do you say?'

Terry wasn't sure whether the man really got it. He seemed to stay blank for an awfully long time. It was a relief when he finally looked up and answered. And answered in the way Terry had been hoping.

'Yes, I'd like that,' Hal said.

'I feel as if I owe you something. A lot actually.'

'You don't owe me,' he replied. 'I owe *you* something. I thought I was helping you out, but I suppose I wasn't as smart as I had to be, I mean to help a cluey fella like you.'

'Well, you did, Hal. But there's one proviso, if I'm to do it.'

'What's that?'

'That you don't close down on me. Don't close me out on whatever happened when I was a kid, that you know about. Keep helping me as much as you can, help me to get my story, my family's story. No matter what it means. Will you do that for me? Is it a deal?'

Hal brooded for a while, then said quietly, 'All right.'

'Good. And you know why?'

'Why?'

'Because you need to hear the truth as much as I do, mate.'

Hal smiled, nodded slowly a few times.

24

A Family Visit

This time Terry was able to speak with confidence. 'We've been conned. I've been conned,' he said. 'It's affected everything, I see that now. I'm asking for your forgiveness. I'm asking for your help. There's so much I want to tell you … stuff about my family that you should know.'

Terry was relived that Jenny heard him out. This was not as hard as he had anticipated; perhaps in the time that had passed since his departure, she had noticed and appreciated the effort he'd been making with Ricky. He repeated that there was something not quite right in what he'd been told about his early life that he wanted to get to the bottom of. His father was the best source of information, but he didn't think he could get him to talk, he explained. Would Jenny please accompany him to visit Stavros? He very much hoped she would see how important it was to him.

'Just this once, Jenny. He listens to you. I might get some answers from him if you come along,' Terry said, ending the pleading.

This was what he had tried to say when he'd called Jenny at work. This time he had spoken with the passion and focus that he couldn't muster in the cemetery.

Jenny sighed down the phone line. 'I'm not sure why, but all right, maybe for old times' sake.'

Terry knew she thought he was making suspicious mountains out of explainable molehills, but luckily she'd always been quite fond of her father-in-law. He had been part of her life for many years. He had been a good *papou* to Ricky, too, an affectionate bringer of gifts and an enthusiastic kisser and squeezer and patter of the little boy's head. That, along with a little manipulation and melodrama every so often to get done whatever small thing he wanted done.

'But listen, Jenny, one last favour. You're also the one who's going to have to get us through the door. He doesn't want to see me, he says. He's not said anything about you being banned.'

'You didn't tell me that straight up, did you? So how? If he doesn't want to see you, how does anyone make him?'

'I don't know ... Take him something, a present? A cake? He's always liked your cakes.'

*

Terry was very pleased that Jenny was prepared to go so far for him. He had not expected her to agree. And he was amazed when, come the day, the idea worked. His father was happy enough to let Jenny in — even though they had turned up unannounced, and much as he was inclined to slam the door once he spotted his son standing behind her.

Inside, Terry soon sensed from the grim way Stavros was avoiding eye contact with him that his father was resolved to keeping the peace. And the old boy quickly relaxed once Jenny adopted her usual positive approach with him. Her peck on Stavros's cheek worked wonders. He was, after all, an inveterate macho who had no qualms about flirting with his son's estranged wife: he repaid her friendliness with a full-bodied hug and noisy smooching on both cheeks. It was all Jenny could do to hang on to the cake.

'How are you, Stavros? Long time no see. I've made a cake …'

'Cake, eh? What kind?'

'Butter cake — I know how much you like it.'

'I like, I like … More than the Greek stuff even!' he said, following Jenny to the kitchen. He watched as she took the cake from its container. 'But,' he went on, 'I don't like what happen between you two. This no good, to break up. No good. But …' He paused to bring out one of his most charming, sweep-away-your-troubles smiles. 'You two here now. And you two together! Maybe something good happen?'

Jenny smiled back at him, if somewhat wanly. 'I wouldn't go that far, Stavros. Don't make too much of it, eh? Terry asked me to come along today.'

'So his idea, you say?' he said, his voice dropping.

Jenny avoided answering, instead opening cupboards and drawers to search for plates and forks. She organised the cake on a tray, turned the jug on and urged Stavros to follow her to the living area, where Terry had already taken up a position on the lounge.

As breezily as she could, she said, 'Well, Anastasia would have been happy to see you eat this, *Papou*! It was her favourite too, remember?'

'I do. I do remember.'

Terry saw little fight in his father today, so took the opportunity to get started. 'I went to Rookwood a few days ago, *Baba*. I put some flowers on her grave. And on *Mama*'s.'

'And for me too? You put some flowers for me too?' Stavros asked earnestly, caught in the moment.

'Yes, I did, for you too,' Terry lied. He was torn by this sudden neediness of his father's, his hurt so obviously close to the surface. He suddenly understood how very hard it would be to push on with what he'd planned. But he had to do it; if ever he needed anything in his life, this was it. He needed to know the truth.

'You go together?' Stavros asked, brightening a little.

The way he spoke removed any doubt: he was angling for a reunion between his son and daughter-in-law. 'No,' Jenny replied neutrally. 'Terry went on his own.' She ate a mouthful of cake, then spoke again. 'I would have liked to have met your wife, Stavros, you know? There are plenty of things I don't know about her. I might have understood things better if I had, I sometimes think …'

Terry shuffled about a bit on the lounge. Surely he had told Jenny more about his family than she was suggesting here? That he couldn't exactly remember what they'd talked about was probably another reason they had finished up where they had.

'Did she work before the cleaning business, Stavros?'

'Oh yes. A bit when Terry was a little boy. But after, no. The cleaning business was good. Plenty money. No problems. Important for the woman to stay home, don't you think, Jenny?'

'Important, yes. And impossible. Don't start me on that. But I know what you mean,' she said. We do what we have to in our lives, don't we? But you, Stavros, you did all right to be able to move to Rose Bay?'

Stavros shrugged. 'I did not bad, not too bad, that's all. In the early days, not so good.'

'So what did you do when you first came out to Australia, Stavros? To survive, I mean. It couldn't have been easy, coming from the old country, trying to start again. I don't think you ever told me the details. Terry hasn't, anyway.'

Stavros seemed uncomfortable at the direction Jenny was taking. He appeared not to believe Terry had never spoken to his wife on the subject in the years they had been married. He stared briefly at Terry, who made sure his demeanour gave nothing away.

'Well, after I first get to Australia I work in factory for a while. I do some odd jobs sometimes, fix fence, fix leaky roof for other people — not bad carpenter me, you know! When they ask me, you know. Extra pocket money.'

Jenny, of course, had no reason to believe that Stavros was hiding something terrible. But for Terry, the responses were not hitting the right notes. He was becoming impatient, and could not stop himself from interrupting the chit-chat between Jenny and his father.

'But you did some other work with Greek people too, didn't you, *Baba*? Do you want to tell us what that was about? Jenny is interested to know, aren't you, Jenny?'

Jenny shot him a sharp look, clearly frustrated by the way he had upset the softly-softly approach she had adopted with his father. Terry knew she was annoyed with him. But he found it hard to stop himself. Although he believed he knew the answers in broad outline, he wanted to hear it all. And he wanted to hear it out of his father's own mouth.

Terry knew he wanted, more than anything, to hear a confession. And if it was way too late for any atonement, he wanted to hear an apology. And maybe a plea for forgiveness. For his sake; and in no small part, he felt, for Jenny's also. If Terry had concluded anything in the past few days it was that the pain his father had visited on him, he, in a twist of the mirror, had bounced on to his wife.

Come on, old man. Put it out there, he silently urged.

But Stavros had detected the tactic behind Terry's last words. He was too clever to fall into his trap. He was not a baby to be cajoled into saying what someone wanted to hear, Terry belatedly realised.

Jenny pushed on pleasantly. 'So, what else were you doing back then, Stavros?'

Terry saw his father's discomfort. He was not expecting Jenny to be so insistent. Jenny was a lady. She was the big dentist lady. Much as Stavros was impressed by her intellectually and physically — she was a good-looking woman — Terry knew she also represented a kind of authority figure for his father. She was the school mistress back at his little village in the Peloponnese, the keeper of the rules. She was the all-mother, the kind who ran households, families — as most women were to him after he had stopped his lusting after them. It was much harder to lie to them, or anyway tell outright lies of the sort that men told each other as part of their daily encounters, forming the very grammar of their

210

relationships. Prevaricating was easy when it came to men, necessary sometimes for sheer survival — whether they were son, brother or father.

With Jenny there in all her femaleness, and with the theoretical honour due women, Terry was conscious that Stavros would tell no outright lies. He knew he was obliged to answer her. But there was still a male in the room, his son perhaps, but another male nevertheless, so the contest would have to go on. But Stavros would say only what was advantageous to him.

'Well, Jenny, I used to tell, to give some information. I used to tell some stories.'

'Did you do that yourself, or —?'

'Myself. Yes. Only myself.'

Terry stiffened. Jenny raised a palm quietly. Terry relented; there would be other opportunities to challenge his father on his lies.

'What kind of stories, Stavros?'

'Oh, something for their life, you know. Something to help them.'

'When you say "them", you mean Greek people, yes?'

'Yes, but some Aussie too. And others — from Europe … you know.'

Now Terry couldn't help himself. He wanted to say, 'You did the Greeks and old Frankie boy emptied the pockets of the Aussies,' but managed to hold back in favour of, 'Just remind me, *Baba* — the bloke next door was named Frank Sargeson, right?'

Stavros didn't blink. Terry wondered whether he'd heard him at all and, if he had, marvelled at how untroubled his father managed to appear. Increasingly frustrated, he lost it completely.

211

'Oh come on, let's stop the charade! You haven't wanted to tell the truth, that's the problem really, isn't it? I know that. And that's why I asked Jenny along today.'

Stavros's face reddened — dramatically, instantly.

'Terry, stop it! Don't upset your father like this, for God's sake! Is this really necessary?' Jenny cut in.

'No! It's not necessary, Jenny!' Stavros shouted. Then, calming himself, he went on more quietly, 'You are right. It's not necessary. Past is finished, everything gone, everything over. My wife, your mother, Terry, she is dead. Your mother-in-law dead now, because of you. And you, you can't even stay with your wife ...' He turned to Jenny, to implore her, 'Why he come here asking me questions, questions? I don't understand.'

Stavros kept his gaze fixed on Jenny. Far from being concerned at his father's attitude towards him, Terry was worried about how Jenny might react. His relationship with his father had been difficult even after she married into the Voulos family. Terry saw her sadness threaten to turn to anger as she got to her feet. When he realised she had had enough, Terry, too, jumped up to leave.

Making for the door, he faced his father one last time and found the most measured voice he had in him. 'Why? Because you haven't told me everything, I'm pretty sure of that. You've left a few important things out, haven't you? I know you hurt my mother. Let alone anyone else.'

But Stavros still would not bite. 'Ha! But you know nothing, nothing ... Go away, please. Go on, get. I had enough for today.'

As usual, Terry realised, it was a stand-off. No winner, no prize-taker, even if a prize could be identified. And all on hold until the next time.

Jenny followed Terry out of the apartment, but took care to say a quiet 'Goodbye, Stavros' as she reached the door. Terry heard his father answer, 'Goodbye, Jenny. You come back sometime please. Okay? I don't hate you.'

In the car Jenny offered Terry a lift back to his place. He had been half-expecting her to explode after he'd lost it in there, and it was a relief she was in such an equable mood.

They said nothing the whole way, until the moment they pulled up at the kerb. Then Terry spoke. 'Thanks for that, Jenny. Really. I'm sorry I blew up. He may not want to tell me any more, but I'm not done with this yet. I intend to find out what Stavros and the neighbour back in Marrickville really got up to together. That's my next job.'

'Do what you want,' Jenny replied evenly, 'only don't expect me to come to anything like that again, okay?'

'I don't. I won't. You've done more than enough.'

'I know,' she said as he got out of the car.

*

Much as he wanted to stay on his father's case in the following days, Terry had other more immediate concerns. He rearranged his garage to accommodate his ever-growing collection of magic gear, including Hal's vanishing cabinet. To solve the transport issue, he bought a beat-up old van out of the meagre savings that he had been carefully nurturing these past months. The idea was that he would be able to ferry his gear around to gigs — 'A magician's got to have wheels,' Hal had chided him. He also attended the first of a series of counselling sessions that Jenny had suggested some weeks before. The initial encounter was not as troubling as he had anticipated. Everything went fine — Jenny was happy, the counsellor content — so long as he kept saying, one way or another, that everything was his fault. He was not resistant: he was coming around to thinking most of it was.

25

Father and Son

Terry woke early on the day he had decided to devote to collating the results of his investigative push into Francis Sargeson. Yet another biography of Houdini was sticking into his ribs. He had fallen asleep reading it the previous night and now turned it over to pick up where he had left off, allowing himself to be diverted from the tougher business at hand. Scanning pages, he thought over what he already knew of Houdini's childhood. The kid — real name, Ehrich — had run away from home at the age of twelve. Somehow or other he got himself from Milwaukee to Kansas City, most probably by train. At thirteen, he was apparently in New York. Terry wondered about the gaps in chronology — what did the twelve year old do during his year in Kansas City, for instance? Once in New York, he rejoined his family, who in the meantime had arrived there themselves.

Ehrich had moved to New York for 'work', the author proposed. Was there not enough money in the Weiss household? This book, like the others, spoke of 'a variety of jobs', mentioning that young Ehrich found employment as a 'necktie cutter'. Having grown knowledgeable about the geography of New York from his reading, Terry presumed that Ehrich must have been toiling in the garment district. In a sweatshop probably. And at that moment his brothers were doing exactly what? Helping how?

With each story of Houdini he had heard from Hal, and through his own reading, Terry felt further drawn to the early life of Ehrich Weiss. He had come to somehow care about the boy's behaviour — his thoughts, dreams, fears, others' expectations of him. When he was living in Kansas City, for instance, did he send money home? Where did he live? Who, if anyone, was looking out for him? Where was the father in the boy's life? Terry was convinced that Samuel Weiss had been a major contributor to this drama, and had no difficulty imagining his type — probably some bearded, hellfire-and-damnation Old World complainer. How could Weiss senior not be unhappy at what he discovered in America? All that money, independence, sheer cheek. A place where women were becoming uppity and sons no longer showed due respect to the patriarchs. And worse, for all his pouring abuse on the heads of the evil-doers and issuing warnings to the members of his various flocks, he was unable to do anything about it. Samuel had moved something like six times looking for a congregation prepared to support him, which spoke for itself.

In the end, if you can't do anything about the larger problem beyond your doors, what do you do? Work on the material at hand, starting with your own family. Bang on about everyone's place, what the progenitors, the ancestors and prophets have determined, what is owed … Not that hard to bend a wife, some young children, to your will, is it? Not then, and not now. For the controlling kind of man there were plenty of precedents — in the holy books, in the sacred writings, for a start. Terry may not have learned much in his experience of fatherhood, but he knew he would not be counted among their number. He had come to see the picture clearly. Men like Samuel, Stavros and, he guessed, Frank were everywhere, and everywhere causing grief.

As to Frank Sargeson, uncovering information on him was made that much harder by having to leave Hal out of it, a decision Terry had come to in the belief that he had to resolve this by himself.

The question was, how was he meant to get to the heart of events and behaviours of the kind that had to be hidden or lied about by their perpetrators? Terry believed there had to be some kind of record somewhere. In a world where the bad as well as the good were usually accounted for, there were numerous ledgers of one kind and another. Churches, police forces, courts, registries of births, deaths and marriages, departments of social security — these all generated records of the ills and travails, the comings and goings of the citizenry, known in this day and age, Terry reflected, as the 'clients' and 'customers'.

But aside from a list created by a bunch of amateur sceptics, there was no formal instrument for identifying, let alone settling scores with, the pedlars of false hope, the psychics and fortune-tellers and other charlatans who took advantage of the weak and confused who lapped up their poison. (And where, Terry wondered, was the psychic register, the emotional ledger? The place that might keep track of the damage that humans did to each other in their hearts and minds and souls?)

It had not taken long to establish that there was no police or criminal record for Frank Sargeson. Nor for his own father. Terry had felt some relief at that, but then wondered if it might not have been better if Stavros and Sargeson had been found out. Caught. Punished. Wouldn't it have been better for everybody concerned?

In the end, after two weeks of more or less concentrated research, he had not been able to add anything further to the case against Frank Sargeson beyond what the spookbusters already had on him and what Aunt Julie had hinted at. Apart from the old woman, there was not a single neighbour left in Jordan Street who had been around at the time. Of those who had moved away and whose names he'd been able to glean from council and land title records, there were only two with identifiable addresses. They were both dead. There was categorically no finding Frank Sargeson.

The personal information Terry had amounted only to what Hal had told him: Frank Sargeson had left home and disappeared one day in the early 1970s, and that was that. Terry had gone to the Registry of Births, Deaths and Marriages on the strength of what was on Sargeson's gravestone to see if he could obtain a death certificate at least, but there was none. 'No surprise in that,' the clerk had told him. 'He could have died interstate, or overseas for that matter,' he explained. Other potential sources of information included the subscribers to Sargeson's memorial — except the cemetery had no record of their names or addresses either. But Terry would not give up on the idea that Hal needed, deserved, to know more about his father.

The few scraps of detail he'd stumbled across so far were those provided by Aunt Julie, for which he was grateful. The only other living person, it seemed, who could possibly have anything to add was Stavros. Although Terry had got nowhere with him yet, that was understandable: if Stavros had been involved in a scam, he would hardly rat on his one-time partner. Terry could not see any way of making progress without talking to his father, and after the last blow-up that would be practically impossible.

Except an excellent reason for landing on his doorstep turned up out of the blue: Centrelink had been trying to contact Stavros. They called Terry to ask whether he might be able to help. It seemed the reprobate had been trying on an old trick.

At the mention of Centrelink, Stavros knew enough to accept help, even if it was from his maddening son. He protested that his having acquired a second address was nothing but an honest mistake, but agreed that there were answers needed, corrections to be made to forms. That was done one grey afternoon at Stavros's flat, after which Terry grasped the opportunity to grill him further.

'So, *Baba*, you really should tell me what went on back then. Might help, you know. I don't hate you so much that I don't want to talk to you, or listen to you. And I've stopped you getting hanged by the government, I reckon, today!'

Whether in reaction to Terry's sarcasm or his mere presence, Stavros set his jaw grimly and shuffled out to his balcony, busying himself with a fern in a pot. He took the plant inside to the sink, where he added some fertiliser, then carried it back outside. Terry followed him.

'Here, *Baba*, let me move things around for you. Tell me where you want the fern to go.'

Stavros bided his time, staring out over the balcony at the block of flats opposite and saying nothing as Terry tried the plant in this then that position. Terry knew very well he would not have been let in at all except for his father's little social security problem. He needed to be careful with every word.

'How many more secrets should there be, *Baba*? I do know a few things already, don't I? I've been talking to Aunt Julie … Anyway, how's the pot look here, do you think?'

Stavros let out a long sigh, then sat down at his little plastic garden table. 'The plant, I don't care, you can leave it anywhere you like. Terry, you listen please. You say you come here today for one reason, to help your father. But you not talking straight.'

'Oh, I'm the one not talking straight?' Terry said mildly. He stopped his fussing to come and sit opposite Stavros.

'You say you went and you talked to Julie, to Yannoula. Why?'

Terry did not respond.

'If you been talking to her, I know straightaway she will say to you things, many things that are not true.'

Much as he tried not to, Terry bristled. More of the same was coming; no doubt there would be further lies and obfuscations. With the greatest restraint, softly, he asked, 'So what would she say that's not true?'

'You worry about this word a lot, this "true" business, don't you?'

'Only ever brought it up because I wanted you to tell me about that fortune-telling stuff, as in did you or didn't you do that sort of thing back then?'

'You say "that sort of thing" like it's something bad.'

'Well, if you take money from people just for telling them made-up stories about their lives and future, it's not the most wonderful thing you can do for them.'

Instead of reacting, the old man appeared to retreat into

thought, furrowing his brow as if he'd been posed a difficult philosophical question. Then suddenly the muscles of his face relaxed, and as if from nowhere he presented Terry with an expression of serene, intimate openness.

'Okay. You listen to me now. Yes, we did tell the "stories" as you call them to the people for money in those days.'

'We?'

'Your mother and me.'

'Frank Sargeson too?'

'No,' Stavros replied firmly. 'I will tell you about him after. But if you want me to talk, I talk.'

'Go on.' Terry was wondering where this change had come from in his father. Maybe he had gone mad at last.

'It all start because your mother liked to read the cups; she learned this in the village when she was a small girl.'

'Did she believe in it?'

'She did. It was my idea to make a little business from this, if possible. But not just for money. Believe me, Terry, not only for money.'

'What then? What do you mean?'

'Terry. *Athanasios*! Think before you talk. You had the easy life, you grow up in the nice house, you not short of anything … You, my boy, are one of the lucky ones. So please think!'

Terry shifted in his seat slightly, remembering countless lectures like this in the past. 'I know that, *Baba*.'

'No, you only *say* you know that. Before you grow up, a little kid, already you were one of the lucky ones. Other people who came out from our country, they were not so lucky. Do you know what life they had?'

'Yeah, yeah, tough. I know, I know —'

'No,' his father spat out, cutting him off. 'You say only words. You never saw what I saw. You never feel what I feel.' He made some show of calming himself before he began again. 'Look, up the street from here used to be a box factory, place for making cardboard boxes. Around the corner, another one was making metal hardware — corners, brackets, angles, such things. Lot of factories, factories everywhere round here. That was Australia in those days. And those days, up and down. For the migrant, one minute work, next minute gone — go on, get out, don't need you anymore. No protection for wogs and dagos, you know. And accidents, accidents all the time — 1950s, 1960s, who cares? Nobody cares. No medical insurance, no compo, nothing. They patch you up at the hospital and send you home. The migrant man goes home, his wife crying, his kids hungry … Terry, you not a bad kid, but sometimes I think you know nothing.'

'Thanks,' Terry said, even managing a faint smile. He was determined not to allow himself to become annoyed, upset.

'You never *experience* these things … To tell you, one time I have no work for eleven months. Eleven months! When you are a baby, I have to ask the church, anybody, for help, for money … And every day I am ashamed. But one man come to me, his own mother and father are dead — killed in the civil war — and his wife sick with the mental problems and she can't have children, ever. And that man, he gave me …'

Terry watched his father begin to mist up, waited as he took a few breaths before continuing. It was impressive how much sheer emotion the man could still call up at his age.

'He gave me fifty pounds to help me and your mother. And he said, "Don't give it back or I will be offended, you need it more than me." Next day, I said to your mother, "We have to do something for them." I said to her, "Why don't you read the cup, tell her a story? Make them, make *her* feel a bit better. To not have a child is a terrible thing. Bad enough to live in a *skata* country and have a *skata* life, but for the woman not to have a baby, this is too much. Tell her something good." That's what I said.'

'So they were the first?'

'The first. And we ask no money of them, we didn't do this for money. Later, from other people, yes.'

'What did *Mama* tell them? What things did she say?'

'Oh, I can't remember exact words, but something like, "Don't worry, I can see that everything's gonna be better … See a trip to the old country … You have a cousin you never met somewhere there, go and find him … So I see you have family there too, go and find them, Christina, you not alone, maybe some money you will find there too, some money you will inherit … everything gonna be better." You see? Things like that — things hard to say is wrong and, who knows, maybe even right.'

Terry had watched his father closely as he spoke, looking for signs that something like this had really happened. He couldn't tell whether this was just a performance.

'How did they react when they heard those words? Can you remember?'

'If you can't work it out, I will tell you!' Stavros hit the table top with an open palm, once, hard. 'They cry with happiness! They say, "Thank you, thank you for this good news. We never expect such good news, Stavros, Eleni. Thank you so much." And they go home happy — that is how they *react*.'

Terry bent over a pot plant, pretending not to have noticed his father's heat. As softly as he could, he said, 'But it wasn't the truth. And if things like that didn't come true, wasn't that like cheating them?' He looked up at his father. 'The people who did pay, what did they say if the promises about the future didn't turn out?'

'Ah! You see? I said you don't know nothing, didn't I? We never promise anything to come true. And you know what? The people don't think we make any such promise, either. They just want the nice story. Just want to hear maybe some good news from somebody else, because anything better than the life they have, what they have to do every day. What they have to suffer. Anything better than the real life where the only words they hear are insult and rubbish, all the bad talk of good old Australia ...'

'Okay, okay, don't get upset,' Terry said finally. 'I only want to know what happened, that's all. But tell me, did you give them any bad news?'

'Yes,' Stavros said in a quieter voice. 'But not real bad news. Maybe your mother said to them, "Be careful, don't go to that place because maybe you find trouble there," or "Don't do that thing because could be danger." But she never promise them bad luck or hurt, if that is what you ask.'

'Pleased to hear it,' Terry said, trying to smile.

Stavros noticed. 'Good. Good you smile. Life is not like you think, my boy.'

'So what did you charge people? How much money?'

'Oh, not much. Peanuts. A few shillings, maybe ten shillings, a dollar today.'

'And did you get many customers?'

'Not too many. This was only part-time thing, remember. Saturday afternoon, Sunday afternoon. Maybe twenty, twenty-five people regular. Other ones come one time or two then we never see them again.'

'And how long? How long did you do this for?'

Stavros did a calculation. 'Ah … five years, nearly six altogether.'

'Six, eh?' Terry was about to stand up when his father scolded him.

'Look, you push this dirt down too hard.' He put his own hands into the soil Terry had been absentmindedly pushing at and clawed it around, loosening it up again. 'Got to be able to breathe.'

'You're right. Look, thanks for telling me all this, *Baba*. The way you've put it, well, it's not so bad, is it?'

'Not so bad, no.' His father grinned at him.

While Terry was encouraged by his father's demeanour and grateful that he had opened up the way he had, there was another person's version of these events. And he could not simply dismiss what Aunt Julie had told him. He would take advantage of this peaceful moment.

'One last thing though. What you're telling me is that Julie, Yannoula, was not telling the truth herself. She doesn't seem like a liar to me.'

Stavros stood up quickly at this. 'Yannoula, Yannoula …' He looked down at Terry who held his gaze.

'I'd like you to explain. What she said was that you were lucky not to have the cops on your neck. That what you were doing was criminal. Her story is different to yours — maybe you can put my mind at rest, eh?'

'Different, *ne*. It is very different. You want to know why?'

'I do.'

'All right, listen to me.'

Once again Stavros sat down at the garden table.

'Yannoula is the criminal. *She* is the lying one, not me. You sure you want to hear?'

Stavros took Terry's steady gaze as a yes. 'Your mother. The blessed one, you think, the saint …' He saw his son fidget, set his jaw, as if this was nonsense and he was irritated to hear it. He appeared to take it as a spur to go on.

'*She* was the not honest one. And Yannoula was just as bad! I never talk to anyone else about this, but now you ask and I am an old man and I don't care anymore. And somebody trying to fool you, so another reason to speak. Look, me and Yannoula … we have an affair. It last, oh, more than one year, then we finish.'

Unable to stop himself, Terry slowly shook his head from side to side.

'Don't do that, my boy — better you hear everything first! And then, after, when your mother find out, she do the same.'

Stavros saw the incredulousness and put his hand up. 'Stop, please, don't be a baby for me now. This is the reality of the adult — doesn't matter if mother or father or anybody else, nobody is perfect, everybody do these things sometimes.'

'With who? What are you trying to tell me?'

'With who? Ha! With "Mr Frank" as she used to call him! With Frank Sargeson, the man next door, that's who.'

Terry got up, ready to leave. 'You're making this up.'

Stavros's eyes quickly locked with Terry's now fierce stare. 'No, I don't make it up. This is the truth. You say you want it, so you can have it. Terry, your mother was like a gypsy inside, believe me. She was more angry than me inside, I tell you. She want to pay me back good — maybe she think, better I do this than stab him with the knife, I don't know.' Stavros paused to spread the fingers of one hand across his breastbone, as if he was feeling ill or to protect himself from an expected blow.

Terry tried to process what he had heard but was finding it impossible. He was meant to take this like an adult — his father was right in his own way about that — but it was he who felt as if he'd been stabbed right now. Absurd, he realised, but he had never considered the possibility that his mother might have done something so seriously wrong. But he stopped himself right there; why shouldn't she be capable of making love to someone other than her husband? What did he know, had he ever known, about what was in her heart? Indeed, about who she even was?

When he understood that Terry had nothing to say, or at least was not going to respond, Stavros looked away and began again: 'I was not a good man. I know that. But I was not a very bad man either … just a man. I never hated your mother. How could I after what I do to her?'

Terry stood still, trying to calm his breathing, to find some way of collecting himself. It was not as if he had that many resources to call on. His father had thrown so many hard balls at him, but none were as hard to handle as the one big lump that had lodged in his head — *these are not the things a parent tells his child, ever. This is too personal, too private.* And yet, why should that be so? Openness and honesty were supposed to be good, not bad things — or so he had heard in counselling.

Terry felt utterly defeated. Eyes closed, he did not notice Stavros had come to his side until he felt a hand on his shoulder.

'Don't feel too bad, boy. Nothing is so bad as you maybe feeling this minute. Every bad thing pass — for your mother, for me, for everyone — in this life. Everything pass for you too. You think you hear too much, yes?'

'You could say that.'

'Phww … your mother was a good mother, you understand?'

'I always thought so.'

'Don't worry too much about the sex business — that is everyday problem for the man and the woman, nothing special. But she look after you, her child, real good. She look after you and, for the first years, me too. But something inside her … always, always she pull this way and then I pull that way. I don't know why. Some kind of fight inside her, something eat her up inside. But I don't say she is the only problem. Me, I am angry too much, too much, when I am young man …

'Terry, she and me, we the wrong people for each other. Sorry to tell you but you say you want to know. Wrong people or in the wrong country, I don't know, maybe that. But we don't fit together good. You know what I mean?'

Stavros intertwined the fingers of both hands and held them up for Terry to see. Stavros himself stared at them intently, then suddenly pulled them apart.

'The first years, my boy, everything good. Believe me. We have the community, the church. Then you come along and even better. Close to each other, you know? We have the picnics and the dances, and the parties. The weddings, the baptism …'

'So what happened?'

'What happened is, like I say, something in Eleni's brain,' Stavros said, pointing at his temple. 'But other things too. If you have money you have good life, if no, life not so good. I told you about that.'

'You did. That's why you did the fortune-telling.'

'*Ne*. But something more than that, too. We not only did it for that reason. Not for money only, and not for make feel better the lonely ones, like I already said to you.'

'Not only? Why else then?'

'I will explain. But must start again, okay?'

'Up to you.'

'Things mess up, many things mess up for us, your mother and me. It was in that time that she have the affair with Sargeson — the man next door, "Mr Frank".'

Terry noted the sarcasm and wondered whether Stavros was angry or jealous, or whether he couldn't have given two hoots. The way he was telling this part of the story made Terry uncertain how much Eleni's affair had ever truly affected him. There was some impregnable defiance, resilience; he could not be entirely precise about what it was, but it was there.

'He was rubbish. But me, I am rubbish too. As I say, I do the same with Yannoula.'

Terry reminded himself not to hurry him, if there were to be no blow-ups. He resisted the urge, too, to draw him further on the detail. He had asked for this, the old man was obliging; the only reasonable response was to hear him out.

'Yes, you said that,' Terry said softly.

But now Stavros shook his head. The small and rueful smile that he had turned on and off until this moment quickly faded. Another few moments and his father hung his head a little.

'Hey, don't go like that,' Terry said. 'You're being very honest. I appreciate it. An affair that happened all those years ago is not going to matter today, is it? Better for you to get it off your chest, I would say. Better for everybody.'

'Better for everybody …' Stavros repeated the words, sounding them out to himself as if they were a strange thing to say. 'I don't know if better, just that I have to say something to you, I believe. I don't want to finish my life and not … Look, this is not the right place. Not the right place and I can't …'

Terry touched his father's arm gently. 'Hey, hey it's all right,' he said, and guided him back to his seat. 'You can tell me as much or as little as you want to. Something else I wanted to ask you — about Hal, Frank Sargeson's boy. Did he know what was going on?'

'I don't think so. If he did, very bad thing for him. He was a young man, that time. Never very happy, that one.'

'Nothing's changed there.'

'Why you say that?'

Terry waved a hand, trying to head off the anxious note that had resurfaced in his father's voice. 'He's okay. You might be surprised but I've seen him recently. Out of the blue.'

'He is all right?' Stavros asked, with more than a little suspicion.

'Yes, fine,' Terry lied as best he could. Much as he wanted to learn about Hal and Frank, he was drawn back to his mother's story. 'But what did you mean when you said *Mama* was a gypsy. Can you tell me?'

Stavros did not answer, but sat up stiffly. He seemed to be seeking the strength of a younger, straighter back as he turned slightly to look out over the street before speaking again. He had the air of a man about to unburden himself of something troubling, but in a collected and measured fashion. Terry wondered at the repertoire of effects his father seemed able to call upon. An ancient and noble tragedian, or a modern comic, it was hard to say which.

'She was not a gypsy, your mother. I said this when I was angry. I said this because I am upset when you ask me about that time. Anyway, it was *she* who was the angry one, like I said. About many things, too. The life we have here, she never liked it. She always want to go back to Greece, be with her family again some day. But really, she change very much because of one thing. One thing only, I believe.'

'What was that?'

Stavros sighed. 'Terry, everything change for your mother when your sister died.'

'My sister? What sister? What are you talking about?' Only when he had finished speaking did Terry understand he had more or less shouted these words. He leaned back against the balcony wall to try to reorient himself. Had he even heard Stavros right?

'You ask for truth. I'm sorry, maybe you don't want me to say any more. I say too much anyhow.'

Without thinking, Terry reached across the table and grabbed his father's hand. He squeezed it tightly. He didn't know what else to do. Not letting go, he said, 'What sister? I didn't know I had —'

His father cut him off. 'You had all right. She live for only three days. But you had, yes. Her name was Fotoula. She die in the hospital. She have problem with the heart and the doctors can do nothing.'

26

A Rotten Little Mafia

Terry knew he needed to see Hal again, and soon. He kept trying to contain the day's revelations, box them off somewhere among all the things that no longer mattered; yet further questions began crowding in, demanding attention. Foremost was whether he had been lied to again. Maybe there really had been a little girl who had died, but what if there hadn't? How to tell, when the man was a known liar, maybe even pathologically so.

By the time Terry was at Wentworth Avenue, the news his father had chosen to share still churning in him, he thought of calling Jenny. But what could he possibly say to her? 'Hi, just called to say I had a baby sister, but she died. Found out today. Fancy that, eh?'

Terry hoped that Hal might know something about Fotoula. He was relieved to find him in a calm, bright mood.

'Hello, mate. You seem happy,' he said in response to the big grin he received at the door.

'Got a new hobby. Come in and take a look.'

Hal led him to where he had arranged a kind of artist's corner. For a drawing board he had a length of pineboard, doubtless scavenged from some back lane. Next to this, on one of his ubiquitous upturned milk crates, he had laid a set of pens and some bottles of ink, along with a few sheets of drawing paper. Looking closely, Terry saw they were nibbed pens and that on one of the sheets Hal had been practising letter forms.

'Like the fancy lettering?' Hal asked.

'Looks good.'

Hal explained his plan to produce hand-lettered captions for the best of his photos. These he intended to mount properly on cards with borders and frames. They needed preservation and some explanatory words, if they were ever to 'go on show', he told Terry.

'They should, too,' Terry replied as he scrutinised the lettering on the topmost sheet. 'And explanations are always good, aren't they? That's what I'm hoping for today, as it happens … Sorry to drop this on you cold but I've been told something that has … I'd like to hear if you know anything about …'

'About what?' Hal asked, putting the question in a way that suggested he sensed trouble coming.

'Oh look, nothing for you to worry about, but tell me first, where did you get this gear from?' He picked up one of the pens and tested the nib.

'Sticking out of a bin, they were. Amazing the things people throw out, don't you reckon?'

'I'll say. Including their pasts.'

At this, Hal decided to pay closer attention. 'Something's up. Go on, what did you want to ask me?'

What Terry did not want at this moment was for Hal to clam up. He scanned his face, looking for clues as to how he might react. About Hal's emotions he couldn't be sure, but on the surface, he wasn't looking that great. His clothes, always less than appealing, appeared to be even shabbier than the last time he'd seen him. There was no sign of any drinking today, but the khaki coat Hal wore had dropped a hem at the back and seemed to be greasier than usual. He noticed also that Hal was barefoot, untypical for him.

Terry quickly glanced around the hall, checking for signs of trouble and was reassured that all seemed to be in order. He stepped a little closer.

'Went to my father's place today, Hal. Stavros, you know … He's been telling me some stories.'

'Oh yes?'

The reply was so guileless, so open, Terry felt he could safely go on. 'Yes. Told me some things about my family that I had no idea about. And also about you and your father … and my mother, too. Some stuff that happened when we were living next door to each other.'

Terry waited for a response, or a cue to continue. He was wary of frightening Hal off. But Hal did not look at him, or say anything at all. Instead, he picked up a fresh piece of paper and arranged it on the board. He sat down and carefully dipped his pen into the bottle of India ink on the crate next to him and began to write.

Terry was impressed by how thoughtful and relaxed he seemed as he worked. He took time after each short effort to ponder what he might write next. He had chosen some ancient-looking typeface to work in, so it was not straightaway apparent what he was writing. All Terry could tell was that whatever it was

Hal was committing to paper consisted of a series of short phrases, one under another in a sort of list.

Terry stood quietly, watching. He was in Hal's place, after all, taking up his time and space. Eventually Hal stopped what he was doing, and when he seemed satisfied with his work, picked it up and took it over to Terry.

'Careful, it's not completely dry yet,' he said. He handed it to him and immediately looked the other way. Terry took the sheet and read it. There, in neat Gothic capitals, were the words:

YOUR MOTHER

MY FATHER

YOUR FATHER

AUNT JULIE

THE BABY

THE BUSINESS

That was all. But it was more than enough. Terry could hear the blood beating in his ears. He looked down the list again. How was it that everyone — everyone — knew more than he did? About everything.

'Hal, what's all this? Why not just tell me what's going on?'

'Why? Because, Terry, I swear to God I never wanted to get down to this stuff with you. Practical help, that was the intention. That's what I wanted for you. Get you up and running. But your old man has given you … has told you some stuff, it seems. Well, here are the issues, as I see them. Let's see what kind of detective you are, eh? Terry, best you find out the answers for yourself …'

Terry resisted the urge to challenge Hal or argue. He folded the sheet of paper and put it in his shirt pocket. 'Okay. Just one thing: what stage of my training does this come under?'

Hal pondered for a moment. 'Preliminary for Levitation. I'm giving you a conceded credit for Disappearance, by the way. But you absolutely need to get started on Levitation, do you hear me?'

'I hear you. And meantime you better start looking harder for those gigs you're always telling me about.'

Hal brightened at this. 'Don't worry, I will. Just that that bloody old booking agent of mine's not answering my calls.'

As Terry turned around and made for the door, another thought arrived: from now on, there would be no more secrets, with anybody. He intended to get to the heart of everything. 'Will you be here tomorrow morning?' he called from the door.

'I will,' Hal replied.

*

Terry cajoled Hal into dropping everything and coming outside. And then, in one movement, he marched him up to the van and shoved him inside, all the while telling him that everything was all right, they were going somewhere nice. He would enjoy it, he promised. Only question was, what size swimmers did he wear?

'Time for a nice indoor dip, old son. Heard of the Ian Thorpe pool, Hal?'

Carried along on Terry's good humour, Hal smiled across at him. 'Couldn't care less about the name. Is the water warm?'

'It is.'

Terry was struck by Hal's going-along-with-it playfulness. They could have been schoolmates, friends, heading out on a prank. For all the older man's grumpiness and obsessiveness, Terry had found a lot to like in Hal Sargeson. He turned on the ignition and headed across Chinatown to Ultimo.

Ten minutes later they stood side by side in the changeroom at the aquatic centre, getting out of their clothes and into the boardshorts Terry had brought along. Hal continued to be willing, as if this was what he did every morning. Terry had decided that getting Hal into the water — and also where he wanted to go next with him — had to be approached as breezily and confidently as possible. In an agreeable, relaxed setting, there was some chance Hal might open up to Terry's questions. And if he didn't, a good wash wouldn't do him any harm, given the odour that was wafting off him at this moment. Not one for fussing overly about personal hygiene, was Hal.

Terry whistled jokingly as Hal turned to face him in his boardshorts. 'Hey, not a bad fit.'

'Been a long time. Is this what they're meant to look like?'

Terry inspected the figure before him. The charcoal-coloured boardshorts he'd bought Hal were the least of his problems. He said, 'They're fine. Made for you.'

What he actually saw was a saggy, aged male body, with grimy white skin except on his weather-beaten face and forearms, both deeply tanned, a paunch on a skinny frame, bandy legs — really, the man's height appeared to be the only thing in his favour. What with the way he carried his head thrust forward, his beaky nose and long neck, he reminded Terry of an ugly flamingo.

'Come on, Tarzan, time for a dip,' he said, slapping Hal lightly on the back.

Late morning as it was, the centre wasn't crowded. Terry steered Hal to one end of the smaller pool then sat down slowly on the edge and waved to Hal to do the same.

Strange how compliant, placid, Hal could be sometimes. Like a good, small child, doing as his parent wished or ordered. Maybe this was just the state he had been reduced to over the years — in moments like these, he appeared to have no fight left in him, entirely happy for someone else to lead the way.

'Those words you wrote for me, Hal … tell me some more. What did you mean by them exactly?'

'You were supposed to find out for yourself, as I recall.' Hal got up and stretched his arms skywards. 'Feels very nice, being here like this, Terry. Thanks for bringing me.'

'Couldn't get anywhere with that list.'

'Maybe you really do need me then, Terry …' Hal looked around at the hip interior of the centre. 'You'd think with my inner-city lifestyle I would have been here before,' he joked.

'Weren't always inner-city though, were you, Hal? Thing is, I can't remember you from when I was a kid.'

'Why would you? I'm older than you, Terry. And you wouldn't have seen me much. I left home when you were little. Not a lot to keep me there, I can tell you.'

Terry tried again to recall a moment, any moment, to which an image of Hal might attach. None came.

Hal sat himself down again carefully, conscious of the wet and hard edges of the pool wall.

'Don't worry about it. What makes me sad is that you know as much as you do about things — now. When I first saw you again after all these years, I wanted something better for you, I did. Do you believe me, Terry?' He looked warily at Terry, as if he more than half expected a negative reply.

'Yes. Don't fret.'

'And I *still* do!'

'Well, best thing is to tell me everything. That's the start.'

For a long while, Hal simply stared at the gentle lapping of water against the pool wall.

'There's not a lot more. You know the worst of it, don't you?'

'If you mean about my mother and your father, Stavros told me they were lovers for a time. That's fact, right?'

'Yes. They were. Hell, Terry, they were … can you believe it? Living next door like that, my father and your mother.'

'But according to my old man, there was good reason. He'd been playing up. It was some sort of revenge on my mother's part, it seems.'

'Maybe. Or maybe not.'

Terry was on the point of asking him about the baby girl when Hal swung his legs into the water. He eased himself in, and once he felt stable on his feet, took a step away from the safety of the wall.

'You coming in?' he said, half-turning towards Terry.

Terry slid down into the water, then moved to stand alongside Hal.

'How long since you and chlorinated water were as one, so to speak, Hal?'

'Bloody long time,' Hal said with a faint smile.

'Thought so. So come on, what else can you tell me? You got

240

as far as my mother and your father. What about Stavros and Aunt Julie?'

'Saw them together. Your old man and that Julie person. Yann-ou-la,' he said, stretching out the vowels, his distaste obvious.

Terry shook his head. 'Where?'

'Started in your backyard, as it happens. Saw them being all friendly-like at some sort of Greek shindig your parents put on. Feast day? Something like that. It was after that when one afternoon ... Yes, I saw them. Through the fence it was, at it in your sleep-out.'

Hal began to shiver, whether from the cold water or something else Terry was not sure.

'Got to get warm,' he said, and leaned forward into the water. He began a slow paddle, stroking away from Terry and heading towards the other side of the pool.

For the moment, Terry wanted nothing more than to drive all this information out of his head. He concentrated on watching Hal, allowed himself to notice the ease of his movements, wondered how someone who hadn't swum for so long could even remember what to do.

Terry set off after him; Hal swam slowly and it took little effort to catch up with him. They arrived at the opposite end of the pool more or less at the same time.

Hal stood up and began pushing the wet hair on the sides of his head — the only place where there was much to push — back over his ears.

'Hey, you know what, Terry?' The words came slowly, in the spaces between gasps for breath. 'I should have come to you ... earlier.'

'Same here,' Terry replied.

'You could have got a lot more guidance from Harry sooner, don't you reckon?'

'That's not what I was thinking, but yes.'

Terry watched him begin to shiver again.

'Can't be a lot left to tell, can there?' he asked.

'No, not too much. Some.'

They headed for the changeroom and the showers.

Dried and dressed, Terry turned to Hal and said, 'Please. Tell me the rest.'

'Look, I will. If it helps get you moving again — you've fallen behind with the training, you know,' Hal said and pointed a finger at him accusingly. He seemed to need to do some more thinking before continuing, nodding to himself a couple of times before he began again. 'Is it a deal?'

Terry offered Hal his hand and they shook. Neither of them spoke again until they were in the carpark.

'So where do you want me to pick up?'

'I know a bit about "the business", that it was a fortune-telling business. They were two of the words, remember? But I don't have any detail. What else can you tell me?'

'What else do you want to know?'

'Did your father have any part in it? Stavros said he was not involved, nothing more than that. And I won't mention that you had another story about him entirely.'

Hal sighed. 'Frank Sargeson, my father …' he said slowly, the contempt unmistakeable. 'He was conniving and he was vicious, Terry. The fortune stuff, the readings, they were only small beer. The big thing was the fake medium act. He took to running that out of your place, you know. The sleep-out. They put up black curtains. I can still hear the women crying, God knows. The things he used to say to them, like their loved ones were waiting for them on the "other side", or they couldn't be reached today. All heartless crap, all for money. Just cruel.'

'And Stavros, what did he do?'

'He rounded up the customers. Then when Frank learned your father was screwing that Yannoula woman, the blessed and sainted widow, he came up with the plan.'

'What plan?'

'I found out later that he had worked up a nice little scheme. He thought he could squeeze money out of Stavros; if he didn't cough up he would tell your mother what he'd been up to with bloody Aunt Julie … But as I understand it, Stavros didn't actually have any dough, other than the miserable few quid he was getting from the factory back then. So then Frank encouraged your mother, poor fool that she was, to put her cup-reading and such to better use … But she doesn't see the money, because your father takes a cut and hands the rest over to my father.'

Terry spent some moments trying to find his bearings. 'Don't know where to start, Hal … You're not serious about Yannoula?'

'I am serious,' he said softly. 'She's not who she says she is. None of them were then. None of them are now.'

'But she seemed …'

'What? Nice?'

'Yeah, that.'

'Nah! No offence, Terry, but I never did think you were very good at sussing things out. Not the bad stuff. You're an innocent, chum.'

'No argument there, Hal. But you're doing me some good, you are. Even if I'm finding all this —'

'Believe it, Terry. It happened. You were a kid, but I wasn't; I was nearly a man myself when this shit was occurring. Took me a while but I figured it out eventually.'

'I can see that. What else did you work out? And I'd like to know how, by the way.'

'What else was on the bit of paper I gave you, again?'

'The baby. My father said I had a sister who died very young.'

Now Hal's demeanour changed. He seemed more wary, anxious even, as if he realised he had maybe gone too far, told Terry too much. He lowered his head before he spoke again.

'Terrible, that. I mean for him to tell you that — bastard then, bastard still, obviously … There was a baby that died. Well, she was your half-sister. Mine too. Terry, your mother had at least one kid by my old man. She died at six weeks. I went and got her death certificate years ago — said she died of "cot death", although I'd like to know what really happened. Never did find out but got my suspicions about that too.'

Terry leaned against the side of the van, feeling desperate. This was not what Stavros had told him. He did not know what to think or what on earth he could say. And there was surely nothing he could do about any of this.

He supposed that he could take this story of a sister as just another of his father's lies. A story put about for spite or punishment or some other twisted reason, later bought as fact by a man who lived in an abandoned hall or temple or whatever it was, who had been a drunk and whose grip on things had never been better than shaky. He supposed he could take Hal's words as mistaken or some kind of mix-up. But he could not. He believed Hal's account to be true — and entirely devastating.

'Hang on, Terry,' he heard a kind voice say. 'Let's go back inside and get a drink, mate.'

Terry had no better idea, so followed Hal back to the aquatic centre cafe, where he sat numbly watching the swimmers doing their laps. Hal pushed a can of soft drink across the table towards him, but he had not the energy to even raise it to his mouth.

'Mind if I stay with you tonight, Hal? I think I need company.'

Hal reached over and patted him on the back.

*

That evening, Terry lay on Hal's old camp bed, as he had so many times before. But he was unable to get to sleep. What a rotten little mafia it had been; a disgusting bunch of cheats and crooks across two families. They had crossed the line — all sorts of lines. Back then Aussies and Greeks didn't mix, back then they were more likely to call each other names than to get together, even for business. Maybe what they got up to was just a new way of hating each other, of punishing each other. They might have been from different camps, and yet something had brought them close enough to get into bed with each other. Maybe there was no other word for that something but 'evil'. It might have been the pleasure of evil — but who was to say it wasn't the pleasure of greed, or of lust, or something else?

At some time during his tossing and turning, he heard a voice say, 'Terry, forget it. Just forget it all … The more interesting problem for both of us, I believe, is what Harry did next …'

Hal's voice was oddly welcome, a cue to stop trying for sleep that was never going to come. Terry sat up instead and turned the light on. Two am. He knew Hal to be not much of a sleeper either.

'What's that you said? Are you awake too?'

Hal was sitting on the edge of his bed, alert and eager to talk despite the hour.

'Look, I want you to start getting serious about the next realm. You *will* became a pro, I promise, if you stick with it. But, as I keep saying, you have to understand more about Harry. The more I think about it, the more I believe coming to Australia was very important to him.'

'I'll accept it as a theory, for now.'

'I know it, Terry. And it's to do with leaving the earth. There's more to be thinking about than that old family vomit, like you've been doing again tonight.'

'You noticed.'

'Bit hard not to. Look, I'm going to keep you to the promise. I'm all dried up, but you're not. As for Stavros, here's my advice — keep away from him. He's more than nuts, he's dangerous.'

PART THREE
LEVITATION

27

Blueprints

The plan was that Terry and Hal would each make their way to Bondi for a lunch of fish and chips and they would each bring a surprise. Terry found Hal seated on a bench above the beach, eating chips from a paper cup, occasionally throwing one to the seagulls.

'Don't do that, you silly bugger,' Terry said as he came over to join him. 'It only encourages them.'

'Exactly,' Hal grinned. 'That's the idea. Seagulls over people any day. So, what have you got in your bag?'

'Steady on. All shall be revealed.'

What Terry had once thought of as a tale told by Hal as part of his training regimen had become ever more meaningful. The story of Houdini had acquired another and more personal dimension. He had discovered a life of strange, sometimes distinct, sometimes muted echoes, which had come to absorb him, full of both warning and instruction. The main issue now was his literary skill, or lack thereof.

Terry reached into his shoulder bag and took out a notebook, which he held on to tightly against the breeze that had begun to pick up.

'Look, I'm not trying to write a life story or anything like that. I'm not a good enough writer. But there's something more to be said about Harry, other than the usual hype. Just remember, don't expect too much. Here goes.

Harry Houdini's behaviour was not that mysterious. The first problem was his father. The second problem was how to handle him. The boy Ehrich Weiss had to deal with the reality of his background and the origins of his family, things he must have felt some shame about. In the Old World, the ghettos of Europe, the rabbis exercised control over the local community. In the New World, that didn't work as well — you had to be very strong to be able to hold a crowd together. It was too easy to ignore a weak rabbi, and a kid could always run away from his father's authority. That's what young Harry did. But afterwards he would have felt guilt and shame … Harry's neglect by his father as a result of his defiance probably made it all worse. In a situation like that, why wouldn't a sensitive kid become troubled and look to escape? Then, later on, why wouldn't someone who felt he could only ever truly rely on his mother look for some way of getting in touch with her after her death?

'See?' Terry broke off. 'This family drama stuff, it's straight from the Greeks, mate.' He turned the page and looked across at Hal. 'What do you think?'

Hal appeared uncomfortable, shifting slightly as he looked for something to say.

'No use mincing words, Terry. We can talk straight to each other, you and I, right? So I'll tell you: it's crap; it's exactly the sort of thing I hoped you *wouldn't* write! You've been reading those books again, haven't you? Psychology and whatnot.'

Far from being hurt, Terry felt like laughing. 'Yep, those books again. Look, I thought you'd say that, so don't think you're upsetting me. I started writing that, then I thought, "Wait a minute, how can anyone know what really went through the mind of a Jewish kid in America a hundred years ago?" And anyway, it's not as important as what the guy actually did in his life.'

'Yes! Exactly! That's the point,' Hal said and gave Terry's arm a friendly punch.

'Writing that was hard. Been thinking more about what I want to do after this, after what's gone down. But you have to come to the flat later for me to show you where I'm up to, okay?'

'Done.'

'Now, what have you brought along today? Or did you forget?'

Hal grinned and put a hand into his inside coat pocket. 'Two tickets to the circus!' He thrust them at Terry as if he needed to prove they were real. 'Adair's Big Top is at Wentworth Park this week. We're going Friday.'

Terry read the blurb on the envelope — 'A night of thrills and fun for all!' — highlighted in red and gold, and smiled to see that they were in fact genuine. 'Where did you get the dough?'

'Pension money. Hey, a circus to the magician is like bread and butter for other people.'

*

251

Terry led Hal by the elbow to stand directly in front of one of the lockup garages at the bottom of his block of flats. Hal looked more than a bit confused.

'Patience, Hal. Got hold of this last week when somebody's lease ended — I want to show you what's inside.'

He slowly raised the roller door to reveal a cave full of magic. Props, tables, even the cabinet he had worked on when he was still living at Ashfield. A magician's workshop.

'Well, well …' Hal smiled. 'Isn't that something?'

'I brought stuff over from the shed. But this is not all I've got to show you.'

Terry flicked a light switch, seeming to expect something to happen. 'Hey,' he called eventually, 'that was your cue! Where are you?'

They heard a crash as a box tipped over somewhere near the back of the garage. Next thing, a half-embarrassed, half-excited Ricky stumbled into view, wearing a proper, fitted magician's outfit, top hat and all, and carrying a wand in one hand.

'You've never met my son, have you, Hal? Hal, meet Ricky. Ricky, meet an old friend of mine, Hal Sargeson.'

The two shook hands.

'Pleased to meet you. Your father's told me all about you,' Hal lied, probably hoping to please the boy. He was successful, judging from the shy smile the boy returned him.

'Ricky and I are going into the magic business together, aren't we?'

Ricky nodded in the right spirit.

'Great idea,' said Hal, 'but aren't you … isn't he …?'

'A bit young? Right now, yes. But we're going into training, him and me, so that later, when he's older …'

'Well that *is* excellent news. But finish school first, eh?'

Ricky didn't look too happy at the prospect, glancing briefly at his father and hoping there might be some reprieve. When none was forthcoming, he nodded reluctant agreement.

'And he's already pretty handy. What have you been practising, Rick? Can you show us something maybe?'

The boy didn't hesitate. He went straight to one of the small tables near the entrance and from it picked up a pack of cards.

'I can do this,' he said, and began to carefully shuffle the deck. Next he fanned the cards across the table. 'Name four cards please.'

Hal grinned at him. 'All right, the four aces.'

Ricky waved both hands in circles over the cards, then with his right hand reached down to pick one up. He held it out. An ace. He did the same thing three more times.

'Isn't that something, Hal?'

'Very good, very good. I'm impressed.'

At that, the boy put one arm across his abdomen, the other behind his back, and took an exaggerated bow.

'Bravo again,' Hal said, and this time gave him a clap. 'Anything else?'

Ricky thought for a moment, said 'Maybe' and went fossicking among the paraphernalia for another trick. He was still searching when they heard a car pull up nearby and a horn sounded.

Terry stiffened. He knew that sound, that car. He looked down the street and sure enough, there was Jenny.

'Sorry, Ricky, we've run out of time today. Mum's here.'

The boy looked torn, finally saying, 'Sorry, Dad, gotta go,' and walked off reluctantly.

'More next time!' Terry called after him.

'Hang in there, Terry,' Hal murmured. 'The boy'll come back to you later. Family always comes back to you one way or another. Plenty of time, plenty of time.'

*

Far too early the next morning, a couple of enormous bangs startled Terry from his bed, so that he was at the door and checking the peephole almost in one leap.

'Hal, for Christ's sake! What's with the noise?'

He opened the door, only to be swept aside in Hal's enthusiasm. 'Hallelujah! Hallelujah is all I can say, 'cause I've found some more.'

'Some more what?'

Hal took some loose sheets of paper from inside his coat and waved them at Terry. 'Didn't know I even had these. They were buried in the stuff at Rosehill. Look …' He spread them out on Terry's dining table.

Terry picked up a page and squinted at it. What he saw was a set of hand-drawn diagrams, some kind of technical drawings.

'What is this stuff?'

'These are Harry's instructions, his plans ahead of his best — his successful — flight in Australia. The one that worked, that got him the record! Terry. Look at it, just look at it.'

What Hal had brought along seemed to be photocopies of some very old documents. Terry didn't know what to say about them. 'Are you sure this is the real deal?' He looked more closely at the material. 'Fuel quantities … wind speed … What's it supposed to mean?'

'It means gold, Terry, that's what it means. It tells here how Harry did it, the first chap to get off the ground properly in this country. You can do this too! Why not give it a go?'

'Aw come on, Hal. That's too hard for us. For me.'

'But this is a real discovery!'

'All well and good, Hal, but it's like finding a bunch of cannonballs, except no-one is making cannons anymore. Sorry, mate, but it's not even an idea for me right now.'

*

Terry spent the rest of the morning, after Hal's disappointed departure, pacing around his flat trying to get a grip. To consider his impossible plan was to make life even more complicated. To recreate a hundred-year-old historic flight with a nonexistent biplane — what was Hal thinking? Still and all, Terry was impressed that he had somehow managed to get hold of those diagrams.

28

The Grand Idea

Concerned that he had dismissed Hal's grand idea too abruptly, Terry went around to see him that evening to make amends. He discovered a strong scent of grog in the air and a Hal who, though not drunk, was not entirely sober either. He had not been prepared for this.

'Hal, I thought you were cleaning up your act.'

'It's not for want of trying, Terry,' Hal croaked as he led him in.

Bad as it was for Hal, Terry took the condition he was in almost as a personal blow.

'Did I upset you about the plane idea —'

'Listen,' Hal hissed angrily. 'I'm the wrong bloke for you. Can't help you, can I? You can see why I had to give it all away, can't ya? Fuckin' useless I am. Hopeless ... So hopeless that I want to tell you something else.'

Terry tried to soothe him. 'You don't need to go on about it, Hal. I think I know pretty well what happened.'

'Do you? I wonder about that.'

'Hal, you helped me get on my feet. A bloke from my past

who came back into my life. You helped me get to the bottom of stuff I never knew about. You told me your Houdini tale. An inspiration it's been too. A great inspiration. Never in a million years did I think I'd ever …'

Hal slowly raised his hand, the palm ending in front of Terry's face.

'Stop right there. You know a couple of things … You never asked me about my name, by the way. What's Hal short for, smarty pants?'

'Harold, I guess.'

'And Harold is also …?'

'Okay, Okay, I get it, but if you named yourself after Houdini, so what? What's your real name?'

'They called me Morris. I hated that. I changed my name to Hal, to remind myself of Harry. Would that make any sense to you? Should do, chap who's had a name change himself.'

Terry took the question seriously, if only to humour him. But before he had the chance to answer, Hal went on, as if letting out a confession he'd bottled up for too long.

'You might reckon me mad — you probably already do. But two things: one, know why I live in this place? Chinese temple, sure, and I love the Chinese because, you know why? They say to the boss cocky, "Yes, Mr White Man, anything you say, sir," and then they do their own thing in their own place and not by the book. Magician's hall? Coincidence, that. And nostalgia … Terry, I've been living here 'cause it was a Temperance Hall! This is a special place of worship. Every day I've spent in here, I sincerely believe has added another day to my life. Between this and AA …'

Hal saw the concern growing on Terry's face and seemed to understand he needed some relief. He smiled at him. 'Don't look so worried, chum. Another thing about this place is it's cheap … But where was I? Yes, point two. Point two is, have you heard of a thing called a role model?'

'Sure. And?'

'When I gave up the grog, or tried to, I realised that wasn't enough. So I ask you — can there ever have been a greater man for a person in trouble than Harry Houdini? There was someone who lived grand. He was brave. He was smart. The more I looked into him the more impressed I was. The more taken I was. I've come to love him and I realised he was a great teacher. Like the Mahatma. Or Nelson Mandela. He was my hero. Do you understand?'

Terry was about to say yes when once more Hal got in ahead of him. 'I'm sure you do. I saw it, I saw what happened, how you reacted. You needed special treatment.'

'Did I now?' Terry was worried by Hal's almost manic fervour, his delusional comparison.

'You did. And the course began with information. Info from libraries, books, magic shops …' Hal lowered his head, his voice too. 'Terry, boy, this is where it gets tough …'

He straightened himself to his full height unsteadily and let out a long, slow breath, then moved to stand beside Terry so that they were both facing the same way. Terry felt awkward and was about to move away when he felt a gentle hand on his shoulder.

'It's all right. Stay there. I did it, Terry, because maybe I sometimes go nuts with the grog — though I'm better than I used to be and not too bad today, as you can see. And I also did it because we are family. And when family find each other they should help each other.'

Terry felt a cold thrill rise up his spine. If he did not know the detail yet, some connection made deep and instant sense. 'What?' he blurted out. 'What are you saying?'

Level and soft, Hal answered him at last. 'You and I are children of the same father. Stavros isn't your father, Terry. Frank Sargeson is.'

It was all Terry could do to stay upright. Wild with hurt and fear, he looked at Hal. Surely he was crazy, he was lying … But he saw instead the benign and gentle expression, the sorrow, on this ageing man's face, and accepted the truth.

'Sweet Jesus, Hal. This is for real?'

'It is. All I can say, brother, is that the things that were done to you and me, they should not have been done to a pair of dogs. That's not what parents do. That's not what love is. I've been looking after myself for years; it came time to help you … Except I turn out to be not very good at it.'

Hal saw Terry's shock and led him to a chair. He stood beside him and waited. After a minute or more, Terry leaned across and put an arm around Hal's legs. He did it without thinking, but continued to hold on, unsure why. He had come to accept there was at least something between them after these few months — but this could not have been imagined. If he let go, there was the danger that he, they, everything would not just sneak out the back of a magic cabinet, but truly disappear forever.

'I'm still … I can't get my head around …' He heard himself speaking while the impossible became ever more plausible. Two families had been bound together, almost a cult, a secret society.

Why couldn't something like this have happened? His mother was submissive, easily led, vulnerable. He had discovered his so-called father to have been even more evil than he had suspected. Hal's father was another kind of lunatic altogether. And they had found each other, cheated on each other, had children with the wrong person. Forget morality. Forget Greek or Australian values. They had made their web and they had entangled themselves in it. The thing was hollowing, gutting, but made perfect sense.

'It'll take you a while, believe me,' Hal said. 'It took me years and years. And I'm still working on it. But, hey, every knock is a boost, right?'

'So they say.' Terry felt his eyes begin to sting, but he held on. There was too much to ask, to say. 'Seeing me at the old people's home. Was that what made you …? The magic act …?'

'You doing magic, that tipped me over. I knew you were around but I couldn't face seeing you. When you've been disappeared as long as I have, you can't face anything.'

Terry saw the enormous tiredness that had overcome Hal. Concerned he might topple over, Terry got up and gently led him to his bed, where he helped him lie down and pulled off his shoes. He pulled up a chair to sit next to him. Hal needed nothing but sleep right now.

Terry needed something else. He would have to try to accept what he had learned about the early years and move on. But to accept what was done did not mean he could just ignore it all. There was no putting off the problem of the man who had been his father. And whatever plans he might conjure — for Hal and for himself — would have to be more than magician's tricks, more than ectoplasm, if they were to survive as a family.

29
Memorial

'Not everything is a trouble in your life, our life. We have some good days we can talk about too!'

Terry heard the light note in his father's voice, the playfulness almost, as Stavros squeezed his shoulder. The combination was disarming, almost soothing.

'Yes!' said Stavros. 'Not such a tragedy, I think, all this … Some bad, some good too.'

Good times, thought Terry. A lunch like this might count as such in other circumstances — but not today. If he tilted his head a certain way, Terry could just make out the Remembrance Pool in front of the War Memorial in Hyde Park. He and Stavros were seated two floors up, in the dining room of the Greek Club in Elizabeth Street where Terry had arranged to meet the old man for lunch. He saw a glint, a sparkle or two bounce off the water; he took up one of the menus and handed the other to Stavros.

'*Psaria, psaria* … fish, fish,' Stavros said, smiling as he squinted through those Coke-bottle reading glasses of his.

'Nothing changes on this menu.' Terry smiled back.

'What did you expect? They Greeks here! Do you remember when I used to bring you here when you were a little fella?'

'Oh yes,' Terry replied. 'Like it was yesterday.'

They agreed on a bit of everything, in the form of *mezethes*. Terry ordered, and Stavros returned to his earlier theme. 'I sit here with you like this … very nice with the park over there and the sun in the window … I don't know. Sometimes I think, "Why this son of mine is interested so much in the black things all the time?"'

'Black things indeed,' Terry said and smiled, keen to give Stavros no cause to fly off or dry up on him.

Stavros shot Terry a look of resignation. He saw a waiter approaching with a couple of plates of appetisers and held off until he had set the food on the table and left again. Terry reached across to spear some whitebait. 'This is good stuff, *Baba*, have some.'

Stavros prodded and poked the fish, looking for the fattest specimens. 'Mmm, good,' he agreed after tasting a mouthful.

'Good as the view,' Terry said, turning to the window again. He was conscious of Stavros watching him as he gazed out. The tactic of avoidance could no longer be sustained.

'Okay, if you're comfortable it's time for me to tell you something, Stavros. I know I'm not your son.'

Stavros screwed up his forehead, making a show of cogitation. He let out a long sigh and lowered his eyes — all before turning a peaceable countenance in Terry's direction. In this theatricalising, Terry had all the admission he needed. The emptiness in Stavros's gesture was as brutal as anything else he had done.

'But here's my question. You belted me. You abused me. You didn't want me, that was obvious. So why did you keep me?'

Stavros looked at him for a long moment and replied calmly, 'You want to know? All right. To keep the peace … Maybe because I feel a little bit guilty, too.'

'Bullshit,' Terry said quietly. 'More bullshit. And there's another question. My sister, my half-sister in fact. What happened there?'

Stavros slapped the table softly with his hand. Eyes narrowed, he did not so much speak as hiss what he had to stay.

'You think you the only one in the world, don't you? Your mother and me, we had a good little business, the two of us. But you, you muck everything up. Eleni always say, "Athanasios sick, Athanasios cold, must look after Athanasios." Day and night I hear this. Well, why I should care so much, why I should listen, when you not my kid anyway? I had the big plan, the big dream! You destroyed everything in that time!'

Pushing his chair back, standing, Terry did not feel anything much for the next few moments — until some sickening sensation arrived in his guts. Then he felt his legs start to move, taking him somewhere, anywhere.

He heard Stavros behind him say, 'Where you going? Terry?' as he walked away towards the doors of the restaurant. He felt white hot now, but when he heard the rhythmic patter of his shoes on the tiles he was glad of the distraction, the effort of trying to walk normally, to slow down, not run. Five, six, seven paces, and the low murmur of the lunch crowd was behind him.

Something, he had no idea what, caused Terry to pause and look back. Stavros was as he had left him, seated at the table, but for one difference. Unless he was seeing things, Stavros had taken up his fork again and was picking at the whitebait. Terry watched as he speared a forkful and raised the mass to his mouth. As he began to chew, steadily, indifferently, shockingly, Terry pushed open the twin doors and took the stairs down to the street. He did not know what his old man — if that was how he should still refer to him — proposed to do, whether he intended to eventually follow him — but now he knew he did not care.

He ran through the traffic and across Elizabeth Street into Hyde Park, stopping on the concrete path between the Pool of Remembrance and the War Memorial. He felt pinned like some exhausted insect, caught, held in the web of ceaseless movements of city shoppers and lunchers and office workers criss-crossing all around him.

He slowly made his way towards the memorial, hoping to get away from the images churning in his head. He went to the gallery and gazed at the sculpture of the slain warrior splayed out on a shield in faux-Greek style. He thought how he had spent his early years avoiding physical blows from his father, now the blows dealt had been of a different kind.

Terry had never felt close to Stavros, but he had never understood what the distance was about either. He had always believed that his not being 'good enough' was the basis of Stavros's anger and criticism, but it was much more than that. It was the fact of being born at all. Not only did he not count as blood, he had got in the road — and that was more frustrating to Stavros and his scheming than anything else. There was nothing personal in it.

This was exactly the wrong place to have come. Terry looked again at the image of the dead warrior and broke into laughter.

Loud, lusty laughter. Greeks killing Greeks, fathers and sons …
He leaned over the railing and shouted at the statue, 'Well, mate,
time for all this to end!'

He left the memorial, walking straight into a flock of pigeons.
He watched them take flight, scattering feathers and dust around
him. How beautiful were their movements as they swooped
upwards and bent through the sky ever higher.

30

Beyond Illusion

Terry retreated to his magic workshop in the garage. It was more than solace he sought; aware that he had not practised at all in the past week, he took up a pack of cards, a standard deck, and turned to face the mirror he had set up against one wall. He would step through the simplest of tricks, finding an audience member's card. There was no-one to play the part but that didn't matter — as with so many tricks, what the participant did or didn't choose wasn't crucial.

Terry held the deck in his left hand and fanned the cards out, their backs facing the mirror, then sneaked a look at the card closest to him, at the bottom of the deck. This, an eight of diamonds, was the key card. To identify the key card was to have all the information needed to be able to pick out the participant's card, preferably with a dramatic flourish.

Terry turned the fanned deck so that the card markings were facing the mirror (these he would not ordinarily see, but the presentation was what he wanted to work on today). As the participant, he chose a card at random.

Next, checking himself in the mirror, but without looking at the card, he cut the deck and returned the card to the top of the cut. Then he reshuffled the cards, making sure to put the eight of diamonds — the key card — on top of the participant's card. He cut the deck once more, then again — knowing this should not break the connection between the random card and the key card.

Now, he turned the cards to face him and looked for the memorised one. Immediately underneath it, of course, was the participant's card. It happened to be a king of clubs. He cut the cards one last time to bring it to the top of the deck.

As there was no spectator for him to ask to name the card, he announced it himself: 'King of clubs …' To finish, he turned it over and revealed it to an imaginary audience.

Terry continued to look at the mirror, satisfied there had been no hitches or glitches. Why should there be? He had practised the thing dozens of times.

Yet enjoying such mastery as there was in this, he also knew it was minor stuff, nothing but trickery. There was surely more on earth for him than this. He had come to accept too many things as given, to believe that change was not possible. What he had confirmed today in the restaurant could be added to that load that seemed to have weighed him down forever.

Conscious of the fading light slanting in from outside, Terry closed his eyes and remained still. The tenuous peace of the moment was destroyed by the screech of birds, a pair of parrots ruckusing past the open door of the garage. He caught the barest of glimpses of red and blue as they disappeared. Feathers, birds, flight brought another memory. A moment with Ricky on a picnic at the Royal National Park, the boy surprised by a noisy, sudden flock of crimson rosellas. The way he had pointed at them, turned to him looking for some reference.

A few years earlier it had been satisfying to name a few colourful birds for his son, and feel the small pride of a father giving his child something new. That kind of pleasure was past, to be replaced by … what? Driving a bus had given him nothing except money, and now, in some dark act — the left-hand path all right, he thought — his own parentage had been thrown up in the air.

As if all that wasn't enough, there was Ricky's situation. For him, what was there but the heartache of his parents' break-up? The kid was hurting. He knew that, to the point where some days it made him feel physically sick.

At this moment, he felt disembodied, floating, looking on at himself detachedly. He saw a bent and stooped old man shuffling down a road somewhere. Someone ready to drop to the ground under the burden he had been handed, accepting that he had been destroyed … But better to believe that wasn't him.

The key card, that was it. All you need to know to pick the seemingly impossible. The fortune-telling business could not have been the whole story for Stavros. But if you thought of that as a key card, what could be discovered from where it was placed? What lay nearby? Terry would take this idea to Hal at their next session.

*

A couple of days later Terry was kicking himself for not having started down this track earlier. Eager to get going, he would first let Hal know what conclusions he had come to.

'I'm convinced there was more to it than Aunt Julie and the rest, Hal. More than the fortune-telling and your old man's fakery too,' said Terry. 'Stavros goes from that small-time stuff to buying a cleaning business with premises and vans and people working for him ...'

'That bit I don't know about. It all must have happened after you moved away,' Hal said.

'If Stavros's business was incorporated there would have to be records of some sort. And even if it wasn't there must have been a registered business address.'

Apart from a trading name listing, the business did not appear on any corporate records. Voulos Cleaners, however, had been licensed under a local council trading law, the premises being located on the Rose Bay strip.

Terry stared at the address he'd retrieved from municipal records and realised he had never been there. Nothing alarming in that, he told himself. He was a kid then, with school and soccer to go to, and his mother on his case to study hard and get into a trade or a profession and thus avoid her and his father's fate. 'I never want to see you a cleaner, *agori mou*,' she had said more than once. After she died and before he'd moved out, he'd had the run of the house after school and on weekends and there was still no reason to visit Stavros's office. Where Stavros worked was of little interest to him; his dark, swinging moods another reason to stay away.

When Terry drove out to the address, he found a print-framing shop, where the proprietors had never heard of Voulos Cleaners. A little further down the strip he came across a tired-looking takeaway run by a husband and wife team well into their seventies, who had to be Greek if the shop's name, 'Santorini', meant anything.

Terry did his best to disarm the couple with talk of the 'old days' and how things had been for Greek immigrants like themselves, taking care not to divulge his connection to Stavros, but assuring them that he too was Greek. 'Must have been more of our people around here? Working in these parts once upon a time?'

There were, agreed the man. 'Some good, some bad,' he added with a shrug.

'Bad too? You're kidding,' Terry joked.

'Yes, for sure,' was the reply. 'Like the bloke who ran the cleaning business that used to be up the street. Fella by the name of Voulos. He no good that one,' the husband said. At which his wife half-turned towards Terry and waved her hand over the frying vat. 'He was hot, like this oil!'

Terry smiled. 'Hamburger with the lot, thanks,' he said. 'And you can tell me the story while you're at it.'

What he heard was simple enough, and it made perfect sense. The pieces clicked together all too well. The 'good little business' that Stavros said Terry had destroyed was not the fortune-telling or cleaning business. It was another sort of business entirely. The story-telling they had done was for money all right, but only start-up money; it was what Stavros used to get the cleaning business up and running. But then the latter became a front, a place through which to wash the contents of brown paper bags, a place of cash in hand. Because what Stavros was really doing was running an immigration racket.

'Everybody knew about it. He find "sponsors" — they say they want to bring in the second cousin, whatever, to help them. But no, the sponsors are crooks like him. They need the cheap labour. The migrant kid, girl or boy, they get here and they owing money — to the sponsor, to Voulos.'

'How was he doing that?'

'He find people in the right places, Australia government and Greece government, and he get the papers. After they come out, if they don't pay up, he send the tough guys around.'

Terry was not at all surprised. He found himself nodding, emotionless, all the while thinking that this might just have been the last straw for his mother. Her health already fragile, a child that had died, all she needed was for her husband to be involved in crime. Stavros had given it all away presumably when it was no longer viable, when immigration from Greece had started to wind up around the early 1980s, which was when Eleni had died. Or maybe he got out when someone threatened him back, said they would go to the cops or such.

Terry left the takeaway considering his options. One was to physically hurt Stavros somehow, as he had hurt others — but he was simply not capable of such violence. The other was to go to the cops. Except that would mean acquiring evidence, facts — of which he had next to none right now. The chances of prosecuting something like this so many decades after the event seemed to him to be nil. What Stavros had done to him compared to what he had likely done to others — demanded their meagre savings to fix their immigrations woes — was negligible. And it was his mother who had borne the worst of it — knowing Stavros was becoming rich by exploiting his compatriots, living with a man who was not the father of her child. About all that, now, he could do absolutely nothing.

Back at the flat, Terry called the man he'd thought was his father.

'Hello, Stavros,' he said calmly. He would no longer refer to him as *baba*, or father; the very last of any feeling he had for him had disappeared. 'I know where your Rose Bay money came from. I'm thinking of going to the police.' There was only a long silence on the other end, then the hard click as Stavros ended the call.

*

A week later, Jenny rang Terry, a sense of urgency in her voice. She had checked in to see how Stavros was doing as he had not answered on the two occasions she had telephoned him. She reported to Terry that a neighbour had emerged from the unit next door, saying that Stavros had left a few mornings before in a taxi, with a bunch of suitcases.

Terry took a couple of breaths, time to organise what he had to say next, then told Jenny everything he had learned. He spoke as calmly and carefully as possible. On the strength of what he now knew about Stavros, it was likely, he said, that the bastard had taken off and would never be found again.

When Jenny asked him whether he could trust what he had been told, he answered, 'Now that he's done that — completely.'

'This changes something, doesn't it, Terry?' she replied.

31

A Night at the Circus

Terry and Hal kept their date for Adair's circus on the appointed evening. But far from any magic, the best thing about that amateurish outfit had been the pachyderms — and not for anything they were made to do in the ring. The usual kneeling, standing on hind legs, trumpeting, the silly hat wearing, Terry thought cruel and depressing. The real pleasure had come earlier.

Before the show started, he and Hal had gone to look at the three Indian elephants in their enclosure. In that darkened corner of the compound, the huge animals had a peculiar impact on Terry. Their round shapes had been silhouetted against the inky night, as if they were shadows on shadow and nothing more, swaying gently from side to side. Terry looked up to the vast, starred heavens above, hoping something up there was looking after them because, here on earth, they stood in mute accusation, forlornly hoping for release. They were chained to the ground, anchored to the earth. But they were also perfect in their being. They were themselves, whatever was done to them.

Heading home later, Terry stopped with Hal near the vaulted brick arches of the railway viaduct that crossed Wentworth Park.

The string of giant fig trees, the ancient wooden coal loader, the fish markets — they were all part of the ordinary, sad world. Terry thought again of those elephants. Then and there he decided. By the time he and Hal had gone their separate ways, the idea had taken ample shape in his brain.

*

Over their next scratch meal together at the hall, Terry brought forth an uncomfortable truth about Houdini. 'He wasn't much of a magician, was he? There were other guys who were more skilful at sleight of hand, more elegant. From what I've learned there were some things he just didn't do at all. Correct?'

'Well yes, some things.'

'Like levitation?'

'If you mean full reversal-of-gravity levitation, large objects and humans, he didn't do those. He hated all that table-levitating, spiritualist claptrap, as you know. But levitation is part of the program. And Harry had his own version — it's called flying. That was another kind of magic, Terry. And what a thing to have done. Right here, in Australia.'

'That's what I want to talk to you about. I think I want to give it a go,' Terrry said plainly.

'True?' Hal looked surprised, and sceptical.

'Yes.'

'At last! Excellent,' Hal said and clapped his hands.

Until now, Terry explained, he had not been able or ready to appreciate the most brilliant of Houdini's achievements. But as Hal had already pointed out, Houdini was not merely an escaper from the known, from everyday shackles and restraints, and nor did his greatest achievement lie in making things appear or disappear, changing one thing into another. The man had launched himself into the skies, he had flown.

Terry tried to picture that flight of 1910. And then what it must have been like for those who witnessed this further amazing act in Houdini's already spectacular repertoire. For an event that had happened and been recorded so long ago, it had come to live vividly with him. He may have resisted, but now it had grabbed him.

That it *had* grabbed him was still concerning, so Terry asked to look again at those plans of Hal's. He turned them this way and that and saw that they were indeed potentially useful. The more he thought about his plan, the more it had a cool kind of inevitability to it. Nothing to get worked up about at all. Sometimes things just made sense.

What if they, he and Hal, could recreate the whole amazing thing again? An old show for a modern audience? The hundred-year anniversary of Houdini's Australian flight was coming up. There had to be a plane somewhere, maybe not a Voisin but at least an original biplane that could serve the purpose.

Everyone loved a historical recreation. Hal had shown he was keen — and he sorely needed a project, in Terry's view. As for himself, there would be something far more important in it. He presumed difficulties, there would definitely be those. Chief difficulty, for instance, was that he had not the first clue about planes or flying.

'So, Hal, it's official … we're getting into the flying business.'

Hal, who had sobered up seriously and seemed to have found his equilibrium, allowed in some doubt. 'Now are you sure? Don't tease me. I'm not a well puppy, as you know.'

'I'm sure. There won't be a Voisin plane about, you can rely on that, but there must be a few old biplanes around and we can —'

'There is, you know,' Hal interrupted him.

Terry stared at him. 'What?'

'There is such a plane. I checked it out. I was going to tell you if you'd let me.'

Terry took Hal lightly by the shoulders, giving him a gentle friendly shake. He was making stuff up again.

'Hal, no kidding now, please.'

'It's true,' Hal said.

Terry began to back away, but Hal immediately grabbed him in a bear hug.

Terry pulled back to look into Hal's eyes. This was the most pleased he had ever seen Hal. His brother even managed a joke. 'Glad you passed over levitating donkeys and elephants, Terry. They shit everywhere you know!'

'I want to do it. I want to do something like this, Hal. Question: how did you learn about the plane?'

'Oh, I did some checking. The internet cafe around the corner, they showed me how to look things up on the computers there. There's still at least one of those Voisin planes around. I'm not kidding, mate. A bloke in Victoria, in some vintage plane club, he's been restoring it. Not done yet, but he's getting there … So, what do you say?'

Terry understood the question. 'Okay, yes. I'll try to get hold of him.'

Hal did a little jig on the spot.

'You can stop the silly dancing,' Terry said, without meaning it. He was reminded yet again of how Hal had long ago left the ranks of the socially acceptable and respectable; he was aware also that he was joining him in his rebellion. 'Did you take down the details?' he asked when Hal was done.

'Ha! I'm not that big a dill, Terry. Right here, mate, right here,' he said and began emptying the rubbish out of his coat pockets. He caught the right piece of paper mid-drop, before it hit the floor.

32

Beyond Diggers Rest

Terry sat in the only chair in this motel room and stared up at the fan. Hal was in the bathroom, loudly brushing his teeth. Had there been an like this expedition ever before in the history of this wide brown land? Ludwig Leichhardt probably had a better idea of where he was headed than he and Hal Sargeson had at this juncture, and look how Leichhardt finished up.

Except that chaos and pandemonium were not the whole story. Terry had spent a full week in Sydney working on the plan, so they weren't venturing entirely into the unknown. He had taken up the offers of sundry credit cards that had recently been shoved into his mailbox — three all up — to finance the trip and all the associated costs to come. The wherewithal was in place. His trawl around the aeronautical associations and magazines had led to the same individual Hal had found — a retired horse breeder by the name of Bannon who had acreage and a home-built hangar up past Diggers Rest, twenty or so kilometres north-west of Tullamarine, and who was deep into a restoration job using parts from all over the world.

Bannon was expecting Terry and Hal to visit him the next morning; presumably he wanted to check them out. Even so, the whole thing was looking more of a possibility by the hour. But Terry was trying for greater than a possibility, he was aiming to make it reality. He *would* make it real. This was the big one for him, the glittering prize, the golden fleece, whatever else you wanted to call it. Crash through or crash, to fly like Houdini had once flown was the test that he had set for himself.

Hal, exhausted from the trip, went to one of the two single beds in the room, where he quickly dozed off. Terry took the opportunity to call Bannon to confirm their arrival and discuss a few questions. He told Bannon that Hal had some early documentation which might be of interest to him.

'I'd love to see it,' said the gravelly voice on the other end of the line. 'But it's not going to help get this baby off the ground, not these days. We've got a whole different set of problems today. Fuel for one. It's different now and the engine's had to be modified. Pretty rough stuff back in 1910.'

Terry was disappointed for Hal's sake that they couldn't use his specs, but he also felt reassured. Better they had lit upon someone who knew what was really needed to get an ancient plane off the ground than some purist worried about following the exact letter of the thing. The material Hal had uncovered and brought down with him in a tatty manila folder still intrigued Terry though. He went through it again while Hal slept.

These were copies of documents that seemed genuine. The drawings were enormously detailed, from the diagrams of the ribs of the wings to the various calculations of fuel usage per airspeed mile. Only shame was they weren't the originals. Should their attempt founder, they could've sold them to pay off the credit cards. Then again, Hal would never sell anything connected to Houdini, Terry mused.

*

Early the next day, Terry and Hal set out in their hire car for parts beyond Diggers Rest. Their first view of Bannon's place was of a few horses roaming in a paddock near the road. Then, as they drove towards the house, a large, metal-clad shed about the size of a small warehouse came into view at one end of the home paddock. A man, who must have heard them coming, stood at the front of the hangar and waved an arm to direct them to go straight there.

Hal eased himself out of the car, stiff from cramming his lanky height into that small space. He dusted himself off as the man headed towards them. Another ancient to be sure, Terry thought, although his hobbling looked very determined. The impression was confirmed closer up. This was a wiry, tough old bird who looked to have a few years on Hal.

He took Terry's proferred hand. 'Hello, I'm Bannon.'

The plane he was rebuilding, he launched straight in, was based on the design of a Farman-Voisin which, as far as he had been able to establish, was a variant on the very early Voisin plane, and was very similar to the one that Houdini must have used. Bannon had bought elements for his restoration from a collector in France, someone who had been gathering parts from all over the world, but who had become ill and was unable to complete the job. He had taken up where the Frenchman had left off, putting the pieces slowly together, making the plane airworthy over the past three years.

'How airworthy is it?' Terry asked the obvious question.

'Well, so far I've given it one run and bumped it up a few metres for a few metres. Maybe fifty all up with the wheels off the ground.'

'Doesn't count as flying, does it?'

'Not according to the rules back then, and not now either.'

'But you're saying it *can* fly.' Terry pushed for confirmation.

'Yes I am.'

They moved across to the hangar doors, each about six metres wide, and Bannon pulled back the bolts. One at a time he slowly swung the doors open. And there facing them on a still, early September morning, in the middle of this dark cavern of space, was something that looked entirely familiar but which Terry had never seen before in his life. An imposing but fragile-looking tube and wood, wire and rubberised canvas biplane. From wingtip to wingtip it spanned the shed entrance to within a metre on either side.

Except there were no wingtips as such. And nor was the propeller or engine immediately to be seen. What they *could* see was a coffin-shaped cabin that Bannon explained was actually the cockpit, set between upper and lower wings, and in front of the cockpit some kind of smaller adjustable wing — Terry guessed for achieving elevation. He took a few steps to the side of the plane and saw that the engine and propeller were located behind the pilot's seat. He wondered at the construction of the wings and went closer to touch one.

'What are these?' Terry asked

'An Australian invention is what. This plane uses a form of box-kite. Do you know who invented them?'

Hal straightaway looked as if he was going to blurt out a response, but Terry waved to him to keep quiet. To Terry this suddenly seemed an important question to be able to answer — if only to convince this chap that he knew enough about planes to be allowed to get into the thing. There was something there from primary school, he had an inkling. And then an answer came: 'Lawrence Hargrave?'

'Dead right,' Bannon said. He patted him on the shoulder. 'Passed the first test, eh?'

For the benefit that Terry perceived might flow, he was more than happy to be patronised.

'A little play,' Bannon then said. He moved around the plane to check that it was fully chocked and tethered. Satisfied that it was secure, he got into the cockpit briefly to make some adjustments, then went to the propeller. A few vigorous swings and the engine fired up. The three of them stood listening to the sound of a motor of a type that Terry imagined had not been used for flying in Australia since Houdini's day. Even at low revs, in such a confined space the engine made a roar that was deafening, but also exciting. Terry felt the thrill go right through him — head, bones, stomach, sinews. It was a wonderful noise. He saw that Hal, standing next to him, shared the feeling: he was practically on tiptoe, and held his clenched hands out in front of him as if praying to some god.

The engine was allowed to run for what was probably less than a minute, filling the air with the stink of burning petrol. Bannon switched off the fuel and allowed the engine to stutter to a halt. Terry was mesmerised, watching the beautiful curves of that metal propeller arc slowly and gracefully until it was still.

Bannon led them outside into the warming air, Terry thinking all the while that for this to work, they were going to be very much in the old horse trainer's hands. Would he co-operate? Was he really interested in going further with this?

He put the question as they headed back to the house: 'Would you really let us fly this plane and try to recreate Houdini's flight?'

'Yes,' was the plain and unequivocal answer.

Terry was mightily relieved, though what Bannon said next was not unexpected: 'I'm willing to get stuck in, yes. As long as we get a few things straight first.'

In the kitchen at the back of Bannon's house, they sat around a small table to talk things through.

'Look, I appreciate what you want to do,' Bannon said. 'Great idea in theory. But what kind of flight hours have you blokes got up anyway?'

Terry and Hal both searched for something to say and, without meaning to, simultaneously took to staring at the table top in front of them. Fact was, Terry thought, he and Hal knew sweet bugger all about flying a plane — any plane, let alone an antique like this. Terry looked up and was about to speak when Bannon got in first. 'Okay, I'm starting to see how things are. I can teach you to fly. That's no big deal with a plane like this. I'm a licensed pilot — or was until they took my licence away. I shouldn't be flying, they reckon, because of the diagnosis.'

'What diagnosis?' Hal asked a bit too quickly. He was not ready for any cracks in the picture so soon.

'I've got motor neurone disease, but it's nothing. Early stages only.'

'If you're not allowed to fly, we aren't either, so how do we get around —?' Terry began.

'Wait. What I want to say is, the Voisin is about as technical as a go-kart. I can teach you. The fact that you aren't licensed doesn't really matter, I say. I just want to know, are you truly willing to have a go?'

'Yes,' Terry said as firmly as he could. 'That's why we came down here.'

Bannon seemed pleased. His shoulders softened and he slumped forward a little, putting his elbows on the table and resting his chin on his hands. 'I would take it up for a full attempt, you know, but I can't. I don't trust myself, truth be told. Strength's just not there anymore in these arms — easy enough to taxi along and get up a few metres, but if you're up there proper and get a cross-wind or a drop in power or something else happens, you need muscles to pull it all back into line.'

Listening to this litany of things that could go wrong, Terry wasn't convinced that he himself had the requisite strength.

'As for the CAA and the others, my position is, do they have to know at all?'

Terry understood the villainy being suggested. Far from being put off, the idea of breaking the rules that held for flying gave him a not unpleasant buzz.

'We could do it private-like, is that what you're saying?'

'Semi-private is what I'm saying. Don't have to invite the world, do we?'

'Not at all,' Terry answered. And was echoed by Hal's own, 'No, not at all, now that you mention it. Too many cooks —'

Terry gave him a quick kick under the table to shut him up.

Working to get onside with Bannon was challenging enough; there were plenty of reasons for him to pull the plug without thinking that Terry had a crazy person in tow as well.

'But someone's got to know, don't they? If you're gonna have a go at Houdini's record, you want somebody to see if you make it, don't you?'

'I do. Very much. And there's one very special young chap in particular …'

Bannon was already too far away in his own thoughts to ask who that might be. Instead, he said, 'All right then, go away and work on your end — who you want to be there and whatever else — and give me another week, max. What about you?'

Terry thought. 'A week sounds good.' He stood up, leaned across the table and extended a hand. He nudged Hal, who did the same.

'Bunch of mavericks, eh?' Bannon said with some pride.

'No other choice,' said Terry with a grin, giving Hal the nod that it was time to leave.

'Where are you staying?' Bannon asked.

'Motel at Tullamarine.'

'Forget that. You can stay here. There's plenty of room.'

33

A Private Enterprise

The following day, Terry agreed on some further points with Bannon. Bannon put it to him bluntly that although he was an untried flyer, he was willing to give him a go at equalling or breaking Harry Houdini's Australian first flight record of seven minutes and thirty-seven seconds — if he showed he could handle the practice runs. If after seeing him in action and concluding he was a danger to himself and the plane, the whole thing would be cancelled. As to other matters, there would be no general publicity about what they were planning. Terry would make contact with a Victorian historic aviation club to secure their interest, if possible, in a hush-hush special project. The event had to be recorded and celebrated by those to whom it truly mattered. Commercial media would be banned — not only for the risk of exposing Terry as an unqualified flyer, but the equal risk that they would take the whole thing as a joke. Mockery and derision were to be avoided at all costs.

The conditions suited Terry just fine, especially the part about being a danger to himself — knowing he was enough of a danger to himself generally speaking, he did not need to plummet to earth in a plane to reinforce the fact.

Terry traced the secretary of the aviation club to his job at a firm of specialist instrument makers. He swore him to secrecy over the phone and told him what was intended; he then asked if there was perhaps a small number of club members who might have some interest in being in on the project. The secretary said most assuredly yes, there would be.

Later, Terry wondered whether the club members might be prepared to put up some money — whether there was some possibility of sponsorship. He mentioned the idea to Bannon, who urged him to pursue it.

When Terry eventually met with a small group from the Classic Aviation Club in Melbourne, he discovered they were the kind of enthusiasts who qualified not so much as eccentrics as out and out cartoon characters. A couple of retired general aviation pilots who reckoned there hadn't been a real plane since the DC3, an ex-airforce man who had been pensioned off, he said, for 'refusing to accept the red tape', even an aged English gent who had flown Spitfires during World War II turned up. All of them loved 'real flying', and all of them reckoned that, fundamentally, the phenomenon had ended a long while ago.

While they debated pet loves and hates over coffee and tea in a Russell Street cafe, Terry was able to scribble on his notepad and firm up some commitments. The cost of this attempt on the record, including his and Hal's travel expenses and Bannon's costs, he estimated at around $4000. If the club members could stump up that amount, the attempt could proceed. If it proceeded and was successful, they would be asked to contribute an equal amount to a charity of common choosing. For their money, they would get to see the spectacle itself; a DVD would be produced for them; and if the attempt on the record proved successful, a certificate would be issued to each member to record their participation in the historic event.

The idea was lauded among the group as an outstanding proposition, an amazing thing to try to make happen. The general consensus was that they all wanted to be involved, but there were some serious questions put to Terry. Given that what was being planned was technically illegal, if the flight was to proceed it would have to be on a private basis — in other words, no-one was to notify the media or any of the authorities of the club's involvment: was that agreed? As Terry and Bannon already wished to keep things hush hush, that was no problem. If the flight did not proceed, the money would not be forthcoming; was that agreed? Terry accepted that as a condition also.

In the end, Terry was more than satisfied with the outcome. He made his farewells and left the group ordering further rounds of tea and coffee and biscuits and feeling that it was the aficionados, the true believers, of the sort whose company he'd just enjoyed, who were the last best hope for a revived world. Who better to imagine other ways, other possibilites, than those whom some might describe as nutburgers or fruitcakes. There was plenty in history to back him up, Terry thought.

Terry and Hal spent the next two days helping Bannon. While Hal carried parts back and forth and wielded a wire brush to scrub them in degreaser, Terry did most of the heavier lifting and toting: he helped pull the manifolds off the engine, then the propeller off its spline, allowing Bannon to check them and pass them as AOK. He helped remove the undercarriage wheels to make sure they were up to taking the strain of a full landing load, not just the small bounces they had endured so far in the taxiing runs along the nearby flats.

Terry was reassured to a degree by this mechanical process, but also needed another kind of reassurance. What he sought, though, was not the sort of comfort that came in words, even if these were positive and welcome.

From the spare bedroom in Bannon's house where he and Hal were in residence, the walk across open ground to the hangar was no more than a couple of hundred metres. One morning, before anyone else was up, Terry was outside in his pyjamas and on his way there.

He pulled the bolts back slowly and just as gently pulled each door aside, taking care to keep the creaking and squealing to a minimum. A low, morning light filled the front of the otherwise large and dark space, and he saw again an object beautiful in its own way.

Dating from the prehistory of aviation, the plane was yet a real pleasure to look at. It was striking from any sort of distance, but up close it was impressive. It was tall, more than four metres from where the wheels touched the earth to the very top of the wings, which were easily ten metres across. This appeared to be a very accurate copy of the plane he had seen in photos. It looked like something a nine-year-old could have whipped up; such design as was evident, Terry thought, was not beyond any clever kid's imagination.

He walked slowly down one side of Bannon's baby, reckoned it to be maybe six metres from front to back. Here was the plane that had first 'afforded flight' in Australia, as it was described somewhere. To 'afford flight' seemed such a beautiful idea, another kind of magic. And of a kind that Harry Houdini must have realised was way greater than any of his escapology and stunts — must have felt so from the first time he got up in the air.

Terry tried to imagine what it was going to be like to control this machine once it had left the earth. It was one thing to get in a modern plane and have it all done for you, but it was he who would have to do whatever needed to be done to fly in this.

And what needed to be done, he saw once he jumped into the cockpit, would be the work of his hands, eyes, muscles. The levers, wires, the steering wheel would do nothing until he made them do it, that was obvious. The thought frightened and exhilarated him. He had never accepted a challenge like this; he was absolutely going to give it his all, however hard it might be and whatever the result. That promise was made. What was less certain and now began to exercise his excited brain was how to get Ricky down here to see it all happen. Or even to see it *not* happen. Convincing his mother to let him come would take about as much effort, Terry felt, as the act of flying itself.

He made the call one morning just before Jenny left for work, knowing she was always at her best then. He said that he had involved himself in some charity work in Victoria (true), a special project in support of MS sufferers (true, as that was the good cause the aviation club had decided on) and wondered if Ricky might be allowed to join him — it would be a great experience for the kid to be involved in such a worthy cause (sort of true). He would only be away from her for a weekend, maybe three days all up.

There had been some silence on the line, but then Jenny said maybe — if Ricky was interested she would agree, so long as he, Terry, would accept some conditions. He heard her clatter down the hall, presumably to Ricky's room, and return to confirm that all was okay.

The conditions turned out to be that Terry would pay for the trip, and that she expected a 'full and proper report' from him after he returned their child home safely — 'and don't just tell me that he "had a great time"'. Terry concurred immediately. Of course he would pay. And a report would be delivered — in audiovisual format, no less.

Terry had not expected anything as simple as appealing to Jenny's social conscience to work so easily. Only later did he consider he should not have been surprised — what had he done but use a tool, a staple of his developing art? After all, so much magic depended on suggesting one thing was happening while planning and arranging to execute another. If it wasn't so important to have Ricky with him for the attempt on the record, he might have felt some shame or guilt. But he didn't.

*

On the Friday before the big weekend, Terry returned to the airport to collect Ricky. He was pretty happy to see his dad, Terry understood from the big hug he gave him. The noise and crush in the arrivals hall, however, meant they could not really talk until they were back in the car. Once underway, Terry was pleased at the enthusiasm that came with the boy's first questions — what were they going to be doing and what was he needed for?

'We're going to be raising some money for people with multiple sclerosis, but … that's not all. Something else really good as well.'

'So where are we going, Dad?'

'Not too far,' Terry said, nodding in the direction they were headed. 'But there's a lot of preparation needed. Because, you see, it involves flying an aeroplane.'

Ricky nodded gravely, as if this needed some serious contemplation on his part. But then he turned to Terry and smiled in awe and wonder.

'Really?'

'Really.'

'What sort of a plane is it? Is it like the one I came here on?'

'Nah, better than that. A very old one, like the ones …' Terry tried to think of an example, but the boy was already ahead of him.

'Like in some old movies?'

'Yes. You got it. It's called a biplane. And we're going to fly it to see if we can beat a record.'

Terry saw Ricky holding his head to one side, the way he always held it when he was struggling with a thought or problem. His heart went out to him — a beautiful young boy, learning to think and understand for himself, rather than be told what was what by parents and teachers. For the moment Terry would leave him with the mystery of what they could possibly be involved in that needed to take place beyond the flat fields and dry grass, the electricity pylons and cyclone fences in the world rushing past. Details would come later, when he showed him the plane and had found some small ways for him to help.

*

The first practice run was scheduled a few days before the record attempt. Hal said they all needed some geeing up and so, on the morning, announced that he had a story about Houdini's own first try on Australian soil, a hundred years before. 'Probably won't hurt,' said Terry to Bannon on the quiet. 'He tells a pretty good story about Houdini, as it happens.'

They settled at the kitchen table around a breakfast of porridge and tea and toast. 'All right, story man. We're listening,' Terry said.

'Okay. What happened — we're talking March 1910 now — was that Harry and his crew started into the flying season proper and, inside a couple of weeks, they were ready for the attempt at the Australian flight record. They were first going to have to practise getting off the ground in the local conditions.

'They made the trip from Melbourne out to the Plumpton paddock at Diggers Rest in convoy. Houdini and Bess in a Model T Ford, for which they'd got a chauffeur, and in a second car were Vickery and Kukol. Brassac, and a man from Melbourne who had once lived in the area and knew it well, were there already; they'd brought the plane up by motor lorry the previous day and camped overnight.

'Brassac had spent most of the previous day assembling it and putting up a big tent next to that of their rival, Banks, to protect the plane. Had he known the Australian chappie Banks was to give up his own assault that very day, he might have arranged for the use of the man's tent; whatever, Brassac was able to get a message to Houdini that the skies were clear for him to try for the record.

'So they get to the meeting point, where they find four other motor cars already parked. This is a big deal, everyone knows. From the roadside, Harry looks across a great big, flat field of dry grass stretching three or four miles in all directions; only a few trees, just what the doctor ordered. He asked the others why the place had been called this odd name but nobody knew — not even the local guide.

'"You don't know and you live hereabouts?" he asks.

'Harry wouldn't have meant to sting him, but here's this yokel staring at his boots, looking sheepish. He pats him on the back, probably says something like, "Doesn't matter, my friend, I'll make the name live forever." Funny thing, but Harry actually noted at the time how often he'd seen these Australians looking embarrassed about one thing or another.

'Next, he turns towards the paddock — this was supposed to be a farm, though nothing looked to be growing — and fixes on the two tents. There's his plane; around it are six or seven men in addition to his mechanic — the only one he could identify from this distance, on account of a floppy straw hat he liked to wear. So they unload the bags and baskets containing the gear from the car, and Harry and Kukol set off towards the tents.

'Rickards would have made the introductions; all these gentlemen of the press had come to record Harry Houdini's exploits. You can imagine, can't you, a bunch of pushy press types all trying to be the first to speak to Mr Houdini! Harry shakes hands with them and then he tells them, or reminds them: "Excuse me, gentlemen, but I would like to pay my respects to Mr Banks who, as you no doubt already know, gave up his own flying attempts yesterday."'

Unexpectedly, at this moment Ricky piped up: 'Mr Sargeson, was the plane like the one that's here?'

Hal looked pleased to receive the question. 'Well, glad you asked, young Rick. I can tell you, yes it was. As to the specifications, well, the motor used petrol and in the old measures weighed 240 pounds; the propeller was eight feet across its two blades of aluminium on a steel shaft, and at full speed it could turn at 1200 revolutions per minute. The all-up weight with Mr Houdini on board was 1350 pounds. By the way, do you know how many men had got off the ground at that time?'

Ricky's brow crinkled. This appeared to be a question he felt he should know the answer to.

'Don't expect you to know, but the answer is hardly any. Fewer than thirty in all the world probably ... Now, what happens next is just as Brassac returns to the plane to start and warm the motor and Harry is about to turn for his own tent to get changed into his flying outfit, Rickards comes up to them quickly with some news. And it's not the news that Houdini would have wanted to hear. Rickards says he's just been told that some bloke had flown in Sydney before Christmas.

'You can imagine that might have been a bit of a shock — to anyone else, but not to Harry. Picture the scene, boys. Harry stares at him hard. Rickards is almost a foot taller than the muscly little fellow in front of him, but the smaller man's gaze is powerful. Intense, in a way that even someone like Rickards was not used to. Not even his fighters could rivet him like Houdini could.

'What does Harry do? He calls everyone over. He asks to be told the story again by the reporter who'd told Rickards, wants to hear it first hand. Harry finds it hard to follow because of the Aussie accent, but the gist of it is that a man by the name of Defries had stayed aloft for something like a minute in December, had covered around a mile.

'"What sort of plane?" asks Harry. And he's told it had apparently been modelled on the Wright brothers' machine, built by Defries based on photographs he'd seen.'

'Yes, well, that'd be right,' Bannon interjected. 'There wasn't any original Wright brothers' plane here at that time.'

'Exactly,' said Hal. 'Banks had the only one and he'd taken possession just the previous month. Well, you might have expected Houdini to feel a bit put out, dismayed even, at what he was being told. But he couldn't have cared less. When the man was done, apparently he just smiled at him.

'I reckon Harry wasn't worried in the slightest, I reckon what he felt was admiration for that fellow. Men like Banks, Defries, what were they but his soulmates? The ones who pushed through. These others, with their city hats and vests, all these sweaty types who either sat in chairs all day, or chased around for stories — he would have pitied them.

'Don't know exactly whether this happened next, but it's on the record that Houdini did have something more to say, something like, "Gather round, boys. I have been told some things I didn't know until today and I could say they might have worried me, those things. But when I was told the details, well, I could see I was still in the game. You see, nobody's hit the home run yet.

'"Give credit where it's due," he probably said next. "That man did take to the air. But what he did, according to the international rules, was a hop. Leaving the ground for less than a minute is not flying, my friends. Nobody accepts that in other parts — and I'm afraid it sounds like you got a bum steer in this.

'"In the US, in France and Germany, they talk of powered flight, yes. But what's more important is sustained flight. That is my aim here. A sustained flight, you've got to stay in the air for more than a second or two. If I make it, then you can say a man has finally flown, actually flown in this country."

'And then, he would have excused himself, because, you know, he just had to fly that plane!'

'Did he go for the record that day?' Terry asked.

'No, he didn't but ...' Hal stopped, turning away as if searching for a memory. 'He did say something more ... what was it again? Oh yes. He was in fact asked the question you just asked, Terry, and his reply was, "We'll see. I'm only a fledgling, after all."'

Ricky surprised them all by clapping when it was clear that Hal had ended his tale.

'Why thank you, young master,' Hal said and took a deep bow.

Bannon was the first to break the ensuing silence. 'Yes, agreed it's a nice story, but we're going to have to do things for real here, cobber.'

He went on to tell them that in the previous month, he had twice raced the Voisin along the kilometre of the flats that made up a large part of his property. But Terry's would be the first attempt to get it airborne since he had returned it to airworthy condition. 'It'll fly, don't you worry about that — question is whether *you* can keep it up there long enough to do the trick.'

Today's go would still only be a trial run, with Terry taking care to do no more than bump off the ground for a few dozen metres at a time. It was important not to tackle the record in any way. It was also important as it would be the very first, and maybe only, practice that Terry would have in flying this ancient craft.

'I hope you're ready to take a knock, Mr Voulos,' Bannon stressed. 'It's going to be like being in a cage made out of wire and steel and trying to jump it into the air.'

'How fast do I have to run?' Terry said, trying to make light of the difficulties. He was already feeling more than a little anxious.

Bannon did not answer, giving him a dark look instead. He wasn't prepared to join Terry in any kind of joking about the project; as he had made clear on many occasions it was the culmination of his life's work as a vintage aircraft enthusiast. This was no laughing matter but a deadly serious undertaking. He got up, explaining that he had to get the four-wheel drive ready to pull the plane to the 'airstrip' for the trial run.

Terry went to get dressed in a pair of grey overalls bought for the occasion. Houdini looked to have flown in something like a regular button-up suit, but that somehow didn't seem right. He unpacked the goggles and helmet he had brought with him, patted Ricky on the head and handed him the gear to carry.

'Right, we're off to where the action is, aren't we, son?'

Outside, they saw that Bannon had already pulled the plane clear of the hangar. At less than a tonne, it was not hugely heavy, but it was awkward to shift around. Bannon was not kidding when he spoke of it as his life's work: he was moving it cautiously and carefully behind the four-wheel drive at no more than walking pace.

'What do you think of it, Ricky?'

'Really good. People did fly in those planes once, didn't they?'

'They did. And I hope to do it again. But just a practice today.'

'Like in the story?'

'Hope so! Now you can help me put this stuff on.'

Terry got down on his haunches and gave the goggles to Ricky. 'Okay, mate, put those on me now.'

Ricky pulled the strap to make a circle behind the two round eyepieces, then eased it all over his father's head. The strap was too loose though, and the contraption fell down Terry's nose, at which Ricky let out a laugh. 'You look silly, Dad!'

'Of course I do,' Terry replied, making an adjustment. He put his helmet in place. 'All right, now we have to get in the car to drive to the airstrip. Make sure you stay with Mr Bannon and Hal while I'm in the plane, won't you?'

Just then Bannon began waving an arm urging them to join him. Terry gave Ricky a quick kiss on the top of his head, hugged him around the shoulders and jogged him along to catch their lift to the flying field.

On a stubbly, hard-packed stretch, Bannon stopped the four-wheel drive and set the plane back from a line of scrub and small trees that screened a dry creek bed. 'Right, this is it. This is where it all starts for you boys.'

They got out and unhooked the plane from the tow cable and put some chocks in place. Bannon led Terry to the cockpit. When he heard the instruction, 'Jump in,' it hit Terry like never before.

'Jesus Christ,' he muttered, and climbed aboard.

Bannon clambered up alongside him. 'Once you're started, I don't want you to hold back. The idea is to get off the ground proper-like today, as we discussed. To give you an idea of what flying is like.'

'And what I've let myself in for.'

'That too. You'll get the hang of it, easy. It's just a mix of throttle and lift, throttle and lift. More to go up, less to come down. Raise the elevator planes at the front, you go up. Lower them, you go down. The wheel works the rear rudder and, when you pull and push it, the elevation. How hard is that? Just remember, low revs at first until you can get moving. Can you remember that?'

Terry nodded. If Bannon was trying to boost his confidence, he wasn't doing a great job.

'Get some lift if you can, then let it straight down again. Try nothing fancy, no turns, no flying. Got it?' Pointing to the far distance, he said, 'See that other line of trees? It's about a mile. Before you get there, throttle off, plane down — couple of gradual steps, not all at once — and you can roll to a stop. We'll drive up to meet you and tow you back.'

The propeller was spun, once, twice, three times and the engine started. Terry was completely unprepared for what happened next. As low as he had the revs, the plane lurched and began to move forward. In no time he was doing fifteen or twenty kilometres an hour. He remembered that he had a steering wheel, and began to concentrate on maintaining as straight a path as he could along the roughly fifty-metre-wide cleared strip.

At first the sensation was like nothing so much as driving down a pot-holed country road in a small truck with no suspension — but sitting about three metres above the road.

After another few seconds, Terry decided to give it more gas.

It did not take long to get to above forty kilometres an hour. A little faster and then he found the courage to raise the elevator planes. And there it was, the sensation of lift-off. He felt the biplane leave the ground. A metre, then another metre, and he was suspended in the air. That was enough for Terry. He immediately eased the fuel off, tipped the elevator plane forward to the descent position and the biplane just as quickly leaned forward and soon after hit the ground. When it was rolling on earth once more, he took what felt like the first breath he had taken since he got into it.

Terry slowed back to a crawl and then, as the wind around him died down, he realised that he felt wet. Once he had come to a complete stop he touched his chest — his shirt and the front of his overalls were soaked through. He had no idea he'd been sweating so profusely.

Not much that could be called flying, for sure, but he'd definitely had the first sensation of flight. He did not want to be cocky, but what was flying except more of what he had just enjoyed? Terry stayed in the plane to wait for Ricky and the others to come up to him. If this was what it was like, then it was wonderful. He would come back for more.

*

Further practice sessions were held over the next two days. With each of these, Terry's confidence grew, along with his feel for what the rudimentary controls available to him could and couldn't achieve. In one run at the end of the second day he stayed aloft for around ten seconds, allowing that he did not go up more than ten or twelve metres. This simple form of elevation was erratic and limited but it was a triumph to get up even that far and exciting to look down for a few moments at the earth whizzing past below.

As the action of a kite still lived very large in the behaviour of this plane, the biggest issue, Terry came to learn, was dealing with the wind, sensing when to throttle back or steering to avoid being blown down or wildly off course. But such progress did he make, and so quickly, that Bannon was moved to pronounce, 'There's a good chance you might still be alive at the end of this.'

34
Flight

Hal insisted that Terry keep right away from the plane and the hangar throughout the morning of the record attempt.

'Don't want you spooked, do we?' he said. 'And there should be a bit of showbiz around this, in my opinion. You got to make an appearance, son, not just be strolling about in the crowd. Gotta give 'em their money's worth. Remember, you're supposed to be the ace flyer!'

Terry hadn't given this side of things much thought, what with everything else racing through his head yesterday and overnight. He had lain awake after three am, listening to Hal snore, but also contentedly watching Ricky sleeping the sleep of the innocent.

Rattling around in the bedroom, trying to get Ricky up and dressed, readying himself for the day's event, Terry decided he would take Hal's advice. The wisdom in those remarks had at first surprised him. Until he told himself he really should stop feeling wrong-footed that the man made sense every now and then; over the months that Terry had come to know him, Hal had without question passed the holy fool test.

At nine-thirty, they had come to the end of another of Bannon's big breakfasts: bacon and eggs and fried tomatoes — 'For strength,' he said. The old horse trainer then stood up and made a sort of speech: 'Okay, youse have been fed and watered. It's time. Now you, Hal, you're to help me with preparations for the spectators, all right?'

Hal nodded eagerly.

'As for you, Terry Voulos, these are my final words: whatever you manage to do today will be all right by me. Except if you crash and wreck my plane — you won't be forgiven that, not even if you die. Do you hear me?'

Bannon smiled as if the remarks were meant in jest, but Terry wasn't at all sure. He noticed that Ricky was looking worried by what he had just heard, so shot him a reassuring look. The last thing he wanted was for his son to be frightened. Ricky kept his eyes fixed on his father, hoping to draw confidence from him.

Bannon saw the exchange and to his credit knew what had to be done. He went to the boy's side and whispered loudly, 'Don't worry, Ricky, I was making a little joke.' He straightened up to speak again to Hal and Terry. 'But I did mean the first part.'

Terry took some comfort from this. He had been unsure at first about this ex-horseman's motives in allowing someone he had so recently met to fly his precious antique plane. But he was committed, as Bannon, too, seemed to be. There was no option but to take what he said at face value.

That they had got so far along with the idea, that Bannon appeared as charged by the process as he himself was, had to be measured as a miracle. A nutter's miracle, some might say, but a miracle all the same. Glancing at Hal and Bannon as they bumbled about clearing away plates, another thought came: *And we're all in it together.* As slowly and quietly as he could, Terry took in a deep breath and just as slowly and quietly let it out again.

Bannon soon announced that it was time for him to get down to the home paddock, then barked out the day's order of proceedings. He would take a couple of Eskies of cold drinks with him as well as some plastic chairs and a couple of umbrellas to keep the sun off the expected visitors. These visitors — all from the Classic Aviation Club of Victoria, the sponsors of the assault on Houdini's record — had been informed that there would be two attempts at the record and two only, the first to be made at eleven am. If that was successful, there would be no other. If both failed, that would be it. The plane simply could not be pushed any harder on any given day; after that much flying time, it would need to be checked and repaired.

'We've got two members of the club officiating as time and record keepers. That's what they agreed, did they not, Mr Voulos?'

'That's what they agreed, Mr Bannon.'

'Good. I'll see you at the plane in half an hour.'

Terry went to organise his kit and make sure Ricky, still in his pyjamas, would be dressed and ready. When he couldn't find his helmet and goggles, he called to Hal to help him.

'Out here, boss!' Hal called back from the verandah.

Terry found him with a bottle of Brasso and polishing cloth in hand, busily at work on the clasps and buckles of his gear.

'What are you doing, Hal?'

'Got to look your best, eh? Remember, Harry always looked right, whatever he was doing!'

Hal passed the gear over to Terry with both hands, a small touch of ritual, as if making an offering to his god.

'Unnecessary, Hal, but thanks anyway.'

'Not unnecessary, never unnecessary.'

Finally ready, Terry set off for the hangar, Ricky by his side. Hal was swishing along slightly behind them in the greatcoat he had brought with him, fearing the Victorian cold — he was happy to wear it even on a day such as this, when the temperature was unseasonably headed for the high twenties. Ricky was in his favourite mock flak jacket and jeans, Terry's camcorder dangling from a cord around his neck. Terry scrutinised the pair of them and felt like nothing so much as a dad on duty.

'Why don't you take that thing off, Hal? It's going to be stinking in a while.'

'Never,' said Hal in a low but kindly growl. 'I'm a knight in shining greatcoat ...'

'So be it, don't say I didn't tell you. And Ricky, have you got the spare batteries for the camera?'

Ricky reached into one of his jacket pockets to triumphantly pull out a fresh packet as proof. He wanted to be seen to be on top of his obligations.

'Good,' said Terry, looking up at the sky. There was some gathering cloud low on the southern horizon, otherwise all was clear blue. And yet that hardly seemed enough. *Wherever you are, Harry, be good to hear from you about now ...*

They got to the hangar to find the gates pulled back and Bannon standing there, staring at the plane. The preparatory tasks he'd had to do were done; he had entered some other space.

'Look at her, isn't she something? All I will say is that she's up to it, Mr Voulos. The real job is yours. Help me hook her up.'

Before moving to the runway strip with the plane, they stopped briefly for a meet and greet at Bannon's designated viewing area. All fifteen invitees had followed the signs posted to direct them from the property gate to the slight rise that would afford the best view of the flying strip. Among the spectators were two in vintage blue flying uniforms. These were the timekeepers; they had dressed as World War II US flyers for a lark, or so they told Terry when he did the rounds and came to shake their hands.

Terry had been unprepared for the general hurrahing that greeted him. 'Three cheers for Terry Houdini!' someone shouted to a good-natured laugh or two and a round of applause. He saw that Ricky was impressed.

'Dad, they're clapping you.'

'How about that,' he said, leaning over to give Ricky a quick hug. 'This is it … Well, reckon I can do it?'

'Course you can, Dad,' Ricky said.

'Try to record this, eh?'

'I will.'

'But it doesn't matter if you can't — Mr Bannon's got a camera too,' he said, directing Ricky's gaze to the camera Bannon held, not wanting the kid to feel such an important job was all down to him.

Hal shuffled over and thrust out his hand. 'Just want to say good luck, Terry.'

'Thanks.'

'Yeah, good luck,' Ricky said and put his arms around his father's waist for a quick squeeze.

Bannon had begun to extricate himself from the gathering and pointed towards the plane. At that, Terry waved goodbye to all, and strode firmly to the car.

'Here's to Harry!' he shouted. The sight of glasses and cans being raised and the shouts of 'To Harry', 'To Terry …' that rang out led him to hold the door open for a few seconds more. This was a moment to be enjoyed.

Bannon started the vehicle, taking the usual care to slowly reduce the cable slack. That done, he began the job of pulling the plane to the end of the strip. It was time.

The plane was set in place pointing north, then unhooked and chocked. Terry paid the greatest of attention as Bannon began his pre-flight preparations. Watching carefully as he turned on the plane's fuel line, Terry checked for drips. He was as determined as Bannon that there be no slip-up of any kind.

He clambered up into the cockpit, nodded to Bannon and raised a thumb. He stared straight ahead at the runway as Bannon moved behind him to the propeller. The usual number of turns and the aluminium propeller kicked the early model V8 into life. Low revs on a low throttle, loud and steady. Terry was sure he could hear each individual explosion in each cylinder, could see every piston rise and fall.

Bannon removed the chocks and moved away to one side. He gave Terry the signal to power up, which he did, slow and steady. The plane began to trundle in a way that already felt familiar. As Terry looked back, the last earth-bound image that registered clearly for him was Ricky, a small boy becoming smaller as he waved to him from the distance.

A couple of hundred metres went by and Terry was confident there was nothing to distinguish this from the practice attempts. A good feeling in itself. He opened up the throttle and began to feel the vibrations in every part of his body as he raced along the flat. Soon, he had to keep his mouth open to stop his teeth from clashing.

Now came the little skips off the ground that Terry had felt previously. But today was about flying and so he gave the plane even more juice. Throttle and elevator and rudder — these, too, were becoming old friends.

He looked ahead, maintaining a straight line as best he could while aware also of the woodland, the trees streaming menacingly past on one side. The job was to get airborne, fly five kilometres, or just a bit over, in a northerly direction, then turn for the homeward run. He would do what needed to be done.

Terry felt the bounces turn into jumps and knew this time that it wasn't the plane or the flying that was going to be the test, but some other thing altogether. As never before he wanted to feel what it was to take an unimagined tool in his hands. He wanted to know how it might be used and what might be altered through its use; he wanted to go to that place where things could be changed and were changed. If Terry knew anything about himself, it was that he was utterly sick of where he had been.

He also knew that something other than thoughts or words was needed to mend the tears and fill the holes he had felt for so long. Whatever his fate today, he'd had encouragement: he'd been told an inspiring story and, more than that, had discovered a new family. He cherished these both.

Terry pulled again on the lever to his right, raising the engine revolutions further. And then, as he was starting to run out of airstrip, there came a much longer bounce and with it a growing lightness in his stomach such as he might have felt in an elevator suddenly jolting upwards at speed.

This lift lasted one, two, three, four, five seconds — the moments kept passing — then way longer than the earlier runs. He dared to look across the fuselage and down. He was up. In the air. If he was not mistaken, this was flight. He was airborne.

But *was* this flight? What Harry Houdini had once known as flight? Hal's story told of nothing like this, for what mattered most, what was consuming every scintilla of Terry's energy and concentration, was the business of keeping the wheel steady and his direction as true as he could gauge by sight. And yet as hard as it all was, with each passing moment he understood that what he had undertaken was not beyond him.

After thirty seconds in the air, Terry was at close to full speed — over seventy kilometres per hour. He turned to see where he was, how far he had come. He realised he had left the small crowd way behind. He tried for a little more altitude and within another half-minute had found what Bannon had defined as the safest maximum possible — some thirty metres, or a hundred feet, above ground.

At this pace, the feeling was of being in a car, a convertible that had somehow become airborne. If not for the helmet, Terry's hair would have been blown about and nothing worse than that. The wind on the part of his face that was exposed was cooling, fresh, almost but not quite stinging.

Exhilaration. There was no other way to describe what he was experiencing. He looked briefly at his watch. At about three minutes, he had been instructed to begin swinging the rudder at the back to create a turn ahead of the run home. If all was going well, he could leave it until the fourth minute. Then, flying back at the same speed would almost certainly mean breaking the original record. Terry looked again at his watch — he would give himself that extra time before turning.

The turn presented no great problem. Terry felt comfortably in charge of the plane and its motion, and now had more of a chance to look around. Beneath him were yellowed or browned-off fields, signs of a long drought; here and there they gave way to patches of green, semi-rural holdings. With Diggers Rest in the distance and from this height, it was a pretty, peaceful scene.

He looked further south, where he could see the outlines of the city, and imagined the blue-grey waters of Bass Strait beyond. No, exhilaration was not the word for it. It was not sensation alone, it was as if some great knowledge had been granted him, as if a long-buried chest had been opened to reveal all kinds of treasure. Gifts not just denied him or that he had denied himself, but gifts that he had never even known to exist.

Was it this, or something like it, that Harry Houdini had experienced a hundred years ago? If he could not exactly know what flight had meant to Houdini, Terry was confident that he had shared with him that same joy of weightless movement that was all his own work. A further glance at his watch showed that he was on target to extend the record. But instead of slowing to stay up longer, he began to increase speed to land sooner. He understood that this flight meant something else to him. The master's record should stand.

Terry pointed the plane downwards, levelled briefly, then inclined down again to reduce altitude. Another few moments heading south and he could see once more the same people who had watched him take off. There they were, gathered at the end of the strip. As to the landing, he felt a small fear but believed he was doing everything as instructed. So long as he kept doing the reverse of what had got him up in the air in the first place, the final approach and landing would present no great difficulty.

Slowing as he came in, losing height, he was nevertheless alert to everything that lay ahead. He wanted to finish the job properly. A couple of hundred metres from touchdown, lining up his run, trying to keep the wings as level as possible, he spotted Ricky. He saw him suddenly break from the group and run off to one side. He was holding the camera to his face with one hand, waving excitedly with the other.

A daring and amazing life, yes, but Houdini had not had the pleasure of seeing a son willing him to safety. The boy in the distance grew larger by the second. Even taken up with the demands of trying to land safely, Terry felt as if they were joined by some invisible current, a bolt of electricity — ground to air, air to ground. He knew very well what Ricky meant to him. There would be plenty of words that would come later and that he would share with him. And later, Ricky would have his own stories to tell.

PART FOUR
METAMORPHOSIS

35

Ta panta rei

The job did not entirely satisfy him. He had too much else going on in that large cranium of his to be happy only with toughing his way out of the tightest corners …

Terry began writing on the plane once they were above the clouds on their return flight to Sydney. He was confident he had learned a thing or two about Harry Houdini — or seen into parts of him more clearly. He was taking seriously his promise to Hal. Whatever Hal made of his work, whether he liked it or not, he would give him the truest version he was capable of. Without question, Terry had acquired something from him, but also without question it was less and more than Hal understood.

Terry kept writing, trying for a style he hoped Hal might appreciate.

Hal took the handwritten page Terry eventually passed across to him. With Ricky next to him and Terry directly across the aisle, Hal read a few lines, looked out the window, read a few more. Once they had got over the border into New South Wales and the Snowy Mountains turned gradually into the dry hills of the south, Terry noticed Hal concentrating a little harder. He shook the sheet out and brought it closer to his face.

Hal was not a speedy reader, but Terry was pleased to see he was making the effort. He kept reading:

The flying was the best kind of release he could find. However many objects and devices he escaped from he probably always felt trapped. As you would coming from a family like his. As a young person Harry felt bad, guilty — about running away, about his father, most of all about his mother. Guilt makes you feel worthless, and once you feel worthless you start running away. Thing is, when is a child really guilty of anything? *Can* a child be guilty of anything? Evidence for theory? It's hardly normal to write to your mother practically every day of your life. Harry was trying to make up for something there. But what bad thing had Harry done that he could have genuinely been blamed for? (Hal, you and I should talk about this before I go any further.)

Hal got to the end and Terry saw his head move up and down a couple of times. He appeared to be re-reading the page. He seemed to be fixed on the last line.

'There's more to say, isn't there Terry?'

'About?'

'Families for starters.'

Hal had never known his mother at all, he told Terry; she was a runaway soon after he was born — a hard little nugget of a fact if ever there was one. Terry was lucky to have had his mother for as long as he had. As for how Hal felt, he appeared way past blaming anyone. You get dealt a hand and you deal with it or you don't seemed to be his view. Bad luck what actually happens. Bad luck what you feel about it.

What Hal knew, he muttered, was that Frank and Stavros were two perfect mongrels, but without them — he pulled himself up to glance at the young boy next to him and Terry nearby — he would, *they* would never have arrived at this. And this was worth something, he said. Now that he thought of it, there *was* someone to blame for something: himself, for not having the guts to go to Terry sooner. Much, much sooner.

'But they say it's never too late.' Hal nodded sagely and retreated into thought.

A few moments later, Hal handed Terry back the page across the aisle. 'What you've said there … there might be something in it. Style's not my cup of tea, but you should keep going.'

'Should I stay on this track for a while?'

'For a while. But you've got to get back to the main story fast.'

Terry smiled at him. If only everyone could agree on what the main story was. 'So you want me to keep going then?'

'I do. Never know, there might be a book in it.'

'Then I will. But there's more important work to do when we get back. Hal, I'm planning something new to add to the act; I want to make a new show. Do you want to be in on it?'

'Well, I'm all for you, Terry, you know that by now. So what is it?'

'I'm not telling just yet.'

'Good, don't tell me. Shows that you're learning.'

*

317

Back in Sydney, other clouds parted. The flying was done. If it was enough for Harry, gave him what he needed, Terry knew it was not so for himself. But after what they had achieved, the rest, if not easy, would not be impossible either. It was time — and he was ready — to launch into the final realm. Metamorphosis, Terry understood at last, could take many shapes.

He called Hal. He had bought him a cheap mobile and Hal's last shreds of resistance to modern technology had given way. Terry had been able to convince him that if he was to play an active role in finding gigs for Terry, he would absolutely have to be available by phone.

'Chief, I can tell you now that I'm looking into metamorphosis.'

A firm 'Excellent' was Hal's only response.

'But I'm not getting inspiration from Harry in this, I have to also I tell you.'

Hal stayed silent for a moment. Terry waited, hoping Hal was taking the view that his half-brother was now making his own decisions. That he was picking up and assessing whatever he believed he could make work.

'If you're talking about what Houdini called "Metamorphosis",' Hal at last said, 'all right, I can accept that.'

'I am.'

Hal was referring to a trick that involved Houdini, with hands tied, being placed in a sack, then a shipping trunk. A curtain would then be raised in front of the trunk by Harry's brother Theo, after which the curtain would amazingly be pulled open by Harry, free of the sack and trunk. He would then reveal his brother inside the very same sack, inside the very same trunk. It was standard fare, an escape and substitution act.

'The substitution trunk is a very tired thing,' Hal agreed. 'Been done to death, with everyone trying to do it faster and faster. I mean, who cares if you get into the *Guinness Book of Records* for how quick you can get your partner out of a box and you into it? So what have you got in mind?'

'Come over and I'll show you.'

*

Hal joined Terry in his garage later the same day. Terry had cleared a space and set up a small work table and chairs, and had some blank paper and pens handy. He asked Hal to watch as he sketched something on the paper. His initial diagram showed a kind of sheet suspended across a stage, and two stick figures standing before it.

'Substituting one person for another is not enough. What I want to do is make one person evolve into another form of themselves, if you get the drift.'

'Real change?'

'Real change.'

'How are you going to do that?'

'I'm not telling.'

Instead of being annoyed, Hal broke into a big grin. 'That's my boy. You really are learning! So, what do you want from me?'

'Get me a spot somewhere, I don't care where but as soon as you can. The show will include what we did last time, plus a new specialty: a mysterious metamorphosis illusion. Say that Copperfield, Angel, the Pendragons, all of them will be eating their hearts out!'

When Hal asked Terry who he was proposing as his subjects, Terry would only say that he had located two willing participants. It would be a surprise, he said. Hal was not to worry his ugly head about it. As requested, Hal took to the phone.

He got on to a small bowling club in Marrickville with a big enough stage and the sort of members who just might turn up for a magician going by the name of Terry Hecate, Transformaster Extraordinaire.

The name had come to him as he began making the calls, he told Terry. 'I remembered the Greek god of magic and change was named Hecate — I didn't tell them that she was a sheila though ...'

Thanks for nothing, Terry felt like saying, thinking that he would have to change it if he was ever hired anywhere else. Too bad if he didn't like it, Hal replied; that moniker had swung the job. And the job was not for one night but two.

Miraculously, Terry had got through to the last stage of Hal's program. They had by now long blown Hal's original twelve-week schedule — but it no longer seemed to matter. This was to be the first performance of Terry's new act.

*

Hal arrived with Terry three hours before start time to help him prepare for the show. Terry meticulously unpacked and lined up his materials backstage, arranging them exactly in the order he would need them. As they worked, he told Hal that Ricky would be coming to watch the show: 'Don't want any stuff-ups in other words ...'

'And here he is,' Terry said, noticing Ricky and Jenny walking towards them. Terry got up to welcome them, and brought them over to Hal.

'Ricky, you know Hal …'

Ricky took the proffered hand confidently, shook it firmly, smiled and said, 'Hello, Uncle Hal.' Hal couldn't have been happier.

'You've never met his mum, though. Hal, this is Jenny … Jenny, Hal's the man I told you about, my mentor and trainer …' Telling her the rest of the story would have to wait.

'Hello, Hal.' Jenny also shook his hand. To Terry's delight, she then said she too would like to stay for the show. Before he could say anything, she took him aside a couple of steps and said softly, 'I want you to know, Terry, that I have more of an idea of what you've been through than you maybe think.'

'And me you,' he replied.

She and Ricky left him to go to their seats. Terry tried to keep an open mind about her presence. He guessed she needed to know more, a great deal more, of what had taken place over the last few months. The previous years. Their previous lives, for that matter.

Terry knew that whatever Jenny thought of how he had behaved in their marriage and more recently, she would continue to involve him as the father of her child. She knew that children hurt. That they carried hurt with them. She was not an emotionally stupid person; she was not a vindictive person either. And if anything could be made better, if not exactly fixed — for their marriage, he held no real hope, but who could say for sure? — then it was imperative for Ricky, if not the rest of them, that they made every effort. Above all, Terry now realised, she wished him no ill or harm.

Hal was less comfortable when introduced to Terry's assistants for the evening — a woman in her sixties, and a young girl of about ten, her granddaughter. They had answered an ad Terry had placed in the local newspaper, looking for 'two ladies who love magic', offering the chance to appear on stage.

Hal looked them up and down and could not say he was thrilled at the choice. The woman wore an old light blue shift, the girl a younger, prettier version of the same. A strange-looking pair, despite the everyday dresses. He was only slightly less anxious when Terry said he had told them what to wear.

Fortunately, nothing much was required of Hal except for connecting with the management and minding the 'talent'. Terry had been working on his metamorphosis act for days on end and was ready to go.

*

What the audience saw was for the most part the show that Terry had developed with Hal's help, an extension of the one he had done at the RSL. Beginning with a sequence of sleight of hand tricks, he next worked his way, after a short break, through three escape routines, ending with the straitjacket escape. Hard work though it was, this caused him nothing like the distress it once had. Terry ended the first half of the show, the first three-quarters, using Hal's excellent disappearing cabinet, with Hal as the victim.

'How much easier to disappear than to have to work your way out of something, eh, folks?'

Terry had allowed about fifteen minutes for the final act, the grand illusion. He had the lights set up to throw a midnight blue, star-spattered-sky effect across the drop at the back of the stage. He waited to evoke a cold, crystal night — dry ice and a blower created a low mist across the floor. When a spot was thrown to the middle of the space, it highlighted a single chair of high Victorian style. There was nothing else on the stage.

Terry entered after a suitable pause to the prerecorded sound of a flute playing three lonely notes: two ascending, one descending, over a couple of minor keys.

He was conscious of Jenny and Ricky in the first row. He knew Jenny wouldn't have expected such a degree of care and attention. Or plain effort either — this had taken some work to organise, whatever followed and regardless of how good it might be. Terry worried, though, about his tux and whether he too obviously looked like a man dressed as a penguin. Was that how Jenny saw him? It was satisfying, however, to see looks of excitement and hear murmurs of anticipation among the audience behind her.

He positioned himself centre stage to announce what would follow.

'Ladies and gentlemen, they say everything changes ... At least the Ancient Greeks said that. *Ta panta rei*, some bearded old ancestor of mine once said. The river flows. Everything flows, everything is in flux. Same for all of us. You're given a life, you live it. Hey, you might be lucky and have a long one. But whether long or short, everything in it alters over time, would you not say?

We grow up, we change, grow old, die. And new life comes along. It's a beautiful thing. What we never get to see because we can't stop time and look, really look, is what happens along the way. Except in photos, and movies or books. And now for the first time through magic. Watch as it really happens, before your very eyes …'

His little speech ended, Terry exited the stage. The flute music swelled in volume and a few seconds later he reappeared with an ordinary-looking woman in a light blue shift with a faded pink scarf tied over her head, peasant-style. The impression was of a woman of southern European or Middle Eastern background — a woman of times gone by, yet, for a new generation of battling immigrants, not gone by at all. In her lighter tones, she contrasted well with the dark blue screen behind her.

Terry led her solicitously to the chair, some kind of cloth folded over his left arm. With his right, he gestured gently towards where she should sit. The woman's face could be seen only in the most general way, the lighting such that her features were indistinct, shaded almost. Expressionless, but apparently looking for guidance as to what she should do next, she eased herself into the chair and looked almost imploringly at Terry. He raised a hand towards her, then lowered it, as if to say, 'Stay calm, everything will be all right.'

Terry next took the cloth in both his hands and unfolded it in one swift motion so that the ends cascaded onto the floor. Spotlit, it appeared a dazzling, shimmery white, as if it was made of satin or silk. Terry rolled it through one more wave and it billowed beautifully. Then, abruptly, he threw it over the woman, as if she were no more than an extension of the chair and his task was perhaps to cover them against the elements, ready them for hibernation through some magical winter ahead. The woman did not flinch or react.

'Ladies and gentlemen, think about the lady who came out here with me ... Is she a person at all? Who is she? It's time to investigate ...'

The cloth suddenly came to life. The section folded over the woman and the chair threw itself upright, the entire cloth straightening in front of the audience to make a single plane of stiff pure whiteness. Terry swiftly moved towards it, took an edge and with a violent tug swung it around as if it was a revolving door. At the mid-point of its revolution he paused — there was not a thing to be seen but an inch-wide pillar of electric white, nothing on either side or behind it, not even the chair. There were gasps from the crowd.

Terry stepped towards the pillar of light, seeming to grasp it somewhere near the middle, and gave another tug. The full sheet reappeared, measuring some two metres across and three in height. The spot lowered and now the sheet appeared to be something like a projection screen.

An ancient windmill, set high on some Mediterranean hill, took form, its cloth sails beginning to turn slowly, lazily against an azure sky. As soon as it could be identified, it disappeared again. To those watching it seemed, perversely, both clear and indistinct, an image in a dream.

A woman with a small girl by her side now stood at a clothes line pegging out some washing. The woman, her face turned away, lifted the little girl up so that she might fix a handkerchief to the line herself. No-one could miss the power of a strong young mother holding up her child, proud of what she, they, could do.

The same woman, older now, her features still lacking clarity, stood to one side at a school — an Australian school — looking on as her daughter took her first tentative steps in a class performance. The woman leaned towards the child, clapped vigorously.

A fourth image, again of the same woman, flashed across the ghostly white surface. This time, now elderly, she raised a camera to take a photo. A young woman stood on a stage somewhere in mortarboard and academic gown to receive a testamur.

And then the low-lying mist was gone in an instant, replaced by swirling volumes of pinkish smoke. Terry stepped through it just as it began to thin out and pulled the sheet round once more to become a streak of light. Two corporeal figures were revealed — the woman and the girl who had featured in the images. The girl had her left arm extended, her forearm crooked into a half-circle. And on that arm sat most peaceably and gloriously a live, white dove.

With great care, the girl gently took the dove in both hands and passed it to the woman, who gladly and graciously bowed as if to honour her as well as in acceptance of her gift. After admiring it for a moment, she took it in one hand to hold it to her chest. The girl then reached for the woman's other hand and together and in step they slowly exited the stage.

Having stood to one side while his players enacted their scene, Terry now bounded back upstage smiling broadly, his arms spread wide. Not only was the applause loud, there were a few cheers with it as well.

He saw Jenny in the front row holding back for a moment. It would not have taken her long to understand what he was doing. Would she be furious? Did she feel set up? So obviously drawn from her own life, her mother's life, the tableau was meant to make her feel better. Perhaps she saw this as he hoped she would, as the best he could do for now. He hoped she didn't see it as the best he would ever do. She knew he had been desperate to find something else, something at all. This was possibly it.

What might be done after this was anyone's guess, Terry thought. If she could make the leap, if he could keep making his own, there might be a way forward.

After scanning the audience and bowing to acknowledge their enthusiasm, Terry zeroed in once more on Jenny and Ricky. They were still clapping. If he wasn't entirely mistaken he thought he saw the faintest of smiles on Jenny's face. Yes, that had to be a smile. That wasn't all. He peered in her direction until she made eye contact, and as he held her gaze he saw her nod her head up and down. A slight, slow nod, but there just the same. That would do for now. It was, he knew, way, way more than enough.

Terry leaned forward and blew kisses, one directly to Ricky, another to Jenny. As the applause slowed he raced off stage for a moment to bring a startled Hal back with him along with the two performers. More clapping followed as he introduced the grandmother and granddaughter team who had been his assistants: 'Mrs Lorrie Armstrong and her granddaughter Hanna.' Then it was Hal's turn: 'And a last round of thanks, please, for my manager, Mr Hal Sargeson!'

*

Jenny and Ricky made their way backstage to see Terry before they left. Terry pulled Hal away from his packing up to join them.

'Wow, so glad to get that done, I can tell you,' Terry said.

Jenny cocked an eyebrow at Terry as he spoke. He was showing off, high, he knew. But he couldn't stop, and Jenny's look was one of surprise, not disapproval.

'This would be all your work, Hal, wouldn't it?' she said. 'Terry said you were very experienced.'

'All his own doing, this time,' Hal said. He had the insight to appreciate there was some sensitivity between them — and the less any third party, let alone him, said right now the better.

'I really liked the way you dressed the woman, Terry. Where did that come from?'

'Lots of places — but I thought, hey, it's Marrickville, we're in old migrant lady heartland here. Wanted to give them something they might recognise ...'

'They weren't the only ones who got it, Terry,' Jenny said with a touch of pretend sarcasm.

She took a step closer, as if not wanting what she had to say next to be heard by anyone else. She added quietly: 'Thank you, Terry, it was great. But it doesn't fix everything, you know that, don't you?'

'I do. Got something else in mind in that regard. Are you interested?'

'Depends,' she said, matter of factly.

She stepped back again to let Ricky come closer. 'You were great, Dad. I didn't know you were going to do that with the girl and her grandma.'

Terry glanced at Jenny, then turned his attention to the boy. 'Makes two of us. I didn't know I was going to do it either.'

'Bye, Terry, Hal,' Jenny said as she took Ricky's hand. She began to move off, seemed to remember something and stopped, turning briefly towards Terry again. 'I mean it, about the thank you part.'

Terry knew they all had a hell of a way to go yet, himself especially, but he couldn't have asked for more than that.

Once Jenny and Ricky had left, Hal deemed it time to give his assessment. 'Very interesting it was too, Terry. Nothing I've seen before. How did you do that?'

Terry touched the side of his nose and with a small smile said, 'Now, Hal, you know I can't say. But for a hint, think George Méliès ...'

Hal knew who Méliès was, as any magician would: 'The French chap who got into films, the bicycle over the moon thing?'

'Did you know that he bought Robert-Houdin's theatre in Paris?'

'I did.'

'Only thing I can say is you've got to go with the times. The times include a hundred years of film technology ... Other than that, I cannot reveal my secrets.'

'What if I were to buy you lunch? Next pension day.'

'Or you could use some of what I'm paying you for today.'

36

New Leaves

The Chinese Gardens were the go, Terry said. Then yum cha. Hal had thought that a splendid idea and so together they made their way down to Chinatown the next fine Saturday afternoon.

Terry remembered where they had sat the previous time they had come here and steered Hal towards the same place.

'Look, Hal, that seat there … under the liquidambar.'

'New leaves, too. Some changes since last we were here, eh?' Hal said once they were settled. 'What's next for Terry?'

'First thing is to keep working on my act. I'm hooked, as you know.'

'And well on your way. Not much more I can pass on, is there? Unless it's water into wine? Pigeons into alarm clocks? Got a million of those if you want. But somehow … Look, I liked what you did. Not kosher, of course — you used a sort of De Kolta chair, I know that, but to your credit you got to another place.'

'Metamorphosis?'

'Conceded.'

Terry was thrilled to hear he had his teacher's approval. 'At last!'

'And something else, you smart bastard. That wasn't Houdini, because you had no substitution trunk … No substitution trunk but getting your people on and off, you handled that terrifically. You got me beat. Only you can't tell me, right?'

'No more than I've told you already — think film.'

Hal grinned. 'Getting the hang of this, aren't you?'

'Seems so, but there are always questions: you can tell me who taught you magic, for one. Don't think I've asked you before. Was it Frank Sargeson? Did you learn anything from him?'

'If you want to know, he taught me nothing, Terry. Learned it all for myself, on the road, here and there.'

Terry appreciated that it would be some time, take further work, to prise from Hal the details of his own history. This was not a subject for today.

'All right, let's move on. Let's talk business instead. Yesterday, it was a few geriatrics at the old people's home, a bowlo …' Terry grinned at him. 'Tomorrow it's gigs at the Canterbury-Hurlstone Park RSL.'

'Did you say gigs, plural?'

'I did. Got a call from your pal, Taylor. Semi-regular, six-week blocks starting next Friday. How about that?'

'Ha, he's come good, has he? I notice he didn't call me direct, the rotten old drunk.'

'But I will need a half-decent manager — I wasn't kidding when I called you that. Are you interested? What about a hit list of local venues and other possibilities? I'll be needing you there, bro. Would you do that for me?'

Hal looked at him wide-eyed. 'Would I ever! Question is, would you want me to?'

'Sure, once I trained you up. But it occurs to me, if you are to become my main man …' he pointed at the shirt Hal was wearing, 'you'll be needing a few good shirts, and they'll have to be regularly washed and ironed, too.'

Hal glanced at his shirt then at Terry. Terry was reminded that his brother was a man whose wounds were not all healed.

'Hey, only joking,' he said. Heaven forbid that Hal should ever become a fully functioning model citizen. He had his own achievements, had made a break — and found a way for Terry to join him. This damaged, clever, stupid, occasionally on the nose man who was his half-brother had already given him more than enough. In return, Terry would help him where and how he could.

'More important is, have you been going to your AA meetings?'

'No need to worry yourself on that score, Terry,' Hal said with some pride. 'And I do have an iron, you know. It's understood that as your manager I will need to look good more often than not. Hey, I like that — "as your manager",' he repeated.

'You will. And as I've resigned from the buses, you're going to be very busy finding us money.'

'Okay. But where's headquarters going to be? With a recent exception, I don't like travelling that much, you know.'

'I've noticed.'

'Would it mean me having to go to your place a lot?'

Terry already had the answer to that. 'Not necessarily … not if you came to live with me.'

Hal lurched across and grabbed his hand, began to squeeze it fervently. Terry felt the change in his grip. He took it that the man wanted this — or did at this moment. 'Good,' Terry said. 'Good.'

'Oh, as for more help, I've now got an assistant.'

'Who?'

'Ricky Voulos, of course. He's meeting us today to seal the deal, along with someone else. They'll be joining us for lunch.'

'Ah then ...'

As if he had practised this too, right on cue, heading towards them were Ricky and Jenny, the boy running ahead to get to them first.

They set off for the Nine Dragons in lock step. Hal walked with Jenny on his right side as Terry and Ricky exchanged updates. All done, Terry swapped places to be next to Jenny. He tilted his head towards her and quietly asked, 'Have you sold the house yet?'

'No. Taken it off the market.'

Terry nodded. That felt like a gift all of its own.

Jenny then turned to Hal. 'I'm interested to hear about your life, Hal,' she said.

'Funny, Terry said that too.' Hal gave a small smile and Jenny gently squeezed his arm.

In a lull, Hal returned to his favourite old theme. 'You know, Terry, there had to be something more in Harry coming all this way ... always thought that. Apart from the flying and the shows. I mean, remember how he was obsessed with spiritualism? And then he wasn't? Maybe there's an Australian connection. I think we should investigate further ...'

'Maybe we will. Maybe we will ...'

How much remained to be done Terry acknowledged most deeply at that moment. He would keep Hal close as family. He had a son, and now a kind of brother, to love. So much more than so many had.

As to the woman who had been, still was, his wife — he knew he wanted her love again. But he also knew that this would call for another kind of magic, the work of months and years to come, the work of learning to love.

For now and from now, what he would ask of himself each morning was what Harry Houdini himself had sought as he continued on the path he had made his own: only the small, continuing adjustments necessary to any art.

AUTHOR'S NOTE

Whereas Harry Houdini occasionally turned to print to expose various charlatans and those he termed 'miracle mongers', writers since his death in 1926 have produced a voluminous body of work on the man himself — and for good reason. The career and significance of this legendary figure have continued to intrigue and his name, as the saying goes, has entered the language. My own forays into the great store of critique and celebration that Houdini has engendered were driven by a fascination that I hope is also apparent in this novel. Among the more valuable texts, and those I would like to especially acknowledge, are:

Ruth Brandon, *The Life and Many Deaths of Harry Houdini*, Secker & Warburg, London, 1993

Raymund FitzSimons, *Death and the Magician*, Atheneum, New York, 1981

Harry Houdini, *Miracle Mongers and their Methods*, E. P. Dutton & Company, New York, 1920,
<http://etext.lib.virginia.edu/toc/modeng/public/HouMirM.html>

—— *A Magician Among the Spirits*, Fredonia Books, Amsterdam, 2002

Harold Kellock, *Houdini: His Life Story from the Recollections and Documents of Beatrice Houdini*, Harcourt, Brace & Co. New York, 1928

Jim Steinmeyer, *Hiding the Elephant*, Carroll & Graf Publishers, New York, 2004

Edmund Wilson, 'Houdini', *The New Republic*, June 24, 1925; 'A Great Magician', *The New Republic*, October 17, 1928

ACKNOWLEDGEMENTS

My warmest thanks to Linda Funnell, Amanda O'Connell and Jo Jarrah, for their skilled publishing and editorial support in the preparation of this book.